TITAN MINE

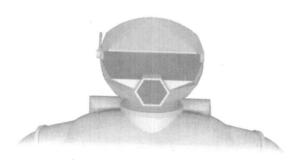

B.L. ALLEY

Lone Peak Publishing LLC

Prescott Valley, Arizona
lonepeakpublishing@gmail.com

This is a work of fiction. Any characters, incidents, or dialogue were created by the author or have been used fictitiously. Any resemblance to actual events or persons, living or dead, is entirely coincidental.

ISBN: 978-0-9863422-4-0 (Paperback)

To my fans. Thanks.

Contents

Titan

ONE

TWO

THREE

TITAN
(Saturn VI)

Distance from Saturn: 1,221,870 km

Distance from Sun: 1,427,000,000 km (9.54 AU)

Diameter (atmosphere): 5,550 km

Diameter (surface): 5,150 km

Mass: 1/45 that of Earth

Average density: 1.881 times liquid water

Surface temperature: 93.7 K (-180 degrees C)

Surface pressure: 146.7 kPa (1.5 times Earth's)

Orbital period: 15.95 Earth days

Atmospheric composition: Nitrogen, methane, traces of ammonia, argon, ethane

I

Isolation

"Can anyone hear me?"

Kem's voice took on a hollow tone inside the helmet of his pressure suit. He knew he wasn't in any immediate danger, but getting a vehicle stuck on a foreign moon was damn inconvenient. "Idiot!" He was about to slam his hands onto the narrow consoles on either side of him until reason took over. Instead, he held his left arm in front of his body and flipped open a small cover on the sleeve, revealing a contoured control pad. He checked his air supply and power levels, then deactivated the radio. With a frustrated sigh he settled back and stared through the faceted bubble of the pod transport cab. It was daytime on the moon, and would be for most of his stay since the mine was positioned at the northern pole, but that didn't mean it was bright out. Kem likened the lighting to an overcast night back home when the city lights would reflect and scatter against the cloud cover to create an even glow just bright enough to see by. Unlike home, however, the color on the moon was somewhere between yellow and orange and the clouds were far less stable. The freezing wind roared outside as it swirled the hydrocarbon fog around the stranded transport, but the low visibility and lack of color variation of the terrain were only partly responsible for Kem's situation. The transport was designed as a transfer vehicle for the hexagonal 4 meter wide by 9 meter long shipping pods, not as a cross-country explorer. The lightweight bed was little more than a tray with a flat bottom and outward sloping sides and was lined with shallow ridges with electro-magnetic grippers embedded in the surface to protect the bed and keep the pods in place. The sides of the bed flattened into fenders to cover the continuous track systems, the design of which also contributed to Kem's dilemma. Rather than utilizing heavy metal plates with aggressive blades, each tread was flat and covered with a soft and slightly tacky material, and like the cargo bed they contained four electro-magnetic attractors embedded in the material. Aboard a cargo ship with no gravity the mild tack of the pads allowed for turning on the metal floor while the electro-magnets kept the vehicle from floating away should it encounter a bump. On the moon, however, the tracks were all but useless, and Kem found himself paying the price for his need to explore.

"Well, Ula, you were right twice," Kem muttered, recalling his chief engineer's warnings. "Without the navigation grid in place I got lost, *and* with the low gravity and nothing to stick to these transports don't work very well." He found himself boxed in by steep hills, and to make matters worse the truck had come to rest in a slight depression. When he tried to look through the rear window his environment suit made it impossible, even with the pivoting driver's seat.

Kem's pressure suit and helmet were identical to those worn by the rest of the mining staff. It was off-white, with gray composite couplers connecting the rigid body to the heavy fabric limbs. The rear half of the helmet was round with a short hexagonal protrusion in the middle. A small round cylinder extended from each side of the helmet just over 1 centimeter, with the one on the right also serving as a base for a short antenna. In contrast, the front of the helmet was mostly angular, with the narrow mirrored lens sandwiched between the extended upper and lower sections. The upper formed a wide flat visor with the underside coated with a gray non-reflective material. The top of the lower section was also coated, but the rest was fuller than the visor and featured a hexagonal extension with an insert that appeared to be a breathing vent, but was really a speaker and microphone combination. That allowed conversations when a normal atmosphere was present, rather than relying on the radios. The extension also housed an eating tube, as well as some of the sensors used to monitor the wearer's life signs, which were both recorded and broadcast in real time. On the back of the suit a modest pack recycled the air and waste. At the bottom it also housed three easily replaceable modules containing fresh gases to replenish those lost during extended periods, liquified nutrients, and the rechargeable battery, which served as a backup to the mini reactor. To make sitting more comfortable the transport seat included a formed recess for the pack. The only real difference between the pressure suits were the interchangeable placards with raised insignias indicating title and department. In Kem's case a gray-colored hexagon represented administration, with three smaller hexagons inside identifying him as the Director. The position was approximately equal to that of the cargo ship's captain. The space below displayed his name. The insignia placards weren't just for visual identification, though, they also stored the owner's personal information electronically and broadcast it along with the suit data, allowing the wearer's identity and approximate location to be determined.

"Maybe they can track my suit telemetry," Kem thought aloud. "On the other hand, if they try to come after me they may get another transport stuck." He wasn't too worried about the latter, though, since he knew if the radio didn't reach the base then the data signal from the suit probably wouldn't either. He activated the reverse view but the image on the monitor only served to confirm that the only way out was the direction he had just come from. He grasped the throttle with his left hand and rotated it to FULL while pulling back on the directional stick with his right, but the smooth treads were unable to gain any traction on the frozen mixture of water and broken-down hydrocarbons. Kem tilted the stick to the right but the truck also refused to turn.

Kem began to feel a bit claustrophobic, but when he reached up to unlatch the collar of his helmet a flashing yellow indicator on the environment display reminded him that the truck's life support was turned off to conserve power. Frustrated, he switched to the suit's external speaker and microphone and activated the transport radio. Hoping there was enough 'air' in the cab to transmit sound he tried calling for help again.

"Transport Two to base. Come in base." He waited a full minute but there was still no response, so he turned off the radio. "Well, Genius, now what?" he asked himself. "Think!" Kem reclined the seat as far as it would go and stared through the tinted roof panel at the constantly shifting patterns of clouds. Since first arriving on the moon he found the practice quite relaxing, especially when construction of the mine didn't always go as planned. After each work day he would spend hours watching the sky while enjoying an aged ferment, and because the moon's atmosphere rotated faster than the surface there was always something new to see. He nearly fell asleep when a brief glint of light caught his eye far above. He focused on the spot and after a few seconds the flash repeated. "That must be the Gemisi."

* * *

The gleaming white cargo ship orbited the orange moon in silence while the ringed gas giant watched from afar. At 750 meters the state-of-the-art ship surpassed even the length of the latest military carriers. The main hull consisted of a hexagonal tube 60 meters wide and was divided into sections. At the front of the ship the hull tube tapered to a flat nose containing an array of sensors, while a small protrusion on the top panel suggested a command bridge, but was merely a housing for additional sensors and multi-spectrum cameras. The bridge was actually positioned deep inside the nose, well protected from impacts or other threats. In contrast, the rear of the ship flared outward, forming a large bowl-shaped tail. As with the short-range ships, the nuclear photonic engines were contained within the space of the main hull, but the more recently developed displacement drive needed for long-distance travel required the much larger shroud. Not to house the reactors, but rather the enormous coil needed to generate the displacement field. The longest section of the ship, just ahead of the tailpiece, contained the gas pods waiting to be filled with liquid methane before being sent home. The ship would have resembled an over-sized projectile if not for the gently rotating 235 meter diameter ring sandwiched between the first and second sections. The ring and main hull were both covered with small hexagonal tiles to protect against micro-meteoroid impacts and radiation. Mounted to the bottom of the hull just behind the ring was the large communications dish, which was aimed at the mine far below on the frozen surface. Directly above the dish, the lower half of the hull housed the shuttle hanger, while the upper half was open on both sides, revealing the 60 meter long landing bay. Inside, one of the cargo shuttles was in the process of being loaded.

"Pod One secure!" The transport driver's announcement crackled as he pulled away from the back of the shuttle.

"Copy that," the controller replied from the inverted six-sided Operations dome mounted to the landing bay ceiling. *"We have one more supply pod for you."*

"Copy Control." The transport shuffled across the smooth

floor toward the front wall, then spun around and backed up to the next supply pod, which was identified by a glowing blue light on the end frame. The pods were housed in 22 individual receptacles built into the wall and were arranged in three rows of seven, eight, and seven, centered between the port and starboard transport berths. Once locked in place the pods could be accessed from inside the pressurized supply room and filled with whatever food and materials the ground crew needed. The pod emerged from the receptacle on a sliding track and the transport's cradle rose to meet it, securing it with the magnetic attractors, then lowered it to the truck chassis. The laden transport then returned to the shuttle and backed up to the open cargo hold.

The white shuttle was 28 meters long and just like the Gemisi was hexagonal in overall design. It had started out shiny, like the cargo ship, but after dozens of trips to the surface the tiles had become dulled by layers of hydrocarbon deposits. The entire angled back of the ship hinged upward and folded in half to expose the cargo hold. Inside there was just enough room for three pods, one centered above the other two. Protruding from the sides of the shuttle were small winglets with control surfaces for atmospheric stability, with the two main engines tucked into the hull below. The front of the engines were enclosed, since they also used nuclear photonic energy, but the shuttle did possess intakes on either side of the fuselage just in front of the engine housings. Those were used to collect additional ions as it flew through space to extend the range. The main hatch was directly in front of the port intake and led into the airlock and eventually the passenger cabin, which tapered down from the cargo hold. Each side contained three small porthole windows for passengers but the front of the craft was capped by a large clear canopy resembling the cabs of the pod transports. Finally, control jets and navigation lights dotted the surface of the shuttle in key areas, allowing precise control and visibility.

The driver raised the pod until the starboard slide latched onto it, then it retracted, drawing the pod into the cargo hold.

"Pod Two secure."

"Before you park we need you to load a gas pod."

"I thought we already sent all of them down."

"Yes, but one of them was damaged and they need a replacement right away."

"Copy that." The transport again scooted across the floor but toward the aft wall of the landing bay, most of which was made up of a huge transparent partition separating the bay from the rear storage block. The block was enormous, nearly 470 meters long, and kept in a vacuum to conserve resources. Entering the area still required passing through an airlock, but it merely served as a containment protocol should any of the filled pods develop a leak. As the driver approached the access hatch it opened on cue. He carefully guided the transport into the cramped airlock and the hatch closed with a dull *'thump'* transmitted through the chassis.

Once the inner doors opened the driver increased the power to the tread magnets and guided the truck out of the airlock and onto the six meter-wide metal catwalk, which was little more than a channel suspended from the surrounding walls. The narrow path stretched all the way to the engineering section at the rear and was surrounded by 100 rows of pods, each consisting of six arranged in a radial configuration pointing toward the center. The sides of the catwalk were only thirty centimeters high, just enough to keep the trucks on course as long as the drivers didn't turn sharply and accelerate. Fortunately, that had never happened, since a free-floating transport could cause serious damage to the cargo pods and the ship.

"Commencing alignment," Control announced.

"Copy Control." The transport continued along the channel as

the pods began to rotate slowly around the vehicle. At least, that's how it appeared to the driver. In reality, the pods were secured in frames which were bolted to the inner hull of the ship, and it was actually the catwalk that rotated, aligning the transport with the next pod designated for retrieval. The driver advanced slowly along the catwalk until he reached the last row of racks that still contained pods. The remaining 5 rows were already empty, as were two of the frames in the sixth row. When the rotation stopped he spotted the blue indicator light and pulled forward, then pivoted the transport ninety degrees until the cradle was properly aligned. A surge of nitrogen pushed the selected pod onto the truck with a muffled *'bumpf'*. The driver activated the cradle magnets, then rotated the loaded transport toward the airlock.

2

Arrival

After emerging from the airlock the laden transport returned to the waiting shuttle and again backed up to the cargo hold. He pressed the button to activate the cradle lift but a yellow light inside the cab indicated the vehicle was mis-aligned. From the driver's rear-view monitor he could tell the variant was only a few degrees to the left, so rather than pull forward and try again he simply deactivated the tread magnets, causing a large flat button on the left console to flash repeatedly. He braced his gloved right hand against the front corner of the cab and threw his weight into it. The transport rocked forward and the treads began to peel away from the metal deck. The driver then slammed his left hand onto the flashing button and the magnets pulled the truck down to the floor. He checked the monitor and activate his com.

"Pod is aligned."

"Copy that," came the response from the shuttle pilot. After loading the last pod the transport driver pulled away and spun around to watch the rear hatch unfold until it sealed the pods inside.

"Cargo hold is secure. Good to go," he reported.

*"Gemisi control to Shuttle Two, you're cleared for departure,"*Control announced. The transport driver spun around and headed toward the starboard side of the landing bay. The possibility of floating off into space was never lost on the drivers,

but all of them felt it was worth the risk. Especially since the lack of doors provided a spectacular, unobstructed view of the huge ringed planet as it watched over the yellow-orange moon directly below the ship. The moon wasn't visible from the bay floor but as the driver approached the edge he was able to glimpse the horizon, revealing a thin purple layer encasing the hazy hydrocarbon atmosphere. He turned to the left and continued forward to the starboard storage berth. Each of them served as garages as well as airlocks. After parking the drivers exited the front of the cab into one of the two pressurized maintenance areas next to the supply room. When the trucks needed service they were pulled forward onto a built-in lift for easy access.

When the driver reached the transparent door he spun the transport around and watched as the shuttle's navigation strobes began to flash, reflecting off of the white landing bay walls and ceiling. The pilot then deactivated the magnetic docking clamps, and with a short burst from the landing jets the shuttle slowly drifted off of the deck while the control jets emitted tiny spurts of vapor as they kept the vehicle stable. Once the skids retracted into the hull the main engines glowed a soft red and the photons pushed the shuttle forward. As it cleared the landing bay the bottom of the shuttle took on an orange hue as the moon illuminated the dirty tiles. Instead of dropping toward the surface, though, the pilot nosed the shuttle upward and flew over the top of the cargo ship in a sweeping arc, waggling the wings for spectators inside the huge ring.

Rather than being a continuous round tube, the ring was comprised of twenty four six-sided segments, with six hexagonal spokes supporting it from the central hub mounted to the main hull. Each spoke also housed an elevator to transport crew between the ring and ship. The outer half of the ring contained two levels of living space, while the inner half contained mechanical systems, laboratories, and the greenhouses. Those were evenly spaced around the ring in six pairs and were open inside. The floor of each agricultural section was 28 by 24 meters and contained soil for traditional farming, while a narrow catwalk spanned the length of the section in place of the normal upper level. They provided access to the suspended hydroponic plants and also connected the enclosed areas on either side where the spokes attached to the ring. Since the agricultural sections were encased in a transparent composite material the catwalks had become a favorite destination for the crew, providing spectacular views of the farms while the moon passed overhead with each revolution of the ring.

The shuttle made a complete circle around the cargo ship, rotating upright as it passed beneath the communications dish.

"That's enough fancy flying," Control urged. *"Let's get those pods on the ground."*

"Copy that," the pilot replied. The shuttle's nose dropped toward the moon and after a few seconds it entered the upper atmosphere and vanished into the orange haze.

* * *

Kem's self-loathing had finally waned as he continued watching for the intermittent reflections from the ship above. He was about to try the radio again when the muted wail of the wind was interrupted by a loud roar. A shadow streaked past the transport, accompanied by the shuttle passing directly overhead in the same direction Kem had been driving. Excited, he watched as the craft first banked right, then left before disappearing behind the hill.

"He must be landing!" Kem shouted. He quickly checked the status of his suit, then reached forward and released the canopy latch. The glass upper and solid lower panels separated, forming a canopy and ramp once they had opened. Kem turned off the lights and shut down the main power, then stepped out of the cab and pushed the panels closed. With the transport secured he stepped forward gingerly, testing the firmness of the frozen ground. It felt solid, but Tam, the mission geologist, had warned the crew about the possibility of hidden pockets of liquid methane lying just below a solid layer of deposits. The suits were well insulated and heated by the mini reactor, but with the surface temperature approaching two hundred degrees below zero, falling into even a shallow pond could mean certain death. Kem walked around to the side of the transport and removed a long pry bar from a slot between the cab and empty pod cradle. Using it as both a probe and walking stick he headed in the direction where the shuttle had disappeared. As Kem ascended the small wind-etched hill he repeatedly drove the bar into the ice to pull himself up. As he did he was grateful for the weak gravity, but appreciated having something keeping him grounded. Many of his crew members missed the ring but Kem never felt completely at ease in centrifugal gravity. There was just something off about it even with the visual cues.

To maintain a sense of continuity throughout the ship even the rooms and corridors without gravity were designed with distinct floors and ceilings. In the early days of space travel the lack of visual orientation caused crew members to experience a decrease in spacial acuity and focus. On ships like the Gemisi, the floors were constructed of coated metal, softening them just enough to prevent injury while still allowing the crews' magnetic boots to stick when needed. The magnets were strong enough to keep them in place, yet still allow them to walk normal, if desired. To float rather than walk a simple toe flex would break the bond. In contrast, the walls and ceilings were well padded with a soft yet slick material, and most of the handholds and control panels had been recessed. Both features made it possible for off-course crew members to skim across the surface and continue on their way, rather than catch on anything that could impede their progress or cause injury. The interiors of the mining base had been designed with the same features, not only for familiarity but also to allow the reusable modular buildings to be installed on worlds with low or non-existent gravity.

When Kem reached the top of the hill he was greeted by the distant planet. Encouraged, he continued climbing until he straddled the narrow ridge, then let out and audible sigh when he found himself looking over a modest methane lake with the mining complex on the opposite side. Other than a small gap on the far side of the mine the entire area was surrounded by low ridges to form an isolated basin. By then the shuttle had settled onto the round landing pad and one of the remaining transports was already backed up to the open cargo hold while the other waited next to the habitat module.

The modest hexagonal building served as an anchor for the slightly smaller operations center balanced 15 meters above atop the narrow elevator shaft. A recess on the roof contained an assortment of sensors as well as the 8 meter tall repeater antenna with a slowly pulsing green light at the top. The antenna was linked to the large communications dish placed on the hill behind the complex to maintain contact with the cargo ship. The rest of the mining complex was made up of the processing station. At the base of the far hill there were two rows of gas pods waiting to be filled, and next to them sat the maintenance building. At the other end of the pods, next to the habitat, was the intake for the processor. From the surface it looked like a simple 50 meter ring with inward sloping teeth arranged around the perimeter.

"Home sweet home," Kem said. He carefully made his way down the opposite slope, which was nearly twice the height of the side he had just climbed, then worked his way around the narrow beach. He tried to watch where he walked but the administrator in him couldn't resist glancing across the lake every few steps to monitor the transfer process. Once the first pod had been extracted the transport carried it to the storage room attached to the back of the habitat. There were four pod racks, one for each access hatch set into the wall. The transport backed up to the one empty rack and the powered rollers transferred the pod until the end rested against the building. It was then secured with mechanical clamps and magnetically sealed so the hatch could be opened and the pod unloaded from inside the habitat. Meanwhile, the second transport retrieved the empty gas pod from the top slot of the shuttle, carried it past the habitat, then transferred it onto the empty rack near the middle of the front row. Kem remembered the radio and used the control pad to reactivate it.

"...parked and meet me at the airlock."

"Copy that." After the hour of silence from being out of range Kem was startled by the sudden chatter. By the time he reached the complex the transfer was complete and two empty pods had been loaded into the shuttle. The last transport waited until the cargo hold was closed, then headed for the storage berths next to the supply room. Like the berths on the cargo ship the three compartments were just big enough for the trucks, but instead of being airlocks the drivers had to back into them, exit, then walk around to the entrance facing the landing pad. It wasn't the most convenient design but it allowed the trucks to be protected without the need for three additional airlocks and the complexity that came along with them.

Kem waved at the transport, prompting the driver to dim the headlights as they passed. By the time he reached the recessed area where the airlock door was located the two drivers had parked the trucks and soon joined him. Kem glanced at their orange insignias and identified them as Nya, the lead driver, and Val.

"Did you forget something?" Val asked. Normally, teasing an administrator would be strictly off-limits but Kem liked to keep his relationships with his team members casual.

"Just a minor issue with the conditions here," Kem replied. "Nothing we can't fix."

"So where did you lose it?" Nya asked.

"It's just on the other side of that hill," Kem explained as he pointed across the lake. "Turns out I didn't get nearly as far as I thought. I still got lost though."

"So how do we get it back?" Val asked. "The shuttle?"

"Not enough space to land. We'll have to come up with another way to retrieve it."

"Hopefully Ula won't give you too much grief," Nya said. "You know how she likes to rub it in when she's right."

"I know, I know." Kem opened a small access panel next to the airlock door, revealing a red T-handle. He grasped it and turned it and the heavy door slid open with a *'hiss'*.

3

The Habitat

Kem led the two drivers into the airlock and turned the inside handle. Once the outer door closed and the status light switched from blue to white he stepped to the display screen, which had a column of buttons on either side, and pressed the upper right one. He waited a moment, but the familiar hum of the equalization pumps never materialized. He pressed the button again but the pumps remained silent. The readings on the screen indicated the system was ready, but for some reason the habitat atmosphere was outside of the allowable parameters. Puzzled, Kem pressed the com button.

"Kem to Operations."

"Go ahead sir." Lue, the Assistant Director responded. Kem could detect a hint of panic in her tone but ignored it.

"What's going on with the environmental controls? We're stuck in the airlock."

"Let me get Ula for you. She can explain it better than I can." Kem looked over at the two drivers, but all they could do is shrug stiffly.

"This is Ula, Sir. Sorry about the delay."

"What's going on?" Kem asked. "We'd like to get out of these suits if you don't mind."

"We're having a slight problem with atmo."

"What kind of problem?" Kem asked. He switched the display

19

back to the habitat environment screen. "According to the computer the pressure and hydrocarbon levels are elevated."

"I'm not sure," the chief engineer reluctantly admitted.

"It looks like we're keeping our suits on a bit longer," Kem told the two drivers before resuming the conversation with Ula. "Is it the processors or do we have a leak?"

"We've already checked the processors and we're scanning the entire building for leaks now. It could be the sensors."

"Wouldn't be the first time." Kem said under his breath as he switched the display back to the airlock controls. "In the meantime, how about getting us out of here? The computer engaged the safety protocol so the airlock won't let us enter."

"We're working as fast as we can."

"What about the manual release?"

"If you sit tight I'm certain we'll have it figured out in a few minutes."

"Who designs this junk?" Kem asked no one in particular. "If we're wearing suits there is no reason we shouldn't be able to go inside." He checked the display again, adding to his impatience. "Screw it!" he finally said and again activated the com. "Ula, we're coming in."

"Are you sure?"

"I'm sure." Kem turned to the two drivers. "Is that okay with you?"

"As long as we get out of this airlock," Val said from behind the mirrored lens of his helmet.

"I'm switching to manual," Kem announced. He pressed the button next to the override icon and deactivated the automatic equalization process. Next he stepped to the opposite side of the airlock and opened a small access panel, revealing a bright yellow handle. He unfolded the grip and grasped it tightly. "Here goes nothing." Kem began cranking the handle in slow circles, generating a muted whirring sound from behind the airlock wall. After a dozen revolutions he looked over at the drivers. "How are we doing?" Nya stepped up to the display and checked the readings.

"You're right at one thousand, Sir." Kem continued turning the crank, slowly pumping inside air into the airlock to displace the moon's less hospitable gases.

"How about now?"

"995," Nya reported as her boss continued cranking. "990...985. Stop!. It's not exactly normal but at least it's the same as inside." Kem let go of the handle and fell to a knee, drawing in several deep breaths while Val stepped over to help him to his feet.

"Out of shape, Boss?" he teased.

"Next time...you get to...crank it." Kem initiated the bio-hazard safeguard and the airlock was instantly flooded with thick white gas.

"Do we really need to go through this every time?" Nya asked. "There isn't any life on this hunk of ice." When Kem didn't respond she grasped the red T-handle next to the inner doors and turned it. The two halves separated with a heavy *'clunk'* and slid open, revealing two more pressure-suited crew members. Kem barely had to glance at their insignias, one yellow and one blue, to recognize them as Ula, and Cas, the Chief of Mining Operations. The Director and both drivers stepped out of the airlock into the main room, which was surrounded by a ring of smaller individual rooms along the outside walls. Those contained operations equipment, storage, and two changing rooms with suit lockers, one on each side of the airlock. An airtight door on the back wall led to the main storage room where the supply pods were unloaded.

"Good to be home," Val said, relieved. Not wasting any time Kem approached his two officers.

"I'm gone for a couple of hours and everything falls apart?

Even with the damaged pod we were four days ahead of schedule and the habitat was functioning perfectly."

"Sorry, Sir," Ula said. "I don't know what happened."

"So where are we with the repairs?" Kem asked.

"As soon as I have something new to report I will let you know."

"Okay." Kem glanced at a small wall monitor displaying multiple images, including a view of the landing pad. "Why is the shuttle still here?"

"Lue had me postpone their departure in case we needed to go look for you." Cas replied.

"Is Lue still in operations?" Kem asked.

"Yes sir. Shall I continue holding the shuttle?"

"They're far enough behind as it is. Let it go."

"Yes sir." Cas headed for the elevator while Kem continued with the update from his Chief Engineer.

"Do you have any theories about the atmo problem?" he asked Ula.

"It's either a breech or a sensor malfunction, but we can't find evidence of either."

"And you're sure it's not the processors."

"As I said we already checked them, but even if they failed the pressure wouldn't increase, just the toxicity of the air."

"Have you checked the readings manually?"

"We can't find the portable monitors."

"What do you mean you can't find them?"

"We've looked everywhere. I have someone going through the pods that just arrived, but so far we can't find either one."

"They must still be on board the Gemisi," Cas suggested before entering the waiting elevator.

"They were supposed to be in the first supply run after the habitat was completed." Kem said angrily.

"Shall I put in a call to the Captain?"

"Not yet," Kem said. The elevator doors closed and the indicator lights began to scroll upward.

"I don't know what to tell you, Sir," Ula said.

"Does the radio still work," Kem asked sarcastically.

"Yes Sir."

"Once we've confirmed the monitors aren't here I'll call the Gemisi and let them know."

"Yes Sir." Without warning Kem punched the wall next to the airlock doors, causing the other crew members to jump.

"Idiots!" he shouted, then turned to the two drivers who were still waiting patiently. "You two. Go help search the supply pods."

"Right away, Sir," Nya replied. She tapped Val on the shoulder and the two of them hurried toward the back of the habitat. Once they disappeared through the storage room door Kem turned back to his chief engineer.

"Do you have any other theories, even wild ones?"

"No sir," Ula replied.

"So what can you do?"

"I've got my team double checking everything."

"Make it quick," Kem said firmly. "After hiking around the lake I really need to get out of this suit."

"Yes sir." Ula did her best to suppress a smile even though it was hidden by the face shield. "Speaking of that, what exactly happened out there?"

"You were right. The ground is too slick for the transports to get any traction on anything but a totally flat surface."

"I hate to say I told you so..."

"Then don't," Kem snapped. He started walking toward the elevator but then stopped and placed a hand on Ula's shoulder. "I'm sorry. I just want to get this place finished so we can get to work."

"Of course."

"Do you know how the grid is coming?" Kem asked.

"No, why?"

"It doesn't look like the radios are going to work well without line of sight."

"Well, we knew the icy surface and constantly changing weather may interfere with communications. How far away were you?"

"Just past that small hill on the other side of the lake," Kem explained.

"That close and you still couldn't get a signal through?" Ula asked, surprised.

"Nope."

"That's worse than I thought," Ula said. "It looks like we're not leaving this basin until the grid is in place."

"Going exploring in a transport without navigation wasn't the most intelligent plan," Kem confessed. "As varied as this terrain is we really need to get the surface mapped so we have detailed topographical navigation."

"We can check the status of the grid when we get to the control room," Ula suggested. "Unfortunately, the shuttles can only carry twelve satellites at a time, and with them still making supply runs it's going to take time to deploy them."

"Two shuttles," Kem said, shaking his head. "The Gemisi's hanger can hold four, so what genius decided this mission would work with only two?"

"It could be worse," Ula said.

"And how is that?" Kem asked.

"We could be in the military."

"True, but at least they get shit done."

"That they do," Ula agreed. "May I ask a question?"

"Sure."

"Why didn't you join? You've never struck me as the type to run away from a fight, and with the war raging back home they could have used someone with your combination of guts and problem solving skills."

"With my engineering and administrative background I felt I could do a lot more good working for the Mining Guild rather than being stuck on a military ship."

"I get the feeling there is more to it, though," Ula said. Kem paused, then continued in a quieter tone.

"Keep this to yourself, but I didn't feel comfortable enlisting because I never fully believed the Council's reason for going to war in the first place."

"Don't tell me you're a sympathizer. That kind of talk will land you in prison."

"No. I'm loyal to my people and will do my job like a good little worker," Kem replied. "I just have some doubts about the accuracy of our history, that's all. Maybe they really were a threat but the logic doesn't add up. Their technology was well behind ours, and only advanced once they started getting their hands on our ships and weapons. That whole 'imminent threat' excuse seems a bit contrived to me."

"Like I said, keep that to yourself."

"You asked," Kem said. "For all the good joining the Guild did me. I ended up in the middle of the war anyway."

"I remember," Ula said. "The attack during your last assignment was pretty bad."

"Yes it was," Kem agreed. "Even if I had supported the decision to go to war I still think mining was the right choice. Besides, have you ever been on those military ships?"

"Only when they were new. I heard after a couple of tours even the larger frigates were pretty bad," Ula added. "Cramped, dirty, no gravity, and if they got attacked you couldn't do anything it about it unless you were a gunner."

"Exactly. No control over your own fate," Kem agreed. "Mining isn't exactly a picnic but at least we can defend ourselves and make a difference. Besides, we get to walk on solid ground."

"Which also means less chance of zero-G dementia. I heard crews on the longer missions were coming home completely nuts," Ula said. "Shaking and drooling and totally paranoid."

"I heard the pacifists started that rumor to scare people out of enlisting," Kem said. "That it was nothing more than normal battle shock."

"Doctor Rue will tell you it's real."

"Probably."

"At least we don't have to worry about attacks way out here."

"Not yet," Kem said.

"I'm sure it will be a long time before the enemy makes it this far," Ula said as she punched Kem in the arm. "That means more time to explore."

"Very funny."

"How do you think it's going?"

"The war?"

"Yes."

"Well, last I heard we were actually making progress," Kem replied. "Getting to new sources of methane before them has helped a lot, and once this facility is up and running our supply will increase considerably." The elevator door finally opened and they stepped inside. Kem pressed the UP button and waited for the doors to close before continuing. "So what can we do about recovering the transport?"

"Well, we could have retrieved it with the shuttle, *if* you hadn't sent it back."

"Val already suggested that but it wouldn't have worked anyway."

"Why not?"

"The area I got stuck in is far too tight for the shuttle," Kem explained.

"What about the rover? We could tow it back."

"Except the rover isn't scheduled to be sent down until the navigation grid is in place, and it doesn't come assembled like the transports. Anything else?"

"Ari had an idea," Ula replied.

"What's that?"

"The magnetic attractor heads were designed to be easy to remove and replace."

"Right."

"So Ari suggested replacing the attractors with spikes."

"And where do we get the spikes?"

"We can fabricate them in the shop. If we machine them with the same mounting posts as the attractors then it's a simple matter of swapping them out and driving the transport home."

"You know, that just might work," Kem said, encouraged. "How soon can you do it?"

"I'll get Ari started on them right away."

"Keep me informed."

4

The Tower

The elevator doors opened and Kem and Ula stepped out into the bustling operations hub. Like the main room below, the glass enclosed space surrounded the elevator shaft, but instead of rooms lining the perimeter a continuous control console occupied the lower half, providing a 360 degree view. The six segments were divided into five departments: Flight Control, Communications, Supply, Science and Exploration, and two sections for Mining Operations. The designed allowed the different departments to interact efficiently while reducing the sense of separation or isolation. In the center of each section there was a free standing computer display table, and the personal facilities were housed in the main support shaft, with restrooms on either side of the elevator and a set of bunks between them for quick naps. The shaft also contained the atmosphere processors for Operations.

"Welcome back," Lue said from behind her face shield. "Did you have a nice drive?"

"What's the latest?" Kem asked impatiently.

"The shuttle is on it's way back but we still haven't found the portable monitors."

"Could they be in the maintenance building?"

"I'm having it checked as we speak," Cas chimed in.

"Now that you're back I'll go down and help search the supply room," Lue said.

"Let me know what you find," Kem said.

"Of course." Once she had left Kem turned back to Cas.

"What's the status of the mine?"

"We're still ahead of schedule, in spite of the shuttle delays and the damaged pod," Cas replied.

"Good." Kem walked over to the control console and looked down at the mine intake. The thick outer ring housed a huge impeller to draw in the atmospheric gases while the inward sloping teeth served to break up the flow and reduce the velocity at ground level. There were two more impellers below the first, each smaller but with more aggressive blades. Once operational they would progressively compress the gases to a consistent density, allowing them to be separated efficiently. All the methane would then be converted to a stable liquid state and routed to the storage pods. Once all but the last set of pods were filled and returned to the Gemisi, the ship would jump home, exchange them for empty pods, then return to the moon. The methane wasn't the only useful gas. Some of the nitrogen would be also captured and stored in the buildings for use in gas-operated devices like the pod lifts and airtight doors. The remaining nitrogen and other gases would then released back into the atmosphere. There was one difference compared to the previous mines Kem had worked on: this mine called for six additional pods to collect more nitrogen.

"I still haven't figured out what the extra nitrogen is for," Cas said.

"I'm sure the Board will tell us when we need to know."

"Or they will just take it and never tell us," Cas added. He led Ula and the Director over to the section of glass overlooking the pods, which were laid out in two rows of 16. Two of Ula's workers were busy repairing the supply lines leading to the pod that had just been delivered.

"Have you figured out why the rollers engaged with the

supply lines still attached?" Kem asked.

"Not yet," Ula replied. "I've already had the safety sensors replaced and my team will test the old ones as soon as we figure out what's wrong with atmo."

"Hopefully that's sooner rather than later. I'm just glad it happened during tests and not after the pods were full."

"Tell me about it," Cas said as he shifted inside his cramped suit. "That's exactly *why* we perform tests."

"Are we sure we're not losing atmo because the same thing happened to one of the supply pods?" Kem asked.

"Doubtful," Ula said, "For the pod to be able to move the latches would have to be released, otherwise, the rollers would simply turn under it. Besides, that was the first thing I checked," she explained. "The latches were all engaged and I closed the inner hatches but the pressure continued to increase."

"It guess it could be anything," Kem said with a sigh. "A micro-meteoroid could have punctured one of the habitat walls while they were being loaded onto the shuttle."

"Except we did a full pressure test as soon as the building was completed."

"What about a meteorite after construction?"

"Theoretically it's possible, but not likely. They simply lose too much energy by the time they hit the ground."

"It has to be something," Kem said, his patience rapidly dwindling.

"Believe me, we are considering every conceivable scenario the engineers came up with when they designed this place. We *will* find it."

"I hope so." Kem said with a sigh. "If this place isn't up and running on time the Board will have my head."

"Speaking of which, I better get back down there."

"Keep me posted."

"Will do." Once Ula left, Cas continued the conversation.

"They wouldn't really fire you, would they?"

"Let me put it this way," Kem said. "The last Director who fell behind got reassigned to the waste recycling system of his own facility. Talk about humiliating."

"That's pretty bad."

"It wasn't even his fault," Kem explained. "One of the pods never got loaded onto the ship before they left home, so they were missing one of the habitat walls and some of the furniture."

"That seems a bit harsh then."

"He should have gotten a medal. They managed to fabricate a temporary wall by using part of the maintenance building and got the mine up and running only two days late."

"We'll do everything we can to make sure that doesn't happen, sir."

"I know you will." Kem stared at the distant horizon as orange clouds drifted past, occasionally obscuring the ringed planet behind a wispy veil. "I'd sure like to get back out there," he said softly.

"Did you find anything interesting before you got stuck?"

"This entire moon is interesting, but between the low light, the dense fog, and getting stuck I didn't have a chance to see much."

"It's definitely different," Cas agreed. "Too bad we have to wait for the rover." The comment made Kem long for the all-terrain vehicle, which would allow for much more detailed exploration of the moon's surface.

"As soon as they send it down we're putting it together and taking a field trip," Kem said.

"That sounds like fun."

"So other than a stranded transport, a damaged pod, and the fact that we're stuck in these suits, is there anything else I need to know?"

"I don't think so. As soon as the damaged supply lines are repaired the mine is ready to go online."

"That soon?" Kem asked, surprised. "I assumed it would set us back at least a day or two."

"What can I say? I'm good."

"Which is why I asked for you to be on my team."

"Actually, we could start the mine now if you really wanted."

"What about the lines?"

"Not a problem," Cas said confidently. "As you know, the system starts at one end and works it's way to the other, filling one pair of pods at a time. Ula's team will have the lines repaired long before the system reaches them."

"And how long will that be?" Kem asked, encouraged by the news.

"They'll be done within the hour."

"That would still put us a full three days ahead of schedule."

"Exactly."

"Starting that much ahead of schedule might help me convince the Captain to send the rover down early."

"Don't forget, we still need the satellites in place to navigate."

"Dammit, you're right," Kem said. At first he felt disappointed but then suddenly perked up. "Unless we use the gyro-tracker."

"And risk getting another vehicle lost? The Captain will never go for that."

"You're right. Speaking of the grid, how far along is the deployment?" Cas led Kem over to the nearest display table and activated it. He entered a command on the keyboard and the horizontal one-meter square screen came to life, displaying an image of the moon and the grid satellites that had already been deployed around the northern pole. "Can we see it in detail?"

"Sure." Cas pressed another key and the flat image began to bulge upward, eventually folding into a free-floating three-dimensional model of the moon's upper half, including the cargo ship and the satellites. The table displays weren't holographic, but instead used microscopic particles that changed color to create the image. Those particles normally laid flat but could also be manipulated magnetically to form a perfectly rendered 3D model. "According to the computer they are at forty five percent."

"Damn. And no way to use the satellites already in place."

"No Sir. Once they are in place they still have to be synchronized to each other, and only then can they begin mapping the surface."

"Well, at least we're ready to start up the mine," Kem said, happy to have some good news. "I'm going down to see where we're at with atmo."

"Shall I initiate the system?"

"Let's wait until the lines are repaired, just in case."

"Yes Sir."

"Besides, if we appear too efficient then the Board will expect us to get everything done early." Kem intended the comment to be humorous, but that didn't make it any less true.

"You're probably right."

"Just keep me updated on the repairs."

"Will do."

"Good work, Cas."

"Thank you, Sir." Kem patted his Chief on the back and headed for the elevator.

* * *

As soon as the doors opened to the main floor Kem stepped out and headed toward the supply room. When he entered the shelf-lined space the two drivers were removing the last containers from the far right pod while a third crew member searched a container that had already been unloaded.

"Anything?" Kem asked.

"No Sir," Nya answered. "No sign of them."

"Damn. Do you know where Lue and Ula went?"

"I think they went down to the machine shop."

"Thanks." Kem started to leave but stopped and turned back to the workers. "When you're done here I want the hatches sealed."

"Yes Sir," Nya replied.

"Carry on." Kem left the supply room and returned to the elevator, then pressed ONE.

* * *

Kem stepped out of the elevator and looked around the dimly lit space. The personnel level was two stories below ground and larger than the medical floor directly above it, which in turn was larger than the main floor. The stepped design served to anchor the tower. The perimeter rooms contained the crew sleeping quarters, Kem's private office and conference room, and the maintenance and machine shops. The main room in the center served as a recreation area with games, tables, and a food dispenser. Like the tower, the elevator shaft contained a restroom as well as the environmental processors. Kem walked around the shaft to the machine shop directly behind. When he entered, Lue and Ula were talking while Ari, one of Ula's junior engineers sat in front of a fabricator. Kem walked over to the bench and peered through the small window on the front of the machine. "How's it going?"

"Good, Sir," Ari replied. "So far I've made enough for one tread."

"Good work. Show me what you came up with." Ari reached into a large semi-rigid bag sitting on the floor and pulled out a small solid metal object. It was hexagonal and about three centimeters across, with one end tapering to a point and the other reduced to a short round cylinder with three equally spaced nubs protruding from the side. "Looks good. Will they work?"

"They will fit perfectly into the attractor sockets."

"Does that mean they will also be magnetic?"

"Theoretically, but unless the frozen ground is covering a solid iron base there wouldn't be much reason to turn them on."

"What do you think?" Ula asked from behind. "Pretty clever, isn't he?"

"That he is." Kem said, sharing his engineers pride. "How soon will they be done?"

"Within the hour," Ari replied. "I also have the other fabricator working on some spikes for the pressure suit boots."

"Wont that make it hard to walk indoors?" Lue asked.

"No, because Ula is going to fix the atmo problem," Kem teased. "Right?"

"Yes Sir," the Chief Engineer replied sheepishly.

"Actually, I designed the boot grippers to be less aggressive," Ari explained. He reached into another bag and pulled out a prototype. Rather than coming to a point it had a flat surface surrounded by a knurled taper. "They won't be as effective as the spikes, but also won't tear up the floors if you use them inside the habitat."

"Sounds good." Kem turned to face Ula. "Let me know when they're ready. I'd like to retrieve the transport after lunch."

"Do you remember where you parked it?" Lue teased.

"Funny."

"What is your plan, exactly?" Ula asked.

"Walk back to the truck, install Ari's spikes, and drive it back to base."

"I'll go with you."

"I think I can handle it."

"There are almost two hundred spikes per track," Ula reminded him. "Besides, you'll still need the extra weight."

"You're right, but I need you here working on the atmo problem."

"Take Nya," Lue suggested. "After all, she's the best driver we've got."

"Is that some kind of crack about *my* driving skills?"

"Did I say that?"

"Actually, you're right. If anyone can handle this terrain it's her."

"I'll make sure she's ready."

"Don't forget to recharge your suits," Ula reminded Kem. "You may want to replace your food pack, too. Just in case."

"I guess that would be a good idea."

"You're also going to need a couple of attractor wrenches," Ula added. "The attractors may be easy to replace but the transports weren't intended to be field serviced, so they don't carry tools."

"Actually, the attractor wrenches won't fit the spikes," Ari said.

"Then how are we supposed to install them?" Kem asked. The junior engineer reached into the first bag again and pulled out two small handles with ratcheting heads.

"I made custom wrenches for them." He handed them to Kem and turned back to the fabricator.

"Thanks."

"No problem," Ari said without looking up.

"So where am I supposed to sit?" Kem asked. "The cabs barely fit the driver."

"We have an extra transport seat in the maintenance building," Ula explained. "The gravity is so light it shouldn't be a problem carrying it with you. All you have to do is secure it in the pod cradle with a few straps."

"Sound's like a plan," Kem said. "Let's get started."

5

Retrieval

With the bulky suit on Kem's arm barely fit between the stranded transport's track and fender, but it was enough room to install the new spikes. While he worked his way along the right-hand tracks Nya did the same on the left side. The two worked quickly thanks to Ari's custom wrenches and before long Kem had reached the last exposed tread. He removed the four flush-mounted attractors and dropped them into the bag, then installed the spikes one by one. After giving them each a quarter turn to lock them in place he pulled his arm out and dropped the wrench into the bag, then stood up. He started to walk around the truck to check on Nya when he remembered his flashlight. He reached back into the gap and pulled on the thick shell, which was stuck to the underside of the fender. Once the magnet relinquished it's grip he turned off the light and pressed it into the custom pouch on his right thigh.

"Almost done?" he asked.

"I'm done," Nya said as her head popped up from the other side of the cradle. Kem closed the bag of parts and picked it up, then scanned the frozen ground around the bottom of the tread.

"I hope this works," he said.

"It'll work," Nya assured him as she finished on the other side. "Ari is a genius."

"Let's hope so. I've had to walk between here and the mine twice now. I really don't want to do it a third time."

"I'm tired after one time," Nya said. "Low gravity or not, these suits are exhausting."

"Having to walk is a little different than sitting in a comfy chair, isn't it?"

"Respectfully, we do a little more than just sit. *Sir.*" She knew he was teasing and was more than happy to play along.

"Still not as exciting as flying shuttles and fighters though, is it?" Kem asked.

"Not exactly, but at least when I'm driving no one is shooting at me."

"You never experienced any actual combat, though, did you?"

"No, but the simulations are very realistic. So is the ass-chewing you receive from the C.O. after getting shot down."

"Do you miss it?" Kem asked as he leaned on the fender.

"The academy?"

"And flying."

"Flying for sure. The freedom of being alone up in the clouds, then hitting the thrusters and taking off like a missile toward space until you're suddenly floating in silence. It's pretty amazing."

"If you say so."

"You flew?"

"Just the standard shuttle training," Kem explained. "Obviously I didn't enjoy it quite as much as you did."

"It's a great feeling," Nya agreed. "I don't think I was cut out for the military. Too many jerks trying to tear you down because they know they aren't good enough, and way too many rules."

"Hey. I have rules." Nya had to suppress her laughter but mostly failed.

"Sorry Sir. I don't mean any disrespect. In fact, working for you has been the best experience I've had."

"Thanks, I guess."

"Seriously. You run a relaxed crew but you get twice as much out of them. That's impressive."

"I learned that from the first Director I worked for. He made us want to work harder for him so I promised myself if I ever became a Director myself I would treat my crew the same way."

"Well, I'm honored to be part of it. Sir."

"I'm honored to have you," Kem said.

"Thanks."

"Well, I guess we should finish up and get this thing home. I just wish we had a lift. That would make this a lot easier."

"That would be nice," Nya agreed. "At least we'll be able to refit the other transports in the maintenance building." The hexagonal building at the far end of the gas pods didn't just contain spare parts and tools, it also provided a full service shop including an airlock bay to work on the transports without suits. The bottoms of the trucks were flat, with a full-length keyed recess similar to those on top of the pods. The long narrow service lift fit into the recess and then expanded, locking the truck in place for safety. The recesses were also used to lock the transports into the back of the shuttles, allowing them to be carried intact rather than having to be disassembled. That meant the pod receptacles couldn't be used, but someone had figured out years before that a single pod could be loaded onto the transport and then both loaded into the shuttle as a unit. The pod needed to be strapped in, since the weak magnetic keepers were never intended to hold them in place during in-flight turbulence, but it was an effective way to avoid wasting all three slots. The practice wasn't officially sanctioned by the Mining Guild but they usually turned a blind eye in favor of efficiency.

"So what's the plan?" Kem asked.

"I'll run the treads backward just enough to install the rest of the studs, then drive us out of here."

"Let's do it." Nya opened the front of the transport's cab and climbed into the driver's seat while Kem pushed the panels closed. When she powered up the little truck he stepped back until until he could see both treads and waited. Nya slowly twisted the throttle and the tracks began to slip across the rollers. Kem watched carefully until the treads that had been on the bottom were on top. "That's good!" he shouted as he held up his hand. She let go of the throttle and powered down the transport, then climbed out.

After installing the remaining studs Kem and Nya got to work securing the spare seat to the front cradle wall using straps looped through the guide rails.

"I think we're ready, Sir."

"One more thing," Kem told her.

"What's that?"

"We need to go over the route. Without NavSats it's really easy to get lost here."

"I've always been a pretty good natural navigator," Nya said confidently. "If I can get an overview of the area I can get us back no problem."

"Then follow me," Kem said, sweeping his arm toward the top of the hill in front of the truck.

"Up there?" Nya asked.

"Sure. I did it before, and without Ari's cleats." He raised his right leg to show off the sole of his boot and the rows of miniature cleats Ari had engineered to replace the attractors. "Like you said, he's a genius." The pair began climbing the steep slope with far less effort than Kem had experienced before.

"Whoa," Nya said when they reached the top. "What a view."

"Isn't it?"

"How did you get out of the camp, Sir? It's mostly surrounded by hills and the only gap is spanned by the lake."

"See the hill where the dish is mounted?" Kem said, pointing.

"Yes."

"Follow it to the right, where it meets the adjacent hill."

"Okay."

"There is a small gap right where those two hills come together. It's hard to see, especially with everything the same color, but it's there."

"So you drove around that hill and ended up in this little boxed in canyon."

"Right. I was hoping I could drive onto the ridge and get a fix on my location without getting out."

"It's probably a good thing you couldn't," Nya said. "You might have driven right over the other side and ended up in the lake."

"Good point." Kem said with a shiver. "Shall we?"

"Let's do it." They returned to the transport and Kem settled into the rear-facing seat while Nya installed one more strap at his waist to keep him from being ejected.

"Good to go, Sir," she said as she gave the strap one last tug.

"Try to keep it smooth," Kem reminded her. "I may be strapped in but my lunch isn't." The comment prompted him to take an extended draw from his food tube.

"Yes Sir. I'll do my best." Nya climbed back into the cab and again powered up the truck. She performed a quick systems check, then engaged the lights. By then the mist had become considerably thicker as is swirled around the transport, so instead of of illuminating the area ahead the beams simply reflected back into her eyes. She shut down the emitters, then darkened the tint on the canopy until it was almost opaque and activated the full-spectrum sensors. A multi-colored wire-frame rendering of the terrain appeared on the inside of the canopy, recreating the unseen terrain. She grasped the throttle and twisted it forward while tilting the directional stick to the right. Instantly the transport responded by rotating in place until it faced the opposite direction. "Heeyah!"

she shouted. "Thanks Ari!"

"Let's go," Kem said anxiously. Nya pushed the directional stick forward and the transport effortlessly crawled out of the depression. As they retraced Kem's path he repeatedly wiped the methane droplets from his face shield, hoping to calculate their position based on the receding view. It was difficult to make out many details, though, so he relied mostly on his memory of the time it took to navigate the narrow space. "You should see a gap coming up on the left. That's where I entered the canyon."

"Copy that." Nya skillfully guided the transport between the steep walls when the vehicle suddenly snapped to the left and slipped through a narrow passage. Kem winced, anticipating a collision, but the fenders never touched the icy walls and they quickly emerged into the large open plain Kem remembered from his earlier excursion. "No problem," Nya announced in a tone that would have come off as arrogant if she didn't have the skill to back it up.

"Now follow the base of the hill and it will lead us back to the mine."

"I'm on it, Sir." Nya said. The little transport bounced along the pebble-covered surface, jostling the director and his lunch, but not so bad as to cause any real discomfort. Kem continued to wipe his shield, more to enjoy the view at that point than to provide any useful navigation. The truck again snapped to the left and he found himself staring at the distant sun. He adjusted his face shield tint from the forearm controls but the shimmering star quickly disappeared behind a bend and they entered the basin containing the mining complex. Nya skirted the maintenance building and guided the truck along the first row of gas pods. She then swung around the habitat and the transport came to a stop just outside the main airlock. "Thank you for traveling Nya's Moon Tours," the young driver said in a sultry tone.

"Funny girl," Kem said with a laugh. "Now get me out of this contraption." Nya exited the cab and stepped into the cradle, then released the waist belt and helped the Director to his feet.

"I'd say Ari's spikes worked pretty well," she said as she began unstrapping the temporary seat.

"Find Val and get the other transports to the maintenance building. I want them retrofitted right away."

"Yes Sir!" Nya set the bundle of straps in the seat and carried it around to the closest berth. She set it on the ground, then rejoined Kem at the airlock. The director turned the handle and as soon as the door opened they stepped inside. Hopeful, he activated the equalization process but nothing happened.

"I guess they haven't fixed atmo yet."

"Looks that way, Sir." Kem reluctantly opened the access panel and used the yellow handle to manually equalize the pressure.

"That's already getting old," he said, out of breath. Nya turned the inside handle and the doors opened to the quiet interior. "Where is everyone?" He asked as he looked over at the driver.

"Game night?" she joked.

"Get those transports modified."

"Yes Sir." While Nya hurried to the elevator Kem was about to call out when he remembered their suits were set to a private channel. He switched to the base frequency and the speaker in his helmet instantly erupted with overlapping chatter. "Kem to Lue."

"Are you back, Sir?"

"I'm on the ground floor."

"You should come up to Operations." Lue suggested impatiently.

"What's going on?" Kem asked, fearing a major delay.

"We've had another pod failure."

"I guess it's a good thing we didn't start the processor. How much is that going to delay us?"

"Well, we can still start the processor early if we transfer a pod from the end to replace the damaged one. As long as they deliver the replacement within fifty hours we'll be fine."

"That's good news."

"There's something else."

"What's that?"

"We found something."

6

Discovery

"Seriously. Why does everything happen when I'm gone?" Kem asked again as he emerged from the elevator. He spotted Lue at the Mining Operations display table and walked over to join her. "Make sure the suits are outfitted with Ari's cleats. They made a big difference."

"Yes Sir."

"So what's the status?"

"Repairs are underway and we're ready to move the pod if you want to start the mine."

"I'll have to call the Gemisi and ask the Captain how soon they can deliver a replacement pod. Since we're ahead of schedule she shouldn't be too upset."

"We may be ahead but I heard the grid deployment is lagging," Lue said. "Probably *because* they keep having to send extra pods."

"So what is it you found?"

"One of the shuttles found it, just to be clear," Lue said as Cas joined them. The assistant director activated the display table and called up a flat image of the moon's surface without the atmosphere.

"Found what exactly?" Kem asked. Lue pressed the 3D button and the image bulged out of the table, forming a half-sphere model showing one side of the moon. A small blip at the edge of a dark region near the equator slowly pulsed, marking the location of the unidentified object.

"Sorry about the low resolution but this was generated from a single pass during NavSat deployment."

"Why were they mapping the surface?" Kem asked. "I thought the scanners were only used to verify the distance between the surface and satellite."

"They are, but they still require low resolution mapping to calculate the distance. The data simply isn't stored unless something unusual is detected."

"I'm guessing they detected something unusual. What is it?" Kem asked impatiently.

"Oh, sorry." Lue increased the magnification to show a flat round object, but the roughness of the image also scaled up, making details difficult to identify.

"A rock?"

"It's too regular," Lue explained. "Otherwise the computer wouldn't have tagged it for storage."

"Could it be one of our probes?" Kem asked.

"It doesn't match any known configuration," Cas explained. "We ran it through the database three times, just to be sure."

"How big is it?"

"About a meter in diameter."

"Can we get a better scan?" Kem asked.

"Not for a while," Lue explained. "The Captain ordered the shuttles to continue working on the grid while their scientists study the data."

"When they didn't have any luck identifying it they sent the data to us," Cas added.

"Right, because we don't have anything better to do," Kem said with plenty of sarcasm. He leaned in and examined the model more closely. "Are you absolutely sure it isn't an extremely uniform rock?"

"Not that uniform," Cas replied.

"Could it be an enemy probe?"

"It's possible, but as far as we know they haven't made it out this far yet."

"And you're sure it's not one of ours?" Kem asked, still unwilling to accept a third explanation. "Maybe something new we haven't been shown yet?"

"No sir," Lue replied. "We didn't deploy any ground probes, and all NavSats and orbital probes are accounted for. Besides, this thing is definitely round, not hexagonal."

"You two do realize what you're telling me, right?" Kem asked.

"I do," Lue said. "What's wrong, are you afraid of little pink men?"

"Have you contacted the Gemisi?" Kem asked, ignoring his assistant's mocking.

"No Sir. I wanted to fill you in first."

"Right." Kem leaned on the table and stared at the object as his mind raced to come up with a logical explanation. After a full minute he straightened up and looked across at Lue and Cas. "Where exactly is it located?"

"It's about ten degrees below the equator," Cas replied.

"Can we get there in a transport?"

"Getting stuck once wasn't enough?" Lue asked.

"We have the spikes."

"True, but even with them the transports are so light you're still going to have trouble getting traction."

"What if we loaded a pod with extra equipment and furniture to add weight?" Kem suggested.

"That would help, but the transports still only carry one person," Lue reminded him. "You would never send someone else on a mission like that alone." Kem was about to argue the point but relented.

"I guess you're right," he said. "Puttering around the base isn't quite the same as trekking halfway across the moon."

"Exactly."

"That settles it," Kem said. "Call the Gemisi and tell them we need the rover."

"The Captain is never going to agree to that," Lue said. "You know what a stickler she is for schedules."

"Mat and I go away back. She'll listen to me."

* * *

No, Kem," the Captain's voice stated firmly. *"We're in the middle of grid deployment here. You know I can't spare a shuttle just so you can go off on some crazy adventure."*

"Are you kidding?" Kem asked. "You saw the data. Unless it's the most perfectly formed block of ice in history it must be artificial, and it's definitely not one of ours."

"I'm sorry, Kem."

"What happened to you?" Kem asked angrily. "You used to be so eager to explore the universe, and now you don't even want to check out one object on one moon."

"That was before I had an entire ship under my command and a career to think about."

"Are we not supposed to investigate any and all anomalies?"

"Not at the expense of mining operations. If we delay the start-up by even one day the Board will have both our asses."

"You think I don't know that?" Kem leaned on the console and took a deep breath. "Look, Mat. The Board can't say a damn thing if we're ahead of schedule, right?"

"Maybe, but you know how they are. These projects are planned down to the last detail. I can't just send a shuttle down

any time you want."

"How will they know?"

"Just a moment" There was a long break before the Captain finally spoke again. *"You can have the rover."*

"Are you sure?"

"I'll send it down as soon as I can."

"Thanks Mat." Kem paused, unsure how his next request would go over. "I do have one more favor to ask."

"And what is that?"

"We had another roller malfunction."

"So now I'm supposed to send you the rover and another replacement pod?"

"Actually, no."

"Then what?"

"Correct me if I'm wrong, but you were already scheduled to send a shuttle down with a supply pod in twelve hours. Then in another twelve the regularly scheduled supply runs begin until the gas pods are full and you start hauling them back to the ship."

"That's right, but the rover requires all three slots on the shuttle, which means I would have to send your supplies on a later flight."

"That flight will only include a single pod, right?"

"Right."

"So, send the rover down on the next shuttle and send the gas pod with both supply pods next time."

"Won't delaying the supplies put you out?"

"We'll be fine." Kem reassured her. "The deliveries are scheduled early anyway to make sure we don't run out of food."

"What about your start-up?"

"Even if we wait for the new pod we will still be ahead of schedule. In fact, we could start the processor now if we wanted," Kem said.

"How?"

"If you agree to this my crew can transfer one of the pods from the far end to the empty rack," Kem explained. "Once that's done we can override the computer and start the processor any time we want."

"That's great, but what happens when you get to the last pod and still don't have the replacement?"

"Are you saying you might be late with the supply run?"

"Well, no."

"Then it won't be a problem." There was a pause before the Captain responded.

"You make a good case."

"That's why I'm the Director."

"One question. How are you going to navigate without the grid in place?"

"We'll use the rover's gyro-tracker to trace our route. Those things are usually pretty accurate."

"But without the mapping you'll have no way to know what the terrain is. You could drive right into a box canyon or a lake and get stuck."

"I'm sure that wouldn't happen," Kem said as he shifted nervously in his suit. "Even so, is there any way you can send us the shuttle scans? I can take Tam along to interpret them."

"We only have the data from the pass that detected the object, so you won't have any mapping until you get close to it."

"That's better than not having any." There was a longer pause as Kem anxiously waited for the Captain's answer.

"If this goes south I'm blaming it all on you."

"Thanks, Mat. I'll owe you."

"You got that right," the Captain said. *"It'll take us some time to dig out the rover, so I'll give you a call when we're ready to send it down."*

"Copy that. We're having a little trouble with our atmo, anyway, so we need to get that sorted out."

"What kind of trouble?"

"We're not sure yet," Kem reluctantly admitted to the Captain. "It could just be the sensors. That reminds me, could you check your inventory for the portable air monitors? We seem to be missing them."

"Those should have been sent down with the first set of furnishings."

"I agree, but we haven't found them yet."

"I'll have the supply team double check and let you know what we find."

"Thanks."

"No problem. I'll let you know when we're ready. Gemisi out."

"Thanks, Mat." Kem thought for a moment, then turned to Lue. "Call Ula and tell her to get that pod moved as soon as possible."

"Yes Sir." While the assistant director took over the com panel Cas pulled Kem aside.

"So you're really going out there?"

"That's the plan."

"Who are you taking with you?"

"Other than Tam I hadn't really thought about that yet," Kem answered. "Any suggestions?"

"You should take the Doctor, just in case."

"I'd prefer to keep Rue and her staff here," Kem said. "Just in case."

"You still need a medic of some kind."

"We've all had basic medical training."

"Take Nya," Lue suggested, having finished relaying Kem's order. "Not only is she the best driver but she went through advanced medical training. Val and Sal can handle pod transfers while she's gone."

"That's a good idea," Kem said. "Anyone else?"

"I don't know who else we can spare," Cas said. "I'll need all hands on deck to start the mine."

"The three of us should be enough."

"If there's nothing else, I need to bring my crew up to speed on the new plan."

"Of course. I should let Nya and Tam know they're coming with me so they can get ready." Kem patted the Chief on the shoulder and headed for the elevator.

7

Special Delivery

Kem managed to get a few hours of sleep while Ula and her team continued to troubleshoot the habitat's environmental issue. After waking up he snapped a fresh food pack into his suit and took the elevator up to meet with Lue for an update. When he reached the tower Cas was busy monitoring the mine while the Assistant Director waited in Flight Control for the shuttle to arrive. Lon, a communications technician, was seated at the console checking readings, pressing buttons, and chatting with the shuttle as it descended.

"Good morning, Director Kem," Lue said cheerfully.

"Are you sure it's morning?" Kem asked.

"According to the system clock," Lue said after glancing at the display. "What's wrong? You don't like living at the north pole?"

"To be honest, no," Kem replied firmly. "I know the concentration of methane is higher up here but I'd still prefer to have proper day."

"Don't forget, this moon is tidal locked to the planet, so even if we weren't at the pole the days would last ten times longer than home."

"I'm not sure that would be any better."

"You could always ask for a position on the Gemisi," Lue teased. "I thought the view from the ring was quite spectacular."

"Sure, if you like fake gravity." While they waited for the

shuttle to arrive Kem changed the subject. "What is the status of the grid?"

"Anxious to get back out there?"

"That, and get the radios to work beyond line of sight."

"Good luck with that. This moon is a harsh one," Lue said.

"You could try the Onslaught code," Lon said after overhearing the conversation.

"What is that?" Lue asked, prompting the tech to turn around and face the Directors.

"When the Mark Ten suits first came out there was a rumor floating around the tech community about a secret code that could unlock all communication channels, including the new encrypted military channels."

"Why would they have that built into the suits?"

"It was supposed to be temporary to allow the suits to be tested more efficiently but it was never removed from the computer code once production began. Either that or the designer deliberately left a back door."

"Even if that were true, how would it help us?" Lue asked.

"In addition to unlocking the channels it's supposed to boost the transceiver by diverting power from the helmet lights and food pump."

"That might be useful," Kem said. "Especially if we get stuck out there."

"Just don't let the military catch you using it," Lue said.

"Exactly," Lon agreed. "If you hate the gravity in the ring, try a moon-based prison."

"Are you speaking from experience?" Lue asked.

"What? No Ma'am," the technician replied nervously.

"Relax. I'm just messing with you."

"It probably doesn't even work," Kem added. "I've heard plenty of rumors like that over the years."

"The source I heard it from is pretty reliable," Lon replied.

"You never tried it yourself?" Kem asked.

"No Sir. Assistant Director Lue is right. Too risky."

"How is it supposed to be activated?" Kem asked. He couldn't see the others' faces but knew both were staring at him nervously. "I'm just curious." Lon motioned for Kem and Lue to move closer.

"All you have to do is open your suit's control pad and enter zero three two five, point one six five five," Lon whispered.

"That's it?" Lue asked.

"That's it."

"How do you deactivate it?" Kem asked.

"You reenter the same code."

"That seems far too simple," Lue said. "What if someone accidentally entered that?" The statement made Lon shake his head.

"The odds of a person randomly entering that exact sequence are..."

"Let's find out," Kem said. He opened his control pad and began entering the code when Lue stopped him.

"Better not, Sir."

"What is the military going to do, show up out of nowhere and arrest me?"

"Arresting you would be nice."

"Copy that Shuttle One," Lon said as he spun around to face his console. "Here they come!" Kem and Lue both looked left across the small lake just as a shadow passed over the far hill and quickly circled the complex. The red domed lights encircling the landing pad increased in intensity and the thick hydrocarbon mist began to swirl even more violently. After a few seconds the shuttle appeared, it's navigation strobes repeatedly lighting up the entire control tower while the stabilization jets fired wildly to keep it upright.

"That is exactly why I hate flying," Kem said. As soon as the shuttle touched down in the center of the pad the strobes ceased and the veil of mist settled around the vehicle. Once the red glow from the main engines finally faded the rear panel began to rise up and out of the way, eventually folding almost in half to form a canopy over the cargo hold. Inside there were two cargo pods resting in the lower receptacles, with the main body of the rover secured in the upper slot. The shuttle's bright service lights came on, illuminating the areas around the hold and cockpit. That served as the cue for the waiting transports, scurrying effortlessly along the frozen ground toward the landing pad.

"Ari did good," Lue said proudly. Before Kem could agree, though, the first transport transitioned onto the landing pad ramp but came to a stop, even though the tracks continued to rotate around the carriages. "I guess I spoke too soon." Lue was about to call the driver when the tracks stopped moving.

"Wait," Kem said as he placed a gloved hand on Lue's arm. They continued to watch when the transport suddenly lurched forward, continuing up the ramp and toward the shuttle. When it arrived it rotated in place and backed up to the waiting rover.

"I'm impressed." Lue said.

"Ari said they would still be magnetic, but I didn't even think about needing them on the ramp."

"That should earn him a nice bonus from the Board."

"I already added a recommendation in my mission log," Kem said. He and Lue continued watching as the body of the rover slowly slid out of the cargo hold, supported by temporary frames bolted to the roof and undercarriage. Without the tracks attached the vehicle resembled a flattened cargo pod with windows lining the sloped upper half. The flat nose was capped with an angled windscreen, which was complimented by the rearward sloping back window. Once the rover body had cleared the cargo hold the transport's cradle rose up to meet it. As with the pods, the tapered shipping frame fit into the cradle with the rover's fenders straddling the transport fenders. The cradle and rover slowly lowered into place and the transport pulled away, quickly replaced by the next.

"Where do you want it?" Nya's voice asked.

"Set the cabin next to the airlock and put the two pods side by side a few meters behind it," Kem instructed the driver.

"Copy that." The transport responded by turning left and driving between the landing pad and habitat before disappearing from view. By then the second transport had retrieved one of the parts pods and made it's way down the ramp, following the same path as Nya. The third transport soon followed with the second pod just as Nya reappeared hauling one of the empty supply pods.

"That was fast," Lue said.

"She's good," Kem replied. They continued to watch as Nya backed up to the shuttle and raised the empty pod, loading it into the upper slot. Once the cradle of her transport returned to it's normal position she pulled away toward the port side of the shuttle and spun around to face it. The lead driver monitored the other transports as they repeated the procedure with two more empty pods. As soon as the last truck pulled away the cargo hold door unfolded and lowered into place.

"Pods are secure," Nya's voice announced as she spun the transport around to leave the pad.

"Copy that," the pilot's voice replied. *"We have one more package for you."*

"Another package?" Lue asked. Kem leaned over and pressed the com button on the flight control console.

"Tower to Shuttle One, what package is that?" the Director asked.

"A passenger." Before Kem could ask who it was a figure

appeared from the port side of the shuttle carrying a modest-sized silver case. The insignia on the pressure suit was colored green, indicating the science department, but Kem couldn't make out their position or name.

"Who is that?" Lue asked as the unknown scientist began walking across the landing pad toward the habitat.

"I don't know," Kem replied. When the visitor descended the ramp and stepped onto the frozen ground their right foot shot out ahead of them and they barely caught themselves before falling. "They certainly don't seem to be comfortable with low gravity."

"That's exactly why I spent so much time in the hub," Lue said. He was referring to the huge cylindrical room on the cargo ship where the six spokes of the rotating wheel came together. Within the hub the six elevator doors were arranged around a large opening in the center, allowing passage between the fore and aft sections of the ship. Traveling to the ring was a simple matter of waiting for the corresponding door to come around, then grabbing onto one of the handles next to it and entering the elevator car. Once inside, the magnetic flooring allowed the crew member to anchor and visually orient themselves before entering the nearly full gravity of the ring. Because of the size of the hub, the outside wall of the surrounding room possessed a low gravity similar to that of the moon's surface. Like the hydroponics catwalks, it had also become a favorite hangout for many of the crew, particularly the miners, since it provided a perfect place to practice walking on the moon's surface.

"They probably don't know about the atmo problem," Kem said. He again leaned over and pressed the com button. "Hey, Nya."

"Go ahead."

"Hurry up and get those transports stowed and show our new guest how to operate the airlock, then tell them to come up to

Operations."

"Copy that."

"After that I need you and the other drivers to start unpacking the rover."

"Yes Sir."

"Who do you suppose they sent?" Lue asked.

"Maybe it's another geologist. Mat was pretty worried about us going out without the mapping done." While waiting for their visitor to arrive Kem walked over to Mine Operations to get an update. "What's the word, Cas?"

"Everything is running perfectly," Cas reported. "Good flow into the separator and the system just started filling the first pods."

"That's good news."

"So they sent someone down on the shuttle?"

"Looks that way," Kem replied. "Someone from the science department."

"Why would they send someone from Science?"

"I'm sure we'll find out soon enough."

"Maybe they're here to help with atmo."

"If that were true wouldn't they send someone from engineering?"

"Who knows." The elevator indicator began to glow so Kem and Lue converged at the doors just as they opened and their guest stepped out.

8

The Consultant

"Ren from the exoscience department, reporting as ordered," the woman stated as she wiped the semi-frozen slush from her suit.

"At ease, Ren. I'm Director Kem and this is Assistant Director Lue." Even though he couldn't see her face Kem could tell the visitor was fairly young.

"Sorry, Sir. The *Captain* is a stickler for procedure."

"I'm well aware of that, believe me," Kem said. "We're a bit more informal here on the ground."

"Yes Sir."

"I apologize for needing the suits. We're having a little trouble with atmo."

"No need, Sir," the visitor replied. "Field work is a necessity in my line of work, so I've spent a good part of my career in pressure suits."

"Really?" Lue asked. "You seem a bit shaky in the low gravity."

"It's not the gravity," she replied. "I wasn't expecting the ground to be so slick."

"We had to fabricate special cleats for the boots," Kem explained. "Before you go out again I'll have a set made for you."

"Thank you Sir."

"So what exactly is your field of study?"

"Exoluinguistics."

"Alien languages?"

"Correct."

"I don't recall seeing you on the ship."

"My team isn't part of the mining operation so we mostly keep to ourselves," Ren explained.

"Team?" Lue asked.

"Every mission is now required to have a team on board with a linguist, a geologist, a biologist, and an engineer. All specializing in exocentric studies."

"And why is that?" Lue asked.

"You never know who may be out there," the linguist replied.

"Are you saying these missions have people like you in case we run into alien life?"

"Not specifically. We mainly come along to handle the situations they can't predict."

"You were sent down because of the object they found," Kem concluded.

"That's correct, Sir."

"I told you so," Lue mocked again.

"Enough with the sir," Kem said to Ren, ignoring Lue for the moment.

"Sorry, Si...sorry."

"Why didn't the rest of your team come with you?"

"We were unable to identify the object from the shuttle scan, so they wanted to collect more data before sending down the entire team. Until then San is trying to clean up the existing scans, when he's not studying the core samples you sent up, that is. Boe is coordinating with the bridge to get a better set of scans."

"So you got stuck with us."

"I wouldn't say stuck. I relish any chance to visit a new world."

"You see?" Kem said to Lue. "She understands exploring."

"Right," Lue said, then turned back to their guest. "What happens if the object isn't artificial, or doesn't contain any writing? Won't your visit be wasted?"

"Not at all," Ren replied. "Linguistics is my primary area of expertise, but I also have a background in engineering," Ren explained.

"So you're performing double duty," Kem said. "You only listed three members of your team."

"You're very perceptive, Director. That's why they sent me first. If I determine the object was made by intelligent life then I'll report my findings and the team will study it in greater detail to establish a possible origin."

"You mean develop a threat assessment," Kem said.

"Well, yes. That too."

"Paranoid much?" Lue said, only half joking.

"We have to be careful but it isn't only about threats," Ren added. "This moon has the potential to yield some significant discoveries. In fact, I volunteered for this mission as soon as I read the preliminary reports."

"What's so special about it?"

"Are you kidding?" Ren replied. Her sudden enthusiasm and lack of formality both surprised and pleased Kem. "This moon doesn't just have an atmosphere, but actual weather. There are lakes of methane replenished by huge raindrops and ground and rocks made of frozen water."

"Tell us about it," Lue said while looking toward the expanse of glass surrounding them. "We're lucky to be on schedule."

"To you the weather is an inconvenience," the linguist continued. "To those of us in exosciences it's the best chance we've had in years to discover new life. Needless to say, San is *very* excited."

"Because of the weather?"

"Partly, but also the ingredients." She hurried over to the nearest display table and quickly brought up a model of the moon before the mine had been built. She waited impatiently for Kem and Lue to join her, then continued as she stared at the display. "This place is fascinating. First of all the methane resides in a nitrogen-rich atmosphere."

"That's kinda why we're here," Lue said. "The nitrogen powers our building mechanisms and aids in the methane conversion."

"Of course, but there are other hydrocarbons present, as well, not to mention a host of more complex compounds."

"And why is that significant?" Kem asked. The linguist walked to the glass panel overlooking the lake and gestured toward it.

"As I said, the lakes are made up of liquid methane fed by the rain." She looked at the two confused miners, then shook her head. "The other hydrocarbons in the atmosphere would suggest the methane is being broken down by solar radiation and yet it's being replenished."

"Which is good for us." Lue stated. "So what's the problem?"

"It's a question, not a problem," Ren said.

"And what is that?"

"Where does the methane come from?"

"The lakes?"

"We believe the lakes are the result, not the source."

"So what is the answer?" Kem asked.

"One theory suggest that at least some of the larger formations we've detected on the surface could be cryovolcanoes, although we've yet to witness an actual eruption."

"Lucky for us," Lue said.

"Maybe your geologist can help Boe with that investigation now that your operation is up and running."

"I'm a bit confused," Lue said. "What does any of this have to do with a linguist or a biologist?"

"Well, the other working theory suggests that the source of the methane is biologic."

"Bugs farting?" Kem asked.

"Probably not insects in this environment," Ren replied as she tried to stifle her laughter. "More likely bacteria or other simple organisms."

"That explains your biologist's interest, but what about you?"

"Let me guess, you're here to talk to them," Lue teased.

"Talk, no." the linguist answered, undaunted. "Language isn't only about audible speech, or even writing. It can be composed of scents, sounds, or even colors."

"You're not really here to study how bacteria communicate, though, are you?" Kem asked.

"Not really, no. If the object is artificial then my job is to look for signs of language and try to translate it."

"And what happens then?" Lue asked.

"That depends on what it says."

"So what's the plan?" Kem asked.

"I was about to ask you that. Until we reach the object I'm just along for the ride."

"Well, I could arrange a room for you but you're not going to do much freshening up."

"I'm fine, Director. I'm anxious to get out there."

"Then the next order of business is getting the rover assembled," Kem explained. "You said you're also an engineer?"

"Junior, but yes."

"You're welcome to help with the assembly."

"I'd be happy to," Ren said. "With your ongoing atmo problem it sounds like you need all the help you can get."

"True, but I'm still putting the entire engineering crew on the rover. I want it ready as soon as possible." Kem paused to activate his com. "Kem to Nya."

"Go ahead Sir."

"Have you unpacked the rover yet?"

"Affirmative. We're going over the parts list now to confirm everything is here."

"Good. Once you're done I want you to stay put. I'll meet you out there with the engineering team."

"Yes Sir."

"Kem to Ula."

"Go ahead," the chief engineer's voice replied.

"Have you found anything?"

"Not yet. There doesn't seem to be anything wrong with the processors, but we still haven't found a leak. Any luck with the portable monitors?"

"Mat says they were sent down with the first load of furniture."

"Nonsense. I helped unload those pods myself."

"That's what I said, but her manifest shows two monitors in pod 332."

"I'll double check, but I'm sure I would remember seeing them if they were in there."

"That will have to wait. I have another task for you."

"What is it?"

"Nya's got the rover unpacked. As soon as she confirms the parts are all there I want you and your team to meet me at the airlock to help assemble it."

"What about the atmo problem?"

"With all of us working on the rover it shouldn't take too long. Then you can get back to troubleshooting."

"Yes Sir."

"She didn't sound happy," Lue commented.

"She's frustrated, just like the rest of us," Kem said.

"Nya to Director Kem."

"Go ahead Nya."

"We've gone over the manifest and everything is here."

"Good work."

"Ask her if they found any portable monitors," Lue suggested with a chuckle.

"If only." Kem replied. "Nya, sit tight, we're on our way."

"Copy that."

"Shall we?" Kem said to Ren as he gestured toward the elevator.

"My pleasure."

9

The Rover

When the outer door opened the wind continued to swirl the orange mist around the complex, constantly changing the visibility. Kem led Ren, Ula, and the two members of her engineering team out of the airlock and joined the three drivers who were finishing unpacking the individual parts containers. The detached tread assemblies were wide enough to stand upright on their own, allowing temporary power modules to be attached so they could be driven with a small wired remote. Nya's team had already rolled them out of their pods and parked them just behind the body of the rover, which still rested on it's temporary shipping frame.

"What's the status?" Kem asked Nya.

"We're ready to go," the driver reported. She stepped over to a large black box and opened the lid, revealing a neatly organized set of matte black tools. "They included everything we need to put it together."

"You two can help me get the tracks into position." Ula said to Ari and Von.

"Yes Ma'am."

"What can we do?" Kem asked his engineer.

"The rest of you can remove the upper shipping frame and start installing the interior pieces," Ula explained.

"Is it okay to do that before the drive system is installed?"

"Sure."

"You heard Ula," Kem said to the drivers. "Start at the front of the cabin and work your way back."

"I'll take care of the top frame," Ren offered.

"Are you sure?"

"No problem." The guest snatched a wrench from the tool case, then used the footholds built into the carriage cover to climb onto the fender and then the roof of the rover. The shipping frame was attached with the same bolts that secured the communications module. The 25 centimeter high module began just behind the cockpit and stretched nearly to the back of the vehicle. The front half of the module was open, like a tray, and housed sensors and the motorized base for the communications dish, which had yet to be installed. The back half, however, was solid and had a tight H-patterned seam molded into the surface. The two sections also appeared to be separate pieces. While Ren got to work removing the bolts, Nya opened the rear-facing door, which separated across the middle just like the transport bubbles. Similarly, that allowed the angled rear window to hinge upward to form a canopy while the lower half swung down and flattened to form a ramp. Sal and Nya each grabbed a cockpit seat and carried them inside, followed by Kem and Val each with a passenger seat. The fixed front seats were bolted directly to the raised area that ran across the cockpit, securing them in place. The passenger seats, on the other hand, were very different. They were mounted on pedestals that allowed them to turn 360 degrees. They also had reclining backs and each tandem pair could be reconfigured into a medical bed. All the seats included a recess for the pressure suit packs, just like the transports. Once the cockpit seats were mounted Nya and Sal began performing system checks while Kem and Val retrieved the last two passenger seats. When they started mounting them Kem noticed a track built into the floor that ran from the right rear seat pedestal to the rear center of the cabin.

"Hey, Nya," Kem said. "Why does this seat have a track?" The driver turned around and peeked between the front seats.

"Oh. That's a just-in-case. Sir." Kem was about to ask her to expand on her answer but she had already returned to her diagnostics. Once they had the seats installed he Val stepped out of the rover. By then the engineers had driven the track assemblies into place below each fender and adjusted them back and forth until they were perfectly positioned.

"Do you need us to get out?" Nya asked.

"No." Ula said. "Once we get these attached I'll need you to raise the suspension so we can remove the lower frame." Ula then stepped back and looked up at Ren. "You may want to hurry up with that."

"Actually, I'm done," The linguist tilted the frame up and slid it toward the back where Kem and Val were waiting. "If someone will hand me the dish I can get that installed." Kem reached up to grab the frame while Val retrieved the dish and mast assembly from the pod. Once the frame had been lowered he Val handed the dish up to Ren. "Thanks."

"No problem." Val said with a slightly flirtatious tone. While Ren attached the mast to the motor assembly the engineers bolted the tracks to the undercarriage of the rover. The dish only took a minute so Ren climbed down and helped remove the bolts holding the lower shipping frame to the underside of the rover body. Once that was done and the four temporary power modules were removed, Ula slapped the side cockpit window.

"Ready when you are," she said to Nya.

"Copy that." Nya activated the ride controls and after a moment the body began to rise, separating it from the frame. Ula and Ren pulled it out and Nya lowered the rover to the resting position. She and Sal climbed out and closed the rear panels, then joined the rest of the team as they gathered at the side to admire their handiwork.

"Now that's more like it," Kem said as he beamed inside his helmet. At just over 9 meters long the fully assembled rover wasn't much larger than the transports, but the low-slung cabin and heavy-duty track assemblies gave it a heft the small trucks simply couldn't match. The rover was also capable of much higher speeds than the transports, with powerful motors driving the tracks on an extremely compliant suspension. The panels covering the track carriages kept large debris out of the rollers, further streamlining the appearance. Even with the vehicle sitting stationary a sense of speed was suggested by the forward-hanging cockpit and sloped back glass. For maximum visibility emission strips all around provided an abundance of light, while large full-spectrum sensors fore and aft could see through even the harshest conditions. Since the rover was never intended to drive aboard a ship the heavy-duty tracks traded the cushioned treads and magnetic attractors of the transports for metal pads with multiple cleats for more aggressive traction. The communications dish Ren had just installed could rotate 360 degrees and tilt a full 90 degrees, allowing line-of-sight as well as satellite communications.

"Shall we take this thing for a spin?" Nya asked.

"Why not?" Kem answered, amused by the driver's enthusiasm while quickly adopting it.

"Have fun," Ula said. "While you're out here playing with your new toy we'll be inside figuring out what's wrong with atmo."

"Don't worry," Kem replied. "Once we're done we'll come in and give you a hand."

"Sure, sure."

"I'll give you a hand," Ren offered and quickly followed the engineers.

"Looks like it's just us four," Kem said to the drivers. "Shall we?" Nya didn't have to be asked twice. She opened the rear panels and climbed inside. The other two drivers waited, but Kem gestured for them to enter ahead of him. Once they boarded the rover he followed them inside and closed the panels. The main cabin was just tall enough to stand up in with the suits on, with room to walk between the four passenger seats. Once Nya and Val had wedged themselves into the cockpit Sal and Kem settled into the row directly behind them. "How much charge do we have?" Nya powered up the rover and quickly scanned the system screens.

"The batteries are almost fully charged. Should I initiate the reactor?"

"No, let's hold off until we're ready to look for that object," Kem replied. "The batteries should be enough for a quick trip around the complex."

"Copy that." Nya engaged the filtration system and within a minute the moon's gases that had drifted into the cabin had been scrubbed, leaving the invisible nitrogen. "That's better."

"Can this thing generate a normal atmosphere?" Kem asked.

"Yes, but only in the case of a suit failure or medical emergency," Nya replied. "Speaking of which, we should have a full set of medical supplies on board so we can perform any kind of treatment including basic surgery."

"Let's hope we don't need that," Kem said.

"Copy that."

"Let's go," Kem said. Nya gripped the control yoke and rolled the throttle forward. With a mild jerk the heavy rover began moving so Nya guided it around the contour of the habitat until the maintenance building came into view at the end of the complex.

"Let's see how she picks up," Kem suggested.

"Yes Sir," Nya said. She happily twisted the throttle all the way and the rover took off like a missile. "Heeya!" the head driver yelled as they quickly reached the edge of the basin.

"Easy," Kem warned. "One good bump and you'll launch us into orbit."

"I think we're safe," Nya said, knowing the Director was only having fun. "This thing is still plenty heavy, even on this moon." She backed off the throttle slightly and spun the rover 180 degrees, then accelerated again, racing across the flat and around the narrow gap between the landing pad and the lake. Her nervous subordinates gripped their armrests tightly but Kem enjoyed every second of the ride his driver was providing. Nya guided the rover around the pad, then steered hard to the left, circling the mine intake until they passed between it and the pad again, making a full figure-eight. When they reached the habitat she stopped in front of the airlock and settled back in her seat. "That was fun."

"Another round?" Kem suggested. Nya raised a gloved hand, but then reached over and touched Val on the shoulder.

"Your turn," she said. Val nervously gripped his yoke and the rover slowly pulled away from the habitat. He followed a similar route, but at half the speed. After passing around the maintenance building he headed back, but opted not to drive around the landing pad. Instead he returned to the starting point and held the yoke for a minute, relishing the brief but satisfying experience.

"It sure doesn't feel heavy," he said.

"Well, we are driving in fifteen percent gravity, so that helps," Nya explained. "Even so, I bet this thing would be a lot of fun in the dunes and canyons back home."

"Sal's turn," Kem announced.

"That's okay, Sir," the junior driver said. "I'm good."

"Are you sure?" Nya asked. "You won't get another chance until we get back."

"I'm sure."

"Sir, what about you?" Nya asked Kem.

"I'm sure I'll get a chance to drive it during the mission." He was about to stand up when Sal interrupted.

"Do you really think it's an alien object?"

"Is that what the crew is saying?" Kem asked.

"Yes Sir."

"Well, we're pretty sure it's not one of ours, but that doesn't mean anything yet. It's probably an enemy probe that we simply haven't seen before."

"It would be amazing if it was from a new species," Sal said. "Scary too."

"That it would be," Kem agreed. "Let's not get ahead of ourselves until we know what we're dealing with. We're still not sure it's even artificial."

"Yes Sir."

"If you're done with the test drives we should get inside and get ready to go."

"Let me get a little closer to the door," Nya said. She pulled the rover forward, then spun it to the right, aiming the back toward the habitat entrance. After backing up to within two meters of the building she set the brakes and shut down the power. Kem turned his seat toward the aisle and stood up, then walked to the back and opened the panels. Once he and the drivers had exited the rover Kem closed the door panels and secured them, then led his crew into the airlock.

10

Solutions

When the inner doors opened the three drivers slipped passed the Director and headed for the elevators.

"Make sure charge and reload your suit," Kem said to Nya.

"Yes Sir." Once they entered the car and the door closed Kem switched to the general channel.

"Kem to Ula."

"Go ahead."

"What's your location?"

"I'm in my quarters."

"Shouldn't you be working?" Kem teased the Chief Engineer.

"If you weren't the boss I might ask the same thing," Ula replied. *"Seriously, though, I had to replace my food pack. I'm not used to wearing these damn suits for so long."*

"Tell me about it."

"How was your test drive?"

"It was good. I definitely feel better with Nya driving. So what's the latest on atmo?"

"I think we figured it out," Ula replied. *"Well, Ren did."*

"That's good news," Kem said, relieved. "What was it?"

"If you want to meet us in the shop I can show you."

"Be right there." Kem stepped to the elevator and pressed the button. There was a low hum as the car arrived and the doors opened. He stepped in and pressed ONE before continuing the conversation. "Is it something you can fix right away, or do you still have to figure out a solution?"

"We're pretty close."

"Copy that." The doors opened and Kem stepped out and went straight to the maintenance shop. When he entered Ula and Ren were standing at the work bench with several sensor modules scattered across the surface. They were 5 centimeter wide hexagonal discs with a small hole in the center. A metal lubrication sprayer also sat on the bench near the back. "Impress me," Kem said.

"As I said, Ren figured it out."

"Well, I can't take all the credit," the linguist began. "I was thinking about the slush on my suit when I first arrived and had a hunch."

"Continue," Kem urged.

"As you know, the walls of these structures are fully outfitted ahead of time, making assembly much more efficient."

"I do know a thing or two about off-world habitats," Kem said as he tapped the gray insignia on his suit. "That's why I get to be the boss."

"Yes Sir," Ren said, unsure if the Director was serious or having fun at her expense. "Anyway, when we set up one of these bases on a body with no atmosphere it's not a problem, but when we come to a place like this the sensors can become contaminated during the time the panels are exposed."

"Which is why procedure calls for them to be flushed with nitrogen."

"Which we did," Ula added quickly.

"I'm still waiting for the part where you fixed it," Kem said flatly.

"Right. Sorry Sir," Ren said. "The thicker atmosphere means the methane takes longer to condense and reach the surface, so part of it ends up being broken down by ultraviolet light into different hydrocarbons and other gases, which are eventually ionized into the mixture that creates the orange color we see. Once that mixture reaches the ground they combine with the water ice in varying percentages, creating regions ranging from yellow to reddish-brown.

"And the geology lesson is important why?"

"Sorry, Sir. The winds then pick up trace amounts from the surface and deposit them on anything that happens to be nearby."

"Like our panels," Kem concluded.

"Exactly."

"But you said you flushed them," Kem said to Ula.

"We did."

"It's really a fault in the original procedure laid out by the engineers back home," Ren explained. "The nitrogen will remove any liquid or rocky dust from the sensors, but on this moon the broken down hydrocarbons become charged, both from the original ionization process and from being dragged across the frozen surface. As it turns out, that makes the particles far more attractive to the membrane inside the sensors. The condensation was removed but it left behind a layer of solids which tricked the sensors into thinking the atmo still contained high levels of the outside air."

"So it was just the sensors."

"Well, yes and no," Ula added. "With the sensors providing incorrect data the processors were trying to compensate for environmental conditions that didn't exist. Once we've cleaned them properly the processors will function normally."

"That's good news," Kem said, relieved. "How will you fix it if the nitrogen flush didn't work?"

"We've been experimenting with several combinations of inert solvents to clean the sensors without damaging them." Ula grabbed the sprayer and held it up. "Once we have the proper formula we can use this to rinse them properly."

"How long will it take?"

"We were about to test another formula. If it works we should be able to restore atmo within two hours."

"Damn," Kem said softly. "I was hoping to get out of this suit before we leave."

"We'll try to get it done by the time you're ready to go," Ula told Kem.

"Get to it." Once Ula left Kem turned to Ren. "I'll have a room assigned to you and have a fresh suit delivered, just in case."

"Thank you, Sir."

"Do you need anything else to help you get ready for our little adventure?"

"Just my case."

"I'll have it taken to your room."

"Thank you. If it's okay with you I'd like to continue helping the engineering team. The sooner we get those sensors cleaned the sooner you'll have proper atmo."

"Of course. I appreciate your help." Kem left the shop and returned to the elevator and pressed FOUR.

* * *

As soon as Kem stepped out of the elevator he looked around the tower until he spotted Lue and Tam in Exploration studying a model of the moon's surface. Before joining them, though, he turned toward Mining Operations and met with Cas.

"How's it going?" he asked the Chief.

"Still humming along," Cas reported. "We're filling the second row now."

"Are you sure we'll get the replacement pod in time?" Kem asked nervously.

"As long as it's relatively close to being on schedule we'll be fine."

"Any idea what cause the failure?"

"Well, after Ula told me about the interior sensors it's certainly possible the same thing happened to the couplers." Cas walked to the display table and called up a model of a pod rack and zoomed in on the corner. The supply lines attached to the pod inside a small recess in the lower corner. "As you know, the fill sensors are built into the pod and the transport sensors use radio waves to detect the presence of a vehicle."

"Right. But the habitat sensors were reading the composition of the deposits and mistaking it for the outside atmosphere. The gas couplers don't work like that."

"True, but the deposits can still affect them. The two halves use a light emitter and receiver tuned to a specific wavelength. When the coupler is rotated into position the two halves are lined up and the receiver sees the light from the emitter. When they separate, though, the light isn't visible and the rollers can be engaged."

"So the deposits tricked the sensors into thinking they were separated."

"Correct. During the test the driver engaged the rollers, but because the sensor was telling them the coupler was open they tried moving the pod even though the lines were still attached."

"Who was the driver?"

"Nya."

"You must be right," Kem said. "There is no way she would have mistakenly initiated a transfer." Kem said confidently.

"None of them would have, but even if she had the system wouldn't allow it under normal conditions."

"So what can we do about it?" Kem asked. "If we shut the mine down then all of your work to get it up and running ahead of schedule will have been for nothing."

"I can help with that." Ula's voice announced. Kem and Cas turned to see the chief engineer approaching them.

"Did you figure out your formula?"

"Our last test appears to have been successful," Ula replied. "I have Ari and Von cleaning the sensors on One right now."

"Good work."

"Thank you." Ula leaned on the table and sighed. "I'm sorry, Kem. I should have thought of that myself."

"Don't beat yourself up. We're all making mistakes with this place."

"So how can you help with the racks?" Cas asked.

"It's going to be extra work, but once the pods start getting transferred we can use the solvent solution to clean the sensors as soon as the couplers separate. Once the new pod is installed and the couplers are engaged the sensors are sealed together, so they should be okay until the next transfer."

"That might work," Cas said.

"Since the sensors are already coated you'll have to manually confirm that the couplers disengage, but after that they should work normally."

"You'll still have to clean them during every exchange, though," Kem added.

"More than likely," Ula agreed.

"You won't have any extra help," Kem reminded the engineer. "Especially if we aren't back by then. With Nya gone the drivers will be extra busy replacing pods and Cas's team will be monitoring the gas separators."

"No problem," Ula said confidently. "It's a fairly simple process so my team should be able to handle it."

"How long do you think it will take?" Cas asked.

"Only a few seconds per pod."

"One more problem solved," Kem said with a satisfied sigh.

"If there's nothing else I'll go help with the interior sensor cleaning," Ula announced.

"Sure, go ahead." Once the engineer left Kem turned back to Cas. "I need to talk to Lue for a minute. See you later."

"Okay Boss." Kem walked around to Exploration and joined Lue and Tam as they continued discussing the expedition.

"...no way to accurately predict the surface conditions," Tam was saying. "All I can do is offer my best guess."

"I feel reasonably confident about your guesses," Kem praised the geologist. "After all, you were dead on about this site."

"True, but I was also able to take my time and extract hundreds of core samples," Tam explained. "It won't be as easy to identify the ground density by looking at it, especially when we're constantly moving. I'm afraid we'll have to take it slow."

"I understand. That's why I want each team member to bring two extra scrubber packs and extra food."

"Speaking of suits, is there any word on atmo?" Tam asked. "I'd sure like to clean up and change before we go. Two full days in this suit is enough."

"They are working on it right now," Kem said. "As long as it doesn't take too long we'll wait until they are finished."

"Thank you!" the geologist said, relieved.

"Just make sure your suit is charged and ready to go."

"Yes Sir."

"So have you learned anything about the geology of this place that will help us?"

"Well, as far as I can tell the darker regions should be the safest to drive over. They are the flattest and appear to be more solid, possibly due to being former lake beds or collection basins for the material being washed down from the hills."

"That's helpful."

"As I said, we still need to be careful," Tam cautioned Kem. "Remember, the lakes here are liquid methane, not water, and I have no idea how deep they may be. If we drive into one we're done."

"I'll keep that in mind. I still think it's worth the risk."

"Oh, I agree." Tam said quickly. "We've been happily trudging through mud just to find single cell life, so discovering evidence of an advanced species is absolutely worth the risk."

"Let's wait and see what it is first," Kem said with a sigh. "Why is everyone assuming this thing is alien?"

"Ula to Kem."

"Go ahead."

"The sensors on One and Two have been cleaned and the processors are working at full capacity." Kem switched the table to display the environmental readings for those floors, which were slowly stabilizing.

"Good work. How long before I can get out of this suit?"

"Atmo should be normal by the time you get down here."

"Then tell our guest to get ready. I want to leave as soon as possible."

"Yes Sir."

"What about the tower?" Lue asked.

"Von will be up shortly to clean the sensors."

"Finally," the Assistant Director said.

"Ula, make sure all the suits we're taking are equipped with Ari's new cleats."

"Copy that." Kem switched off the com and turned to Lue.

"Call Nya and make sure she's getting ready to go."

"Will do," Lue replied. Kem nodded, then turned to Tam. "Is your data ready to load into the rover?"

"Yes Sir."

"Then let's go."

"Clean uniform here I come!" the geologist said enthusiastically. The two men entered the elevator and rode it down in silence, both contemplating the upcoming expedition. By the time they reached the bottom floor the computer readout indicated the atmosphere was normal, just as Ula had promised. As the elevator doors opened Kem reached up and popped the latch on his collar with an overwhelming sense of relief.

II

Departure

"Are you ready?" Kem asked himself as he stared into the mirror through the helmet lens. He pressed the latch tight against the collar of the freshly cleaned suit, then turned around and walked out of the bathroom. A suit support case beckoned from the main door. It contained spare gas and food modules, a patch kit, and a few tools. Kem checked his glove joints one more time, then walked to the door and picked up the case. After one last deep breath he pressed the button and the doors snapped open with a soft *'schwip'*.

* * *

"Is everyone ready to go?" Kem asked as he stepped out of the elevator. The rest of the team had already gathered outside the airlock, each with a support case at their feet, along with two additional cases. One he recognized as Ren's and the other had a medical symbol on it.

"Ready Sir," Tam said as he gyrated in an attempt to remove the kinks in his new suit.

"At least we got to clean up and change," Nya replied. "I hadn't spent that much time wearing an environment suit since training."

"It wasn't my suit that was the problem," Kem added. "It was me stewing in my own juices."

"That's gross."

"Why the extra medical supplies? Didn't you say the rover is well stocked."

"Just in case," Nya replied.

"Shall we?" Kem asked while looking directly at Ren.

"Ready when you are, Sir," the linguist answered excitedly.

"Let's do it." They each picked up their cases and entered the airlock, then Kem turned the red handle and the doors slid closed. Nya initiated the depressurization sequence and the pumps began to hum softly.

"It's nice not to have to operate them manually, isn't it?" she teased Kem. The hum stopped and the light above the outer door changed to white. Kem turned the other red handle and the door slid open, revealing the howling wind as it swirled the orange mist around the waiting rover.

"There's my baby," Nya said lovingly. She picked up her support case and the medical case and carried them to the rover, then set them down and opened the back panels. "Everyone aboard!"

"*Your* baby?" Kem asked with a chuckle. He picked up his own case and led the others out of the airlock.

"After you, Sir," Nya said with a sweep of her arm.

"Actually, Tam is going to sit up front," Kem replied. "He needs access to navigation and I want him to have the best view of the road ahead."

"What road?"

"Exactly," Kem said. Nya stepped into the rover and set her case down, then made her way to the front. As soon as she settled into the left-hand seat she powered up the vehicle, then opened the cover on her forearm control pad and linked it to the rover, allowing basic control of the auxiliary systems. Once the interior lights came on Kem placed a hand on Tam's shoulder and took the case from him. "After you." The exogeologist stepped in and joined Nya in the cramped cockpit. While he struggled to wedge himself into the right-hand seat Ren stepped into the rover, then Kem followed and closed the rear panels. With the wind outside suddenly silenced his breathing echoed hollowly. The hydrocarbon mist trapped inside the cabin quickly lost momentum but remained airborne, so Nya engaged the filtration system. While the gases were being scrubbed Ren and Kem stowed the extra cases in the side compartments and took their seats. Ren sat behind Nya and Kem settled into the seat being Tam. The geologist slipped a small hexagonal data stick out of the pocket on his right sleeve and plugged it into the navigation console in the center of the instrument panel.

"What are you loading?" Nya asked.

"The scan data from the shuttles as well as the scans from the Gemisi's preliminary sweep," Tam explained as his fingers danced across the console buttons. "After they discovered the object I had the Captain save everything from that point on and send it down. It's not much, but I figured it's better than nothing."

"I'll take any help you can give me," Nya said with an unseen wink. "This place isn't exactly friendly to vehicles. Right Director?"

"You know, Cas was telling me about a position in maintenance that just opened up," Kem replied. "I think scrubbing the inside of separator tubes would suit you." Ren looked over at the director with genuine concern for Nya until they both began laughing.

"You were right," the linguist said. "Things are a lot more casual down here than on the ship."

"On a ship everyone is on edge all the time," Kem said. "You are always conscious of the possibility of a leak or some other catastrophic emergency."

"That's for sure."

"That's why regular down time isn't just important to let the crew recover from zero G, it allows a regular release of that tension. My methods may appear casual, but that is by design," Kem explained. "We have a limited crew working much longer shifts. The danger may not be as great but fatigue can make even a simple problem escalate out of control, including personal disagreements. By creating a sense of family it keeps everyone as relaxed as possible and able to stay focused when something goes wrong."

"Which it usually does," Nya added.

"Maybe next time I sign up for a mission I should take advantage of my engineering background and join the ground crew," Ren said. "All that switching between no gravity and full gravity gives me a headache."

"If the rest of you would like to strap in we can get this party started," Nya said. The passengers responded by engaging their seat restraints, which consisted of four short semi-rigid straps; one on each side of their waist and one above each shoulder. Keyed clips on the ends fit over the small collared studs mounted to the waist and shoulder joints of the pressure suits. The straps were then tightened by turning two large knobs, one on each side of the seat cushions where the occupant could easily reach them. Once they achieved the proper tension a light on the outboard armrests glowed blue, and once all of the occupied seats had been engaged another blue light on the instrument panel also lit up to let the driver know they were secure. Once the passengers were strapped in Nya switched on the forward light panels, then gripped the yoke and gently twisted the throttle. The rover began moving toward the landing pad until she rotated the yoke to the left and the rover snapped around to face the lake.

"Easy," Kem said softly. "I'd like to keep my neck."

"Sorry Sir." Nya advanced the throttle slowly and followed her test drive route along the lake until they passed the maintenance building. From there she guided the rover to the spot where the two hills came together and slipped between them. The passage was barely wide enough for the rover but they emerged on the other side without a scratch. After crossing the clearing she and Kem had driven through before they approached another mound twice the size of the rover. "Which way now?" Nya asked Tam.

"South."

"Didn't we just come from the south?"

"Yes."

"Just tell me how many degrees left or right. I always get confused driving near poles."

"Go left until we get around this small hill." Tam instructed. "Then follow the long hill for about one klik. There should be a break where we can get through to the valley beyond."

"You're the boss." Nya steered around the hill, then straightened out and followed the base of the ridge. The rover bounced softly back and forth as it occasionally ran over the larger rocks of frozen water, but overall the vehicle always felt solid and sure-footed. When they reached the gap Tam had described the wind suddenly picked up, creating an opaque curtain of orange gases. Nya hit the brakes and the rover rocked to a stop.

"Problem?" Kem asked, already knowing the answer.

"No Sir." Nya engaged the sensor arrays and the cockpit windows darkened as a multi-colored rendering of the landscape appeared. The image was similar to those generated by the pod transports, but with far greater detail and depth. Nya turned off the cabin lights and proceeded forward, guiding the rover through the narrow gap. When they reached the other side the display expanded again, revealing a huge valley with only fist-sized or smaller rocks littering the ground.

"Straight ahead," Tam said. "All the way across this flat area to those two hills on the far side."

"Are you sure it's solid?" Kem asked.

"Pretty sure. Remember what I said about the darker areas being that way due to deposits left behind after the lake dried up?"

"Not exactly a firm answer."

"Well, it's our best guess. It's possible there are lakes with layers of hydrocarbon deposits over them, but we haven't found any evidence of them yet," Tam explained. "Just to be safe, it would be prudent to keep an eye out for them."

"Got it," Nya replied with a nod.

"Let's go." Kem said. Nya twisted the throttle gently and the rover inched forward. She slowly added power, but when they reached the lake bed the vehicle suddenly dropped 10 centimeters.

"Whoa!" Tam shouted as he gripped his armrests tightly.

"I think you were right," Ren said calmly as everyone stared at the image. "It's definitely a thin layer of something."

"Over what?" Nya asked. She twisted the throttle back until the rover reversed enough for their tracks to be visible. "There isn't a lake underneath."

"Fascinating," Tam said as his training and curiosity took over. "Make sure you image our journey."

"Got it." Nya reached over and switched on the display recorder. "Now what?"

"Increase the sensor penetration. We should be able to see through the ice and spot any deep spots." Nya adjusted the image and, as predicted, the later of deposits became translucent green while the ground below appeared solid blue. "Okay. Let's go."

"Maintain a reasonable speed," Kem ordered. "You need to be able to stop in time if you spot a hole."

"Yes Sir." Nya eased the throttle forward and the treads began carving a path through the thin layer, allowing the rover to drive on the solid ground. As her confidence increased so did their speed until they were again traveling at a moderate pace. Even so, all four occupants stared intently at the shifting image displayed across the front windscreen.

12

First Obstacle

"Fascinating," Tam said again as he marveled at the sensor images of the passing landscape. "I could spend years studying this moon."

"It's an amazing place," Ren agreed. "The atmosphere, the gravity, the solid water and liquid methane."

"But we use liquid methane all the time, and it's not even cold," Nya said.

"Yes, but it's processed and compressed," Ren replied. "The methane here is all natural and cycles the way water does back home."

"It's not just the composition of the atmosphere that is intriguing," Tam added. "It's the very existence of an atmosphere that is most interesting."

"What do you mean?" Nya asked as she steered the rover around a large rock.

"We've never before encountered an atmosphere on a solid body with such low gravity and no magnetic field. Even if they start out with one it get's blown away by solar winds relatively quickly. This moon is fortunate to be protected by the planet's magnetic field. I believe that's why it's so thick in spite of the moon's size."

"It's also more dense than it should be, in case you didn't notice," Ren added.

"It's a rare combination, that's for sure," the geologist said.

"Do you really think there could be life here?" Nya asked.

"That's what I hope to find out while I'm out here." The rover slowed and everyone shifted their attention from the conversation to the screen.

"We've reached the other side," Nya announced. She drove onto the lighter-colored shore and up a shallow slope, but as they approached the ridge the image showed a two meter high vertical wall blocking their path. "We're not getting through this way." Nya spun the rover to the left and examined the sensor image, then turned 180 degrees to the right. "There!" she said, pointing at the windscreen. "It looks like part of the wall has fallen. We may be able to get through."

"How far?" Kem asked.

"About five hundred meters," Tam answered.

"Let's go." Nya gripped the yoke and guided the rover along the wall. When they reached the breech she turned to face it.

"Not so much fallen as naturally formed," Tam guessed. Nya eased the rover forward and the explorers found themselves overlooking an expansive valley surrounded by steep cliffs. "It's a huge depression. Spectacular!"

"Hard to tell, but I'd guess it's at least thirty meters to the valley floor." Nya added. "What now?"

"Tam?" Kem asked. The geologist scrambled to review the scans, paging through them as quickly as possible.

"Nothing, Sir. The data is just too crude and incomplete."

"How wide do you think it is?"

"If I had to guess I'd say it's close to one hundred kliks."

"I'd like to avoid going around if possible," Kem said. "Nya?"

"Sorry sir. The sensors can't penetrate this wall and if get any closer to the edge it may collapse."

"That wouldn't be a fun ride," Ren added.

"No, it wouldn't," Kem agreed. "Does anyone have a suggestion?"

"We can get out and take a closer look," Nya replied. "If we can see the interior maybe we'll find a way down."

"Isn't that just as dangerous?" Ren asked.

"I'll lock the tracks and we can use the rover as an anchor."

"How will we secure ourselves?" Tam asked.

"We can connect our suit tethers to the tow cable," Nya explained.

"Will we even be able to see out there?"

"There's one way to find out." Nya switched off the display and adjusted the tint of the glass to CLEAR. To the occupants' surprise the weather outside was fairly mild, with only occasional wisps of orange mist passing vertically in front of them.

"Well okay then," Ren said. "Let's go."

"Sir?" Nya said to Kem, seeking his authorization.

"Why not?" Kem said. "Like Ren said, we may as well learn everything we can while we're out here." He reached down and slapped the restraint knobs inward, releasing the tension. After detaching the clips he let the belts retract into the seat and stood up.

"Grab the helmet scope from the bin," Nya said. "If we can't get down here we'll need to find another way."

"Okay." While the others unbuckled, Kem opened the forward right hand bin and removed a small case, then set it on the floor and opened that, revealing the helmet scope. He removed the device and turned it over a few times, then handed it to Tam.

"Why don't you let our driver use it," the geologist suggested. "Using those things always makes me dizzy."

"Sure." Kem reached past Tam and Nya took the scope from him. "Let's go." He stepped to the back of the rover and opened the panels. There was far less wind than when they had left the mine and visibility was very good. "Everyone check your power and your heaters. It's a bit chilly out."

"Funny, Sir," Nya said. "I'll get the cable ready." She walked to the front of the rover and opened a small door between the two main sensor arrays. Inside there was a metal loop with a red button next to it. She pressed and held the button until it began to flash, then used the control pad on her left forearm to activate the winch. As the tow cable slowly played out she reached down and popped the recessed clip out of the small hexagonal housing on the front of her suit, then began pulling out the thin cable attached to it. After clipping her tether to the tow loop she began backing up as the cable continued to spool out. When she approached the edge of the crater she stopped the winch just short of her being able to reach the edge, then walked back toward the rover where the rest of the team was waiting. "It'll be a little awkward being tied to the same cable but at least we won't fall in." Once all four explorers were securely attached to the cable they walked as a group to the edge and took in the view.

"Amazing!" Tam said as he visually scanned the basin from side to side. "It looks like a giant impact crater."

"Or a super-volcano," Ren added.

"Not likely on a body this small," Tam replied. "However, it's not entirely out of the question."

"Let's find a way across," Kem suggested impatiently. "Then you can argue geological theory all day." Nya slipped the helmet scope on, which fit between the visor and chin area, completely covering the lens. When she activated the device it provided the same range of vision but added multiple layers of data. With the weather fairly clear she selected normal optics and turned on the range finder. After looking from rim to rim the scope displayed the results.

"You were close," Nya said to Tam. "Ninety seven kliks."

"Do you see a way to the bottom?" Kem asked.

"And a way out the other side," Tam added.

"Hang on." Nya stepped forward until her tether was tight. "I can't quite see the edge. Step back so I can let out a bit more cable." Once the other three explorers moved toward the rover she let out a bit more cable and stepped to the very edge.

"Be careful," Tam urged. "Even if it's stable it's still ice."

"That's why we're cabled to the..." Nya suddenly dropped straight down as the ice collapsed under her. Her helmet struck the edge, knocking the scope off and sending it sliding toward the group as she disappeared.

"Nya!" Kem yelled as he cautiously stepped to the broken edge and looked over the side. Fortunately, the cable held and he found her hanging vertically against the crater wall. "Are you okay?"

"I'm...fine." She kicked at the side repeatedly trying to get a foot hold, but was unsuccessful.

"Let me help you up." Kem reached down and grabbed her by both hands and started to pull her onto the rim.

"Wait!" she said, "I think I see something." She let go and rolled onto her right side.

"What is it?"

"It may be a way down."

"Where?"

"To our west, about one klik or so. Hand me the scope." Kem picked up the device and handed it down to her. After reinstalling it she adjusted the settings and scanned the area in question. "It looks like a road," she said calmly.

"A road?" Tam asked. "Here?"

"Well, a partially fallen shelf that we can use as a ramp to the bottom, if you want to be technical."

"Right. What about a way out?" Nya turned so her back was

against the ice wall and again adjusted the scope.

"It looks like a spot on the far side has collapsed into the crater. We should be able to get out there." She slipped the scope off and handed it to Kem. "Stand back, Sir." Once Kem moved away Nya activated the winch and it pulled her up onto the flat area. Kem then grabbed her by the waist and helped her to her feet.

"Are you okay to drive?" he asked.

"Oh, sure. I was more startled than anything."

"Then let's go find your road." The team moved away from the edge and unhooked themselves from the cable, then Nya retracted it while the others re-entered the rover. While they strapped themselves in she closed the back, then climbed into the cockpit, cleared the cabin, and activated the sensors. She spun the rover to the right and after cautiously driving along the edge of the crater they reached another gap that seemed to correspond with the ramp she had seen. Once again she turned toward the crater and locked the treads. "Nya, Ren, you stay here," Kem ordered. "Tam and I will check it out." He moved to the back and again opened the panels.

"Oh, joy," the geologist said, louder than intended. "After you Sir." After exiting the rover they hooked onto the cable and Kem waved.

"Let it out," Kem instructed Nya. "Slowly."

"It only has two speeds, Sir," Nya replied. "Here we go." She activated the winch and the two men led the cable to the edge. Kem raised his hand again and Nya stopped the winch.

"That's good," the director said. "Stand by." Kem and Tam stepped to the edge and looked.

"I think Nya was right," Tam said. "It looks like a narrow section of the cliff separated and slipped down to form a ramp."

"It may not be a road but do you think it's passable?"

"It's barely wider than the rover. I'd prefer to go around, but if Nya can keep from driving off the side it should be possible." Tam replied. "The only question is the density. As long as it's the same as the crater wall it should remain stable."

"I'm sure it shifted thousands of years ago and has been like this ever since."

"Or, it just happened yesterday and is still settling."

"There's one way to find out."

13

The Crater

"Everyone ready?" Nya asked as she stared at the glowing blue light. The question wasn't so much about the passengers' restraint status as it was their willingness to remain on board for such a risky maneuver.

"It's now or never," Kem said. "Let's go." With visibility much improved Nya left the sensors off and the windows clear.

"Here we go," she announced as she eased the rover forward. All the passengers held onto their arm rests, but as the ground ahead slowly disappeared beneath the overhanging cockpit Tam's fingers sunk much deeper into the padded material. With nothing but empty space in front of them Nya carefully rotated the vehicle to the left and eased it forward until it tilted down, bringing the narrow ramp into view. "So far so good,"

"Nice and easy," Tam urged with an abundance of anxiety in his voice. Nya nodded and continued forward as the cliff face gradually rose to eventually fill the left-hand windows.

"Well, at least we can't fall that way," Ren said with a nervous laugh.

"That doesn't exactly make me feel any better," Tam said. "This whole shelf could break away and fall over with us on it."

"You could have kept that to yourself."

"Sorry. I analyze when I'm nervous," Tam replied. "I remember this one expedition..."

"Everyone shut up so I can focus!" Nya shouted. The passengers instantly fell silent and stared straight ahead as the rover continued to descend. After a few minutes Nya appeared to relax somewhat and loosened her grip on the yoke. "Halfway there," she said softly. With that announcement the passengers all breathed a sigh of relief until the right side of the rover dropped slightly.

"Whoa!" Tam yelled. "Are we falling?"

"Take it easy!" Nya shouted. "It's just a rut." The entire rover suddenly dropped 30 centimeters and tilted so far to the left that the distant horizon was no longer visible.

"That's no rut!" Kem yelled as he spun his seat around to look out the rear window. "Tam was right, the entire shelf is pulling away for the wall!"

"What do we do?" Tam shouted. Without a word Nya tilted the yoke to the left and twisted the throttle to FULL. The rover leaped forward and slammed against the cliff, then continued scraping along the ice as it descended rapidly toward the crater floor. "What are you doing?" Tam asked desperately. "As the shelf continues to separate we'll fall into the crevice!" Nya flashed an angry glare at the engineer but said nothing as she fought to maintain control. The rover continued down the ramp as the gap between the shelf and crater wall continued to grow. "See?"

"Shut up!" Nya snapped. To the passengers' surprise she continued to hug the cliff face rather than remain centered on the ramp. The left-hand treads no longer had anything solid to ride on and the rover rolled to the left and slammed hard against the wall. Nya released the throttle and waited patiently while the passengers stared at her with both panic and confusion. The rover continued to roll until the roof was resting against the cliff face with the left side facing straight down. As the ramp continued to fall away, though, the rover began to roll to the right and level out. Nya twisted the throttle to FULL again and as soon as the tracks settled onto the inside face of the ramp they began crawling forward. Nya fought the twisting yoke as the vehicle bounced in all directions, testing the limits of the seat restraints. Eventually, they reached the section of ramp that was still intact, clearing the collapsing shelf and speeding away from the ensuing cloud. "Heeya!" Nya yelled in triumph as she spun the rover around for a better view of the devastation. Other than the last few meters the entire shelf had fallen away and ended up on it's side on the crater floor. As the passengers stared in stunned silence the wind picked up and swirled the icy cloud into a funnel stretching well above the rim of the crater.

"Is everyone okay?" Kem finally asked.

"I...can't believe... we survived." Tam said, still in shock.

"That's why I had Nya drive," Kem said proudly. "She's the best."

"Aww, thanks Sir," Nya said with a surprisingly casual demeanor. "Unfortunately, I think I may have broken the dish." She drove around to the middle of the former ramp and turned to face a pile of ice blocks larger than the rover. The surprisingly intact mesh antenna protruded from the top of the mound like a flag marking a newly claimed summit.

"I'd definitely call that broken."

"Sorry, Sir."

"That's okay," Kem reassured her. "Between saving us or the dish I'm glad you picked us."

"I second that," Tam said as he reached across and gently placed his hand on Nya's forearm.

"Besides, without the grid we didn't have much chance of communicating with the base anyway."

"It's a good thing you didn't listen to me," Tam said humbly as he stared at the pile of frozen rubble. "That would have been us."

"Don't worry about it. Just another day on an unknown moon." Nya spun the rover around to face the far side of the crater. "Shall we?"

"Hang on," Kem said as he turned his chair toward the aisle and looked up at the ceiling.

"I don't see any damage in here but we should go out and make sure the antenna didn't cause any when it was torn off."

"Right." Nya shut down the main power and started to undo her restraints when Kem interrupted.

"You stay here. I'll go out and take a look."

"Yes, Sir."

"I'll do it," Ren said.

"Are you sure?" Kem asked.

"Sure. It'll only take a minute."

"Be my guest."

"Make sure you take a patch kit," Nya added. "They should be in..."

"The right-hand forward bin," Ren said. "I know." She released her belts and stood up, then walked to the back of the rover and opened the bin. She pulled out a small tool case and stepped to the back of the rover. After releasing the latch she pushed the rear panels open and stepped out onto the frozen ground. By then Kem had gotten up and joined her.

"I want you back inside as soon as possible," he said.

"Yes Sir." Ren pushed the panels closed and walked around to the right side of the rover, then used the foot-holds to step onto the fender. After climbing onto the roof she looked into the recess where the antenna had been. "It looks like the cable disconnected cleanly but the entire motor assembly came off with the antenna. As far as I can tell all six sets of threads have been torn out of the metal."

"Is the damage just in the module or the actual roof?" Kem asked.

"It looks like it's just the module."

"We're not getting any new gases inside," Nya added.

"I'm going to patch it anyway," Ren said. "We don't need this mist to get into the electronics."

"Make it fast," Kem urged. "I want to get going."

"Yes Sir." Ren opened the tool case and removed a small hammer, then closed the case to keep out the mist. After tucking the cable and connector inside the hole she repeatedly pounded on the torn metal. As she worked her way around the hole each blow resonated throughout the interior of the rover. Once the edge was slightly below the surface Ren reopened the case and removed a small square piece of metal with a temporary backing on one side. She peeled off the backing, then carefully aligned the square over the hole and pressed it into place. The moment the adhesive touched the metal it reacted, becoming super heated and fusing the patch to the tray. "That should do it," Ren said. As she climbed down Kem opened the panels to let her in, but even after she reached the ground she didn't appear at the back of the rover.

"Where are you?" Kem asked.

"Hang on."

"What are you doing?"

"I'm going to get the dish. We may need it."

"Forget it. Get inside."

"Almost got it."

"Ren."

"Aaah!"

"Ren!" Kem raced out of the rover and over to the mound of ice, but there was no sign of Ren or the dish assembly. "Where are you?"

"Down here." Kem carefully climbed onto the largest block of

ice by using the smaller blocks as steps. *"Careful, Sir."* When he reached the top he crawled forward until he found himself looking into a two-meter deep hole. Ren was lying at the bottom on a fresh pile of ice, with the dish assembly resting on top of her.

"Almost dying in the rover wasn't enough?" Kem asked.

"Just get me out of here. *Sir.*"

"You're the engineer. Any ideas?"

"We could try to move the block but it'll probably be easier to just throw the tow cable over and pull me up."

"I'll be right back." Kem climbed down and walked to the front of the rover. "Nya, release the tow cable."

"I heard. Here it comes." Kem opened the cover and grabbed the loop, then walked slowly toward the block of ice as the cable spooled out. After coiling an extra meter of slack he climbed back up and lowered the loop down to Ren. She clipped her tether to it and Kem pulled out the slack.

"Okay Nya, slowly."

"Copy that." The cable began sliding through his gloved hands and after a few seconds it began to lift Ren from the hole. Once she was close enough he grabbed her arm and helped pull her onto the top of the block.

"That's it!" Kem yelled. He detached the clip and waved. "Reel it in." While the loose cable snaked it's way back into the front of the rover Kem picked up the antenna, then helped Ren to the rear and opened the panels. "Good work."

"No problem." As soon as they entered the rover Kem closed the panels and strapped the dish assembly to the floor using the recessed tie-downs. While he and Ren buckled themselves in Nya purged the hydrocarbon gases and once the cabin was clear she glanced back at the passengers.

"Ready?" she asked.

"Let's go," Kem said. "I just hope you're right about the other side being open. We can't exactly go back the way we came."

"I'm sure the rest of the trip will be smooth," Nya said as she eased the rover forward. "We're already past our glitch quota."

"Even so keep a sharp eye out."

"Shouldn't we use the sensors?" Tam asked.

"If you like," Nya said. "Set them to warn of any hollow pockets but I want to leave the windscreen clear. As long as we have decent visibility I'd like to enjoy the view."

"Got it." While Tam activated the sensors Nya increased the speed and the rover glided along the pebbled ground while the passengers took in the interior of the frozen crater in silence.

14

The Final Leg

When they reached the far side of the crater most of the wall remained intact, except for the section Nya had spotted earlier. It was less than one kilometer long but dipped dramatically, with a mound of dirty ice spilling into the crater.

"Looks like you've already been here," Kem teased his driver.

"You're lucky you're the boss," Nya replied. As they approached the mound they could see a series of grooves cut into the semi-translucent surface, snaking their way from the crater floor to the flattened rim above.

"They look like drainage channels," Tam said, forgetting all about their recent near-death experience.

"Wouldn't the crater be full of water then?" Nya asked as she aligned the rover with the groove.

"Methane, you mean," Tam corrected her. "It's possible during heavy rains the methane drains into the crater but then evaporates. As deep as the channels are I'd guess the process has been repeating for a long time."

"That's a lot of rain," Kem said.

"It could be." Before they could continue their discussion the sky quickly darkened.

"Maybe we should get out of here," Kem said. Nya nodded and released the brake just as a series of dull thumps echoed inside the cabin and the windows became dotted with thick raindrops.

Nya turned on the front wipers, which slid side to side on tracks built into the window frames, then lined the rover up with two of the wider ridges and slowly eased the tracks onto them. "As fast as you can," Kem urged as the rain increased in intensity.

"Good thing I installed that patch," Ren added.

"Can everyone stop talking?" Nya asked impatiently. "I really need to focus so we don't get stuck." The passengers again complied as she worked her way up the slope by carefully following the shifting ridges. The left side of the rover dropped a few centimeters and the back began to slide sideways but Nya gave the throttle a quick twist and the rover crept back onto solid ice. When they finally crested the edge of the crater the mist suddenly cleared, revealing the planet directly ahead but much higher in the sky. The rain stopped just as suddenly and the weak sunlight struck the raindrops on the left-hand windows, creating a shimmering light show throughout the cabin. "Looks like we won't need the artificial imaging," Nya said as the rover leveled out. "It's really clear now." She sat back in her seat and grasped the yoke. "Which way," she asked Tam.

"Head straight for the lower tip of the planet's rings," the geologist answered. Nya twisted the throttle and steered the rover toward the moon's captor while the passengers settled back and tried to rest.

* * *

Kem woke up with a start when the rover pitched sharply to the left. He looked over at Ren but she appeared to still be asleep. He then turned to the cockpit for an update, which had been switched back to sensor imaging, but Nya's seat was empty. Tam, on the other hand, also seemed to be enjoying an extended nap. Kem sat up straight and looked toward the back of the cabin and was surprised to find the driver sitting behind Ren holding a small control pad. She seemed to notice Kem but remained focused on the screen as she tilted it back and forth in tiny increments. Kem reached back and tapped Nya on the knee. When she glanced over he held up two fingers and they both accessed their suit controls and switched the radio channel to avoid disturbing the others.

"Sorry for the bump, Sir. For frozen water those rocks are hard."

"Tell me about it."

"The good news is I'm finally getting the hang of this."

"The hang of what?"

"Remote driving."

"Remote?" Kem asked.

"Sure." Nya tapped the screen, then held the small control pad up and wiggled it. "It's all in the wrist."

"Whoa!"

"Relax, I put the rover on AUTO." Kem took the pad from her and realized it displayed the same sensor image as the windscreen.

"Where did you get this?" Kem asked.

"It was in the center console," Nya replied. "I thought since the terrain was going to be flat for a while I'd give it a try."

"I wasn't aware they had outfitted these things with remotes." Kem handed it back and Nya disengaged the auto pilot and resumed driving.

"We practiced with them at the academy, although mostly with fighters," she explained. "All next generation vehicles will have them, including big ships like corvettes and frigates. Personally I'd be too nervous to pilot one of those by remote, but a shuttle would be fun."

"As long as I'm not in it." Kem said. "So each vehicle has their own remote control?"

"Yes, but any pad can control any vehicle. They just have to be paired and then off you go."

"Fascinating. How long was I out?"

"Just over an hour," Nya answered as she focused on the screen.

"Do you need a break?"

"I'm fine," she replied. "Maybe I'll take a nap once we reach our mystery object."

"If you weren't such a good driver I'd insist," Kem said.

"I appreciate that, Sir." Nya tilted the pad to guide the rover around a dark patch of ice, then leveled it to straighten out. "So do you really think it's an enemy probe."

"I know the idea of discovering an intelligent species is exciting, but logic says it's either one of ours or one of theirs."

"I hope it's not one of theirs," Nya said with a sigh. "I quit the military and joined the Mining Guild to get away from the war."

"You and me both," he agreed, amused by the parallel to his own career decision. "It certainly wouldn't be the same having warships in orbit around us. Even if they *were* ours."

"I bet Ren will be happy if it's not one of ours, but not for the same reason."

"She's definitely passionate about the possibility of discovering new life."

"Not just that," Nya said. "There's something off about her."

"What do you mean?"

"It's just a feeling, but if I didn't know better I'd swear she's military."

"Why do you think that?"

"For one thing she is really formal. Even when she's just standing it looks like she's at ease."

"What's wrong with being comfortable and relaxed?"

"I don't mean at ease," Nya replied. "I mean *at ease*."

"How can you tell that when she's wearing a pressure suit?" Kem asked.

"Like I said it's just a feeling, but she also can't stop calling you 'sir', Sir." Nya steered around a spire slightly taller than the rover and headed for a gap between two small hills.

"I think you're letting your time at the academy get to you."

"Maybe."

"Did you ever think that maybe she also went to the academy but ended up quitting?"

"I suppose you're right." Nya stopped the rover and deactivated the control pad. "It's getting a bit tight. Time for the real thing." She removed her restraints and returned to the cockpit, kicking Tam in the process. As he began to emerge from his slumber she engaged the throttle and the rover began moving forward slowly. When it entered the narrow gap the right fender scraped the icy wall, sending a shudder through the entire cabin.

"Maybe you should have stuck with the remote," Kem teased. Both passengers were stirring so Kem and Nya switched their suit coms back to the previous channel.

"Did you two sleep well?" Kem asked cheerfully.

"How long were we out?" Tam asked.

"Almost an hour," Nya replied.

"How much farther?" Ren asked groggily. Tam checked his navigation data, then looked up at the windscreen image.

"Hang on," Tam said. "Nya, turn five degrees to the right."

"Got it." When she made the correction a small flashing dot appeared on the right side of the image.

"There it is," Tam announced. "I'd guess twenty minutes if we don't run into any more obstacles."

"What's the procedure when we get there?" Nya asked.

"We keep our distance and perform a detailed scan," Ren explained before Kem could respond. "Then if the sensors don't detect any biological, chemical, or radiological threats we can take a closer look and try to figure out who made it."

"Let's not get ahead of ourselves," Kem warned. "It could still be a natural formation."

"If it's artificial will you be able to determine the origin?" Tam asked Ren.

"Well, if that's the case then at least we'll know it's not from here," Ren explained. "If it turns out to be an enemy probe I'll be able to identify it for certain. Otherwise I will do my best to figure out what it is and where it came from by translating any writing we find."

"Are you sure you can?"

"Absolutely! I don't just study theoretical forms of language and their structure, I'm also fluent in all enemy languages."

"That's impressive," Tam said.

"Like I said, if it's one of theirs I'll know."

"I'd rather have it turn out to be a rock than an enemy probe," Nya said. "The last thing we need out here is the military." Even with their eyes hidden Nya turned and flashed Kem a knowing look, then turned around and guided the rover through another narrow passage. Once they emerged on the other side the image revealed another dry lake bed.

"Can we go around?" Kem asked his driver. Nya spun the rover a few degrees to the right, then to the left, revealing steep ridges on either side of the vehicle.

"We'd have to backtrack and find a route around the whole area," Nya explained.

"Maybe this one isn't hollow," Kem suggested. Nya pulled to the edge and adjusted the sensors.

"It sure looks the same as the first one we encountered."

"We'll just have to go slow again," Tam suggested.

"How deep do you think it is?" Nya asked the geologist.

"It doesn't appear to be more than ten to fifteen centimeters."

"And the deposits are the same thickness."

"Actually, they appear to be significantly thicker. Why?"

"I have an idea." Nya reversed the rover until it was completely within the passage, then turned to her passengers. "Tighten your belts."

"What are you going to do?" Nya answered the question by twisting the throttle to FULL and the rover leaped forward and sped toward the lake bed. As they approached the edge the passengers braced themselves, but instead of falling through, the rover simply glided on top of the crust.

"Heeya!" Nya yelled. "Keep an eye out for thin spots." The rover skimmed across the bed with only a mild vibration cause by the cleats. At their high rate of speed it only too a minute to cross the bed and as they approached the other side Nya began visually scanning the shore. "Find me the smoothest way off this thing," she said to Tam.

"A few degrees to the left. It looks pretty flat there and I don't see anything large beyond it."

"Got it." Nya adjusted their heading and when they reached the other shore the rover transitioned onto it with a subtle bounce and slid to a stop. "That was fun."

"I can't believe that worked," Tam said as he caught his breath.

"Which way?"

"Six degrees right," Tam replied. Nya adjusted the heading again and guided the rover toward their destination as the groups' excitement and apprehension began to grow. After another kilometer they reached a cluster of small hills and icy rocks. "Through that gap," Tam said as he pointed at the wire-frame image.

"I hate this imaging system," Nya said. "It never looks quite right to me." She turned it off but fortunately the weather and cleared again. Nya followed Tam's direction and ended up facing a clear spot in the center of the formation, but the object was nowhere to be seen.

"Where is it?" Ren asked impatiently. "You said it would be right here." Tam again scrambled to double check his data.

"As far as I can tell it should be right in front of us," he said. He held his portable display up and pointed to a very low resolution round blob with a larger curved blob next to it. "*This* is that small formation right *there*." He pointed to the two-meter tall mound ahead and to their right.

"Hang on," Nya said. She backed the rover away from the hill and steered around it. Once past the formation they emerged onto a large plain littered with rocks 10 to 15 centimeters in size. She drove for almost a kilometer when a brief glint of sunlight caught her eye. She steered toward it and a flat cylindrical object with a metallic surface came into view. "Is that what we're looking for?"

15

The Object

"It's definitely not a rock," Kem said.

"How did you know where to find it?" Tam asked. Nya reached over and tapped the directional pad on his display, shifting the image to the previous grid.

"I recognized that formation here." She pointed at the spot in question, which clearly showed the circle of rocks and hills. "See the ground there? No small rocks." Nya then shifted the image to their current location. "This area is covered with rocks, and if you look closer there are long patches without rocks and low narrow rocky areas only a few centimeters high. That is what you were seeing as a hill on the low-res scans because it looked different than the surrounding surface."

"That's embarrassing," Tam sighed. "Instructed in geology by a driver."

"Don't beat yourself up," she said. "We all have geology training, and these scans are terrible compared to NavSat topographics."

"Still, I'd appreciate it if you kept this between us."

"Whatever you say," Nya agreed with a laugh.

"If you two are done patting each other on the back I'd love to find out what that thing is," Kem said with some urgency.

"Yes sir."

"Can we get a closer look?"

"Hang on." Nya eased the rover forward until the object was only a few meters in front of them and increased the intensity of the forward light bars. The round object appeared to be tinted yellow and was comprised of upper and lower halves, each slightly tapered inward from the middle. A series of silver-colored rods and shelf-like appendages lined the perimeter, while on top there was a small silver box accompanied by a number of short cylindrical pieces. Two were black and tapered, while three of the silver-colored posts were arranged along the outside edge and had cables attached to them. Those cables led several meters away from the object but whatever they were attached to at the other end had been covered by deposits.

"Is it really that color or is it reflecting the atmosphere?" Kem asked.

"It's hard to say," Tam replied. "The other parts seem more polished but they are far less tinted. I'd say it's that color."

"What do you suppose the cables were used for?"

"Maybe they were used to secure it during transport," Nya suggested.

"Or carry it," Tam said.

"But this thing is tiny," Nya said. "Surely they would have put it inside their shuttle."

"It would help to know who built it."

"Ren, do you recognize it?" Kem asked the linguist.

"No Sir."

"Nya, perform a full scan," Kem ordered.

"Yes Sir," the driver replied. She activated the sensors and set them to perform a complete analysis. "I'm not picking up and power sources."

"What else?"

"It's just over one meter across and partly hollow. I can't tell what it's made of but there are definitely multiple alloys present."

"Any markings?" Ren asked.

"None that I can see from here," Nya replied. "You may be using your engineering background more than your language skills on this one."

"What about radiation or explosives?" Kem asked.

"Faint chemical traces, but nothing known to make explosives," Nya reported. "I am picking up some minor radiation but I'm not sure what the source is."

"If I had to guess I'd say you're picking up residual solar radiation." Tam said. "We see that with both ships and natural bodies like asteroids after long term exposure without electromagnetic shielding."

"That's why our ships are covered in protective tiles now," Ren said. She released her restraints and stood up between the cockpit seats. "They absorb the radiation, then slowly release it back into space."

"Surely this thing would have been protected somehow," Kem said.

"I'll know more once I can have a closer look, but if I had to guess I'd say this thing didn't arrive on a ship."

"You think it was shot here?"

"Possibly. That's how we used to do it."

"But why?" Tam asked. "Our adversary may not be quite as advanced as we are but I doubt even they would deploy probes and bombs that way."

"There are still a lot of things we don't know about them."

"I don't think it belongs to them," Nya said.

"You're still hoping it's from an entirely new species, aren't you?" Kem asked.

"It's an exciting possibility."

"Pure speculation," Ren said. "It must be an enemy probe. They probably designed it to confuse us, which is exactly what happened."

"Nya, is your scan finished?" Kem asked.

"Yes. As far as I can tell it poses no immediate threat."

"Unless whoever it belongs to is looking for it," Tam added.

"Don't worry," Ren said. "I'll protect you." The linguist walked to the back and retrieved her case from the storage bin, then set it on the rear seat and opened the lid. While the others watched, confused, she removed a small pistol and snapped it into the tool clip on the right thigh of her suit.

"See?" Nya said to Kem.

"Care to explain why you have that?" Kem asked Ren.

"It's just a precaution, Sir. You don't like guns?"

"Not particularly," Kem said. "They remind me how much I hate war."

"No one likes war, Sir, but sometimes it's necessary."

"Is it, or do our leaders only tell us that to justify their actions?"

"What about protecting our people and way of life?"

"From an enemy who was decades behind us and posed no immediate threat?" Kem asked as his anger began to swell.

"No, from an enemy who clearly had the means to blow us up any time they wanted to," Ren argued. "If we hadn't attacked first it may have been too late."

"Can we save the political and moral discussion for later and focus on identifying this thing?" Nya asked hastily. "I'd like to get out of here."

"Of course," Kem said.

"I'm sorry, Sir," Ren said. "As I said, the weapon is just a precaution."

"I think it's safe to say we're alone out here," Tam said.

"And yet here we are looking at an object that could be alien," Nya said. "I hate to say it but Ren has a point."

"I didn't say it's alien," Ren insisted again. "It must be an enemy probe."

"Just make sure you keep that thing on SAFE," Kem told the linguist.

"I will. Sir," she assured him. "Shall we take a look?" She opened the rear panels and stepped out, then surveyed the landscape in all directions while the others followed. Kem closed the panels and the group walked toward the object, excited yet cautious. Once they reached it they gathered around it, leaving a gap to allow the rover lights to illuminate it.

"Look for anything that can identify it," Kem ordered. The group moved closer and examined the surface thoroughly.

"I don't see any markings," Ren said. "There is definitely a buildup of deposits on the surface, but not enough to suggest it's been here that long."

"How long would you guess?" Kem asked.

"Maybe fifty years." As she leaned over the top of the object she suddenly stopped and straightened up. "I know what the cables are for."

"Not to carry it?" Tam asked.

"No. It was definitely shot here along time ago, which negates my theory of it being a decoy." Ren followed the tangled cables to the spot where they ended, then reached down and grabbed them.

"Careful," Kem warned. "We have no idea what they might be attached to." Ren ignored his warning and pulled them out of the ground, along with a large circle of light-colored fabric.

"What is that?" Tam asked.

"It's a parachute," Nya said. "We learned about them at the academy. We used them to deploy people and equipment before descender technology was developed."

"So you're saying it's one of ours?"

"It could be."

"That would make it hundreds of years old," Kem said.

"I don't know what to tell you."

"You went to the academy?" Ren asked, ignoring the latest speculation.

"For a while, but I dropped out to join the Guild," Nya replied. "You too?"

"Me? No, I was just curious."

"It must have been scary relying on something like that," Tam said. "What if it didn't work?"

"Then you fell like a stone," Nya said. "Splat!"

"Charming."

"How did you know?" Kem asked Ren.

"Sir?"

"About the parachute."

"Look at the top of the probe," Ren said as she walked over and knelt next to the object. "The top of the rectangular box is open but looks like it was covered by that flexible material at one time."

"A container for the parachute."

"Correct. The open cylinder in the center was probably use to deploy it somehow."

"How do you know that?"

"To understand languages I studied a lot of history, both ours and that of our enemy. I remember seeing similar systems on very early craft"

"But you said it's only been here fifty years," Nya said.

"True, but if it was launched a long time ago it would have taken decades to get here. That would make it very old yet still fairly new to this moon." Ren turned to Kem. "If it isn't ours that would mean our enemy was more advanced than previously thought."

"This doesn't prove anything," Kem said.

"I disagree," Ren said. "This is definitely not ours, which means they had high speed delivery systems capable of launching probes great distances much earlier."

"You know, I hate to say it but I think she's right," Nya agreed.

"This proves we were justified in attacking first."

"And how did you come to that conclusion?" Kem asked.

"We attacked them sixty years ago, right?"

"Right."

"We know this probe is much older than that, which means they could have easily launched attacks on us sixty or even a hundred years ago."

"Maybe. But they didn't."

"Because we struck first to prevent that."

"Even if you're right, it's still possible they never would have attacked."

"We could argue about this all day," Nya said. "Regardless of who made it, the question is what are we going to do about it?"

"We need to call it in," Ren said.

"Why?" Kem asked. "What's the rush?"

"No rush," she said. "It's procedure to let the Captain know as soon as we have something to report."

"Procedure or not, even if the grid was finished we're not calling anyone with the dish snapped off," Nya reminded her.

"Then we will have to repair it," Ren suggested.

"Sir?" Nya asked Kem.

"It would be nice to have communications in case the grid is completed before we get back," he said. "Ren, if you think you can repair the dish go ahead."

"Yes Sir." The linguist looked back to Nya and swept her hand toward the rover. "Care to help?" Nya again looked at Kem and he issued a subtle nod of approval.

"What the hell." the driver said with a sigh. "Alien or not, anything is better than standing around staring at a piece of space junk."

16

Communications

Nya followed Ren back to the rover and opened the panels, then stepped inside and opened the right rear storage bin. While she retrieved the tool case Ren unstrapped the dish and carried it to the side of the vehicle.

"Hand me the tools and the dish," she said when Nya emerged from the cabin. She lifted the case up to Ren followed by the dish assembly, then climbed up herself.

"What would you like to do first?"

"We need to remove the six bolts holding the front half of the tray so we can lift it up and remount the dish. Then we can reconnect the cable," Ren replied. "Hand me a wrench." Nya retrieved two wrenches from the case and they began removing the bolts.

"Have you done this before?" Nya asked.

"Done what?"

"Worked on a rover in the field. You seem to know your way around it pretty well."

"I could say the same about you. By the way, that was some amazing driving back there."

"Thanks."

"So with that kind of skill why did you leave the academy?" Ren asked.

"I never felt like I fit in there," Nya said. "I tend to be

spontaneous, which doesn't mesh well with a structured environment."

"You mean you didn't like taking orders."

"I take orders all the time, just not from arrogant jerks who think they are superior because of the symbol on their chest or who don't respect my abilities."

"I'm guessing that isn't the Director."

"Not at all. He may seem soft, but he knows how to get the best out of us while making us feel valuable and appreciated."

"You admire him."

"I would do anything for the Director."

"That's good to know," Ren said. "People can definitely develop a complex, superior or inferior, depending on which end of the ladder they find themselves."

"I thought you said you didn't attend the academy."

"The academy isn't the only place where you find those types," Ren said.

"I guess that's true." Nya agreed. "If I hadn't joined the Guild, though, I wouldn't be in the middle of nowhere on a strange moon repairing a communications dish."

"You never know," Ren said.

"I definitely get to do more driving out here."

"Speaking of driving and feeling superior, I heard about a guy aboard the Gemisi who thinks he's the best driver in the universe, but I doubt even he would have gotten us out of that situation."

"I bet his name is Mac."

"I think so," Ren said. "We've been here so long I forget sometimes that all of you were on the ship. With us, I mean."

"It's only been six months. Even so, this place has definitely become home," Nya said with a sigh. Once they had removed all six bolts she sat back and stared at the shallow tray containing the sensor equipment. "Now what?"

"We need to disconnect the module harness."

"Do you know where it's located?" Nya asked.

"On the old two-eights it's near the back."

"Then this one is probably at the front," Nya said facetiously. "Engineers love to change things. No offense."

"None taken." Ren crawled to the front and grasped the handholds built into the border of the tray. "When I lift it up see if you can see the harness."

"Copy that," Nya said as she pressed the side of her helmet against the roof of the rover.

"Ready?"

"Go." Ren pulled up but the tray refused to move. She applied more force and without warning the tray suddenly jerked upward. Startled, she lost her grip and fell backward but Nya grabbed her arm to keep her from going over the side.

"Thanks," Ren said as she caught her breath. "What happened?"

"I was right about engineers," Nya said. She grasped the loose tray and raised it, revealing a large multi-pin connector near the front. "There is no harness."

"I guess that makes sense," Ren said. "It saves cable and avoids having to reach under to plug it in. They never made those harnesses long enough for field repairs anyway."

"We better hurry," Nya said. The two of them moved to either side of the tray and tilted it toward Ren just as a gust of wind caught it and almost ripped it from their hands. "Whoa!"

"That was close," Ren said. "Hold it steady."

"I'll try."

"The patch I installed should be strong enough, so all we have to do is drill new holes for the cable and mounting holes."

"We should flatten the original hole first," Nya suggested as she ran a finger along the jagged edge.

"Good idea." Ren removed two hammers from the case, one small and the other slightly larger. While she pressed her body against the top side of the tray she held the head of the larger hammer against the patch while Nya used the small hammer to flatten the metal against it. Using the original hole as a guide she then drilled a new one through the patch the same size. After switching to a smaller bit she then drilled six new mounting holes for the motor.

"That should do it," Nya said.

"How are we going to install the bolts without the threads?" Ren asked.

"If you look in the lid of the tool kit there should be a separate container of small parts."

"Got it." Ren removed the flat container and opened it while Nya removed the threaded posts from the screws still attached to the dish base. She handed one of the screws to Ren, who then began trying different nuts until she found one that fit. "That's it." She removed five more nuts and snapped the parts container back into the tool kit lid.

"I'll hold the mast while you install the nuts." Nya pressed the motor bracket against the patch, then slipped a screw through one of the holes and held it while Ren installed a nut. After repeating the procedure they tightened all six, securing the bracket to the patch. Ren grasped the mast and applied pressure in multiple directions. "It feels solid."

"How's it going?" Kem's voice asked. Nya and Ren both looked around until they spotted him standing on the right side of the rover.

"Good, Sir," Nya said. "As soon as we connect the cable we should be ready to go."

"Good work, both of you."

"Thank you, Sir."

"Thank you," Ren repeated. "I don't know what you're paying her but it's not enough."

"That's for sure," Kem agreed. Another gust of wind caught the tray and again tried to tear it from Ren's hands. "Can I help?" Kem asked.

"You're welcome to steady this thing," she replied. Kem climbed up and stood on the fender just in front of Ren and grabbed the edge of the tray. "Thanks."

"No problem."

"Got it!" Nya said from the other side of the tray. "Let it down slowly." Ren and Kem pushed the edge over carefully while Nya supported it from the other side. Once the tray was lying flat on the roof she moved to the front and pushed down hard to engage the main connector. "That should do it. Stay clear." She pressed a button on her suit's control pad and the dish instantly tilted up and spun around until it locked into place. "I guess it found a NavSat."

"Can it do that with the grid incomplete?" Kem asked.

"Sure," Nya replied. "Any time a satellite is present the dish will lock onto it, but there isn't any data to transfer yet." Encouraged by the successful repair she and Ren began reinstalling the tray bolts.

"I guess I could try contacting the Gemisi, just in case," Kem said.

"I'll do it," Ren hastily volunteered. She handed Kem the wrench, then jumped down and ran around to the back, then opened the panels and climbed in.

"Okay then," Kem said with a chuckle and began installing the bolts on his side. "While she's doing that why don't we figure out what we're going to do with that probe?"

"We could take it back to the shop," Nya suggested. "It would be a lot easier to study indoors."

"Are we sure it's not dangerous?" Tam asked nervously as he

approached the rover.

"No radiation and no explosives, so I'd say it's safe."

"What about biological?"

"You think something moved in?"

"Or was placed in it by whoever sent it here. It could contain genetic material to reform or repopulate this place. Maybe even a bio-weapon."

"Tam is right," Kem said as they climbed down. "We don't know what this is so we need to take every precaution."

"We need to bring it back right away," Ren said as she rejoined the group.

"You got through?"

"No Sir," Ren replied. "I just mean it's too important not to. We need to return it to the mine so a full assessment can be performed."

"Okay, but we're putting it in the maintenance building, not the habitat."

"How long do you think it will take for them to finish the grid?" Tam asked.

"They should be done within a couple of hours." Ren's answer prompted Nya to check the status indicator on her control pad.

"I guess we better get this thing loaded," Kem said. "Nya, grab an isolation bag from the rover."

"Yes Sir." Nya returned to the rover and opened the left rear storage bin. She removed the largest specimen bag, which had handles attached at the corners, then rejoined the group. When they returned to the object everyone stared at it. "How are we going to get it into the bag with all those parts sticking out?"

"Maybe they retract," Ren suggested. She knelt down and began pushing inward on the protrusions but nothing happened. Frustrated, she then pushed sideways on one of the longer rods with a circular piece on the end. At first it resisted but then rotated until it rested against the side of the object. She successfully repeated the procedure with the matching rod on the other side, then stood up. "Everything else seems to be fixed in place."

"Well, that should help," Kem said. He grasped the cables and wadded them up with the parachute and placed it on top. "Let's get it into the bag." Working together they managed to slip the specimen bag around the object and sealed it, then with Tam and Nya at the front and Kem and Ren behind they carried it to the back of the rover. Once everyone was inside Nya climbed into the cockpit and activated the main power while the others tilted the object onto it's edge and secured it to the side wall with two straps. After giving them one last tug Kem reached back and closed the panels. "All set!"

"Everyone strap in," Nya replied. While the passengers settled into their seats and secured their restraints she purged the cabin, then initiated a bio-hazard cleanse. Once the rover had filled with the thick fog she purged it again and grasped the yoke. "Here we go." She spun the rover 180 degrees and began following their tracks though the rock formations until they reached the dry lake bed. As they glided across the flat landscape heavy methane raindrops began to thump against the windscreen. Nya focused on the terrain and the tracks leading them home, but with nothing else to do the passengers contemplated what the object could be, and who it belonged to.

"Maybe Ren was right about it being a diversion," Tam finally said. "Something the enemy made to keep us occupied."

"Either way it's definitely an enemy probe and we need to treat it as such," Ren said.

"I guess it wouldn't be the first time we underestimated them." Kem said.

"It makes the most sense," Ren said. "I prefer to study the facts and draw scientific conclusions, not speculate."

"Surely you've at least considered the alternative, though," Nya said.

"That it's alien?" Ren asked. "That's a bit far fetched, don't you think?"

"Not as much as it used to be."

"Why are you so determined to conclude it's alien?"

"Why are you so convinced it's not?"

"That's enough," Kem said. "Both of you." He expected more bickering but instead Nya abruptly brought the rover to a stop. "What is it?" Kem asked.

"We're back at the crater."

"You're not thinking about going back down there, are you?" Tam asked nervously.

"Of course not."

"So go around. What's the problem?"

"The problem is, since we can't go through the crater that means the gyro tracker is useless, so which way do we go?"

"Oh." Tam began scrolling through his scan data while shaking his head. After a minute he looked over at Nya. "I just don't know. The scans are incomplete but the terrain appears flatter to the right."

"That's not very encouraging."

"I'm sorry, but I simply can't give you a better answer."

"Then we'll do it the hard way," Nya said. She backed away from the crater and rotated the rover to the left, paused, then turned to the right.

"What are you doing?" Tam asked.

"Looking for a path." As the rain resumed bombarding the rover she repeated the scan one more time. "I can't tell which way to go."

"Pick one," Kem finally said. "I doubt one way is significantly better than the other."

"Go right," Tam suggested.

"Why right?" Nya asked. "I thought you couldn't tell."

"It's simple logic. We know the mine is closer to that edge of the crater, so that means it's a shorter drive."

"Unless we run into another crater."

"Or a canyon, or mountains, or a lake," Ren said.

"Don't forget, there is only one way into the complex," Kem said. "If we go right we'd still have to drive all the way around the basin."

"Right through your old neighborhood," Nya teased. "Sir."

"Ah, memories."

"You're the boss," Nya said. "You make the call."

"Being the boss means trusting my people. Whatever your instincts tell you I'll support your decision."

"Yes Sir." Nya gripped the yoke and twisted the throttle as she turned the rover to the left.

"I hope you're right," Tam muttered.

"Me too." They had barely begun to move when an indicator on the center console began to flash. Nya stopped again and activated the large center screen.

"What is it?" Kem asked.

"Someone must be looking out for us. We're receiving a download from the NavSats."

"They finish the grid!" Tam shouted, prompting Kem to lean to the side for a better view of the screen.

"How long will it take?" he asked Nya.

"A couple of minutes, Sir. It's a lot of data."

"Let's contact the base while we're waiting. I'm sure they are anxious to know where we are."

"Yes Sir." Nya activated the com and sent a pairing command to the suits. "Accept the link and you'll be live." Kem opened his sleeve panel and tapped the flashing green button.

"Rover to base. Come in please," Kem called. After a few seconds he tried again. "Rover to base, come in."

"This is Mining Complex Alpha. Stand by for the Assistant Director."

"Is that Lim?" Nya asked. "He always sounds so formal."

"He's new," Kem explained.

"Nice to hear your voice," Lue said. *"We were starting to wonder if you had fallen into a crater."*

"Not quite," Kem replied as everyone looked at each other and laughed. "In fact, we'll be heading back as soon as the Nav data downloads."

"The Gemisi just informed us the grid has been completed for about an hour. I'm surprised we didn't hear from you sooner."

"We had a little trouble with our antenna."

"I see. Did you find what you were looking for?"

"We did."

"What is it?"

"Some kind of probe, but we haven't been able to determine it's origin."

"So it's definitely not one of ours."

"We don't think so. We're bringing it back for further study."

"I know a few engineers who will be thrilled to get a closer look at it."

"What's the status of the mine?"

"Everything is running smoothly."

"That's good news."

"The replacement pod will be here in about an hour, but we're still three rows ahead of the empty rack. Plenty of time."

"I'm glad that worked," Kem said. "What about atmo."

"Our visitor's solution did the trick," Lue replied. *"After a thorough cleaning the sensors are working perfectly."*

"That's good news." A beep from the Nav console interrupted

the conversation, prompting Kem to mute his call to the base. "What is it?" Kem asked Nya.

"The download is complete," Nya reported. "We're good to go."

"Good job." Kem reactivate his com. "Lue, we've received the navigation data so we're heading back now."

"I need to go, too. Have a safe trip and we'll see you soon."

"Rover out." Kem sat up straight and tightened his restraints. "Ready Nya?"

"Almost." The center screen came to life, displaying a full-color image of the moon's surface including a glowing dot showing the rover's exact location.

"Got it!" Nya announced.

"Can you find us a route home?" Kem asked.

"No problem." She pulled out the tethered stylus and touched it to the rover blip, then used the directional pad to scroll the image until the mine appeared. She touched the screen again and within a few seconds the computer calculated a route and displayed a pulsing line between their location and the base. "Everyone ready?"

"Let's go." Instead of referencing the console screen Nya touched another button and the wire-frame sensor image on the windscreen was replaced by a fully rendered photo-real image of the landscape, minus the weather. The same pulsing line also appeared as a virtual three-dimensional guide projected along the path. Nya pressed another button and let go of the yoke and the rover began following the route automatically.

"I thought you preferred to drive," Kem said.

"Normally I do, but sometimes it's nice to sit back and enjoy the ride."

"I can't argue with that. How far is it?"

"Just over a hundred kliks," Nya replied.

"How long will that take?"

"A couple of hours as long as we don't run into any more obstacles."

"Keep me informed." Kem reclined his seat and did his best to relax in the bulky suit.

"Taking another nap, Sir?"

"No. I'm just going to relax for a bit."

17

Breakdown

The rover jerked sharply to the right with a heavy metallic *'clunk'*, waking Kem.

"Dammit!" Nya shouted as she brought the rover to a stop and powered it down.

"I thought you weren't going to remote drive any more," Kem said. After a quick stretch he raised the back of his seat and realized she was still in the cockpit. He released his restraints and leaned forward.

"I think we lost the right track," Nya said. "I don't know what happened. I've been doing my best to avoid the larger rocks."

"Don't worry about it. You've been doing a great job."

"I appreciate that, but it's doesn't make me feel any better."

"Is it serious?" Tam asked anxiously.

"I don't know yet," Nya replied. She took a deep breath, then addressed Kem again. "Sir, if it's just a pin we can replace it, but if one of the treads or rollers broke then we're stuck here."

"I thought these rovers were built for harsh environments," Tam said. Kem could sense Nya's frustration and placed a hand on her shoulder while he addressed the geologist's comment.

"In case you forgot, other than losing the dish we came out of that shelf collapse unscathed," Kem said calmly. "I'd say this thing is pretty tough. Our driver, too."

"These rovers may be tough but this extreme cold will make

any material brittle," Ren explained. "Don't forget, unlike most of the moons you've probably explored this one has an atmosphere to draw the heat out of objects much faster."

"I meant no disrespect," Tam said.

"Where are we?" Kem asked.

"About 50 kliks from base," Nya replied.

"How long was I out?"

"About an hour. Do you want me to go out and have a look?"

"Not yet. Call the base. Maybe the shuttle is still there," Kem ordered. "Being one driver short it may have taken them longer to transfer the pods."

"Yes Sir." Nya sat up straight and activated the com. "Rover to...Mining Complex Alpha. Come in." There was a moment of silence before Lim's monotone voice responded.

"This is Alpha, go ahead rover."

"Base, this is Director Kem. Is the shuttle still there?"

"No Sir."

"How long ago did they leave?"

"About twenty minutes."

"They've already made it back to the Gemisi," Nya said.

"Uh, base, is Lue available?" Kem asked.

"She's talking to Chief Cas. One moment, Sir."

"Do you think a transport could reach us?" Kem asked Nya even though he already knew the answer.

"I wouldn't recommend it," she replied. "They weren't constructed for cross-country travel on rough terrain."

"Meaning even if it didn't get stuck it'd probably break before it reached us."

"Very likely, Sir."

"This is Lue," the radio crackled. *"What's going on, Kem?"*

"Lue, we have a slight problem," Kem explained.

"Is everyone okay?"

"We're fine, but it looks like we've thrown a track."

"Can you repair it?"

"We're not sure yet. I called you first hoping the shuttle was still there, but Lim said it left a while ago."

"That's true. You can thank Nya for training her drivers well. They did a heck of a job."

"Sorry, Sir," Nya said.

"Don't be," Kem said. "Lue, is there any chance we can get a shuttle down here?"

"You know what the Captain is going to say. Between the high winds and already having to make unscheduled trips already she's not going to be eager to send another if she doesn't have to."

"Maybe we won't need it," Kem said. "If it's just a pin Nya thinks we can repair it here. If not, I'll call you back."

"I'll ask Ula if she has any ideas, just in case. We have your location, so that won't be an issue."

"Talk to you soon." Kem settled back in his seat and stretched again. "Nya, let's go have a look."

"Yes Sir."

"Mind if I tag along?" Ren asked.

"Not at all," Kem said. "More minds on the problem will get us home sooner." He stood up and moved to the back of the cabin. While he retrieved the other tool kit Nya removed the remote control pad, then she and Ren released their restraints and joined him.

"What should I do?" Tam asked.

"Monitor the radio," Kem suggested even though all their suits were capable of doing so. He handed Ren the tool kit and opened the rear panels as a blast of wind swirled around the cabin.

"Just don't touch anything," Nya added, prompting the geologist to turn forward and cross his arms. With tools in hand the trio stepped out and Kem closed the panels.

"There's your problem," Nya joked. The entire right-hand track was laid out several meters behind the rover, with the carriage rollers resting directly on the frozen ground. She bent over and walked the length of the track, examining every segment. Once she reached the end she repeated the procedure from the opposite side until she returned to the others. "The brackets appear to be intact." Kem looked past the end of the track and spotted several cylindrical pieces. He walked over and picked them up, then returned and held them out for Nya and Ren to examine.

"The pin sheared," Nya said. "That's good news. It should be easy to fix."

"How do we get the tracks back onto the rollers?" Kem asked.

"I can try backing the rover onto them. Hang on." She activated the remote pad and set the drive to REVERSE. As she eased the rover backward, though, the lack of traction on the right side caused it to rotate in place. Nya drove it forward and returned it to the original position. "Looks like we're doing this the hard way."

"What do we do?" Kem asked.

"We need to pull the track onto the carriage." Kem reached down and grabbed the end tread and pulled but it didn't move.

"It's too heavy," he said.

"It can't be heavy," Ren said. "We're in fifteen percent gravity."

"It's probably frozen to the ground," Nya guessed. "I noticed every time we stop there was a slight jerk when we started moving again. The treads must heat up on the rollers, then slightly melt into the surface. As long as we are moving it doesn't matter, but once we stop they refreeze."

"Then we need to thaw them or use pry-bars."

"Or we use the puller," Ren said.

"Where are we going to get a tread puller out here?" Nya

asked. Without another word Ren opened the tool case and removed a thick cylinder 20 centimeters long and the diameter of the tread pin, then walked to the front of the rover and opened the tow cable cover. Then she moved to the right corner and grasped a recess on the end of the nose panel. She pulled it out to the side, revealing a heavy open-framed arm 30 centimeters long with three rollers mounted on a bracket near the end; two vertical and one horizontal.

"Let out the tow cable," Ren instructed Nya.

"Copy that!" Nya said as she activated the winch. "When did they start including those?"

"This is the first generation to have it," Ren replied. She guided the cable over the first vertical roller, which was mounted sideways, then around the horizontal roller, and finally under the last roller, which was in line with the center of the carriage. As the cable continued to spool out she walked it all the way past the rover until she reached the far end of the track assembly. While holding the cable loop between the two brackets she pushed the cylinder through all three, then twisted the end, causing it to expand and lock it in place. "Okay! Take it in!"

"You don't have to shout," Nya said as she reversed the winch. "We're using radios."

"Sorry." Ren held onto the cable as it pulled the end of the track up and toward the rover like a snake obeying it's charmer. When it reached the rear drive wheel at the top of the carriage, though, it caught on the cogs and the winch whined in protest. "Hold on!" Ren shouted again. Nya stopped the winch and shook her head. "Sorry. You need to disengage the drive."

"Hang on." Nya used the remote pad to release the brakes. "Ready."

"Reel it in." When the cable began moving again it glided over the roller effortlessly, pulling the track over the top of the carriage.

Once it had reached the puller arm Nya stopped the winch while Ren removed the temporary pin and let the end of the track hang. Once the cable had fully retracted Ren closed the cover, then folded the roller bracket and shoved the arm back into the nose.

"That was easy," Kem said. "I'm impressed."

"We still have to loosen the drive wheels, then feed the track under the carriage and join the two ends," Nya explained.

"So how do we do that? Another built-in gadget."

"Unfortunately, we have to do that the traditional way," Ren replied. "We need to muscle it under while driving forward, all while avoiding getting your hands crushed."

"That doesn't sound like fun."

"I have an idea," Nya said.

"What's that?" Ren asked.

"As you said, normally someone would have to guide the track manually while the rover is driven forward."

"Right."

"But the rollers on these are so efficient it shouldn't take much effort to push it in this low gravity."

"You're right," Ren said.

"So what's the plan?" Kem asked the two women.

"Get ready to push it forward," Nya said.

"Will it really be that easy?"

"Are you kidding?" Ren asked. "Sorry, Sir. I meant no disrespect."

"Don't worry about it. I yield to your expertise." Kem moved to the back of the rover and waited while the two women got to work. Nya removed a replacement pin from the tool case and set it on the fender, then removed a socket wrench and handed it to Ren. The linguist knelt down and began removing the bolts from the center part of the carriage cover. Once it was loose she grasped each end and turned to face Kem.

"Sir, can I get you to set this inside?" Kem reached out to take the panel from her when a gust of wind ripped it from Ren's hands, sending it flying toward Nya. Before the driver could move out of the way her helmet was struck by the panel, cracking the lens and sending her to the frozen ground.

"Nya!" Kem shouted as he and Ren ran over to help. "Are you okay?"

"I'm fine," Nya said as they helped her up. "The ground broke my fall."

"Always the comedian." Kem looked up just in time to see the wind carry the panel over the side of a small ridge. "Can we drive without it?"

"Yes, but we should leave it behind," Nya answered.

"Then once we're done we'll try to retrieve it."

"We better hurry."

"I'm sure it won't get too far."

"That's not it," Nya said. "My helmet is leaking."

"What?"

"It's not bad, but I'm definitely losing air."

"You better get inside and let us fix the track then."

"That won't do much good until we can establish cabin atmo, and we can't do that until *everyone* is inside the rover. I'm better off staying here and helping."

"She's right," Ren said. "It will be faster with three of us."

"Are you sure?" Kem asked Nya.

"Yes Sir. My pack is keeping up for now."

"Then let's get this done."

"Get ready to push, Sir," Nya instructed.

"Just tell me when."

"Stand by." Nya crouched at the front of the carriage while Ren did the same at the back. They loosened the drive wheel tensioners, then moved around to face each other and pushed the wheels toward the center a few centimeters. Nya then pulled the front end of the tread down and wedged it under the lower front roller while Ren walked to the back end of the track and knelt next to it. "Okay, Sir, start pushing. Slowly." Kem placed his hands on the rear panel and applied gentle pressure. As Nya had predicted the rover began rolling forward. She gripped the edge of the front tread to keep it in place while Ren kept the back end straight as the rover pulled it closer. Once the front end became trapped by the weight of the rover Nya stepped back and watched carefully until it emerged from the lower rear roller and Ren ended up next to Kem holding the loose end. "Stop!" Kem stopped pushing and peered around the linguist.

"Everything okay?" Kem asked.

"Yes. That should do it." Nya use the pad to set the brakes, then picked up the lower end of the track and raised it toward the upper end as Ren pulled her end down tight. "Sir, can you push the pin in?" Kem retrieved the pin from the fender and pressed it into the first hole in the tread bracket. As the two women held the ends together he began pushing it in until it passed through the first two brackets, but after a few more centimeters it stopped.

"It's stuck," Kem said as he wiggled the pin.

"That should be enough," Nya said. The women let go of the treads and they stayed in place.

"I'll get the hammer," Ren said. She removed the larger one from the tool case and began pounding on the pin while Nya and Kem held the treads straight. Once it was all the way in Ren grabbed the socket wrench and handed it to Nya. She pressed the socket into a small recess in the inside end of the pin and began turning it. As she did a set of cams slowly rotated outward, locking the pin in place. After one last turn she pulled her arm out and handed the wrench back to Ren, who then placed both tools back in the case.

"That's it," Nya said as she stood up and raised her fist triumphantly. She turned toward the others when the crack in her helmet lens suddenly expanded across the entire width and the air began escaping more rapidly.

18

Return

"Nya!" Kem shouted again. He knelt next to her and placed his hand over the lens but the crack was too wide. "We need to get her inside!" Ren opened the back and helped guide the others into the rover.

"They're in!" Ren shouted as she closed the panels. Tam quickly activated the purge, clearing the cabin.

"We need to get atmo in here now!" Kem ordered.

"No!" Nya said as she gripped Kem's arm tightly. "We need to find that panel."

"What are you talking about?" Kem asked as he placed both hands over the crack. "You're losing air."

"If we don't retrieve it the wind could carry it back to the mine," Nya explained calmly. "Imagine how much damage it could do."

"You're right." Kem sighed and turned toward the cockpit. "Tam, let's go before it gets too far."

"Yes Sir." Tam released the brake and gripped the yoke tightly. Once they were underway Kem turned his attention back to Nya.

"What can we do about your suit?"

"There should be a stack of bonding strips in the forward bin. Try using a couple of those to seal the leak."

"I'll get them," Ren said. She hurriedly searched through the bin until she pulled out a small black case and spun around to face

Kem. "Here you go, Sir." She opened it away from herself and Kem pulled out two semi-transparent strips 4 centimeters wide and 15 centimeters long. He removed the backing of one and pressed it over the crack.

"Hurry, Sir," Nya said. "I'm almost out of air." Kem quickly applied the second strip, then pressed both against the broken lens as firmly as he could without cracking it more. "I think that's it," she said. "I need to replace my gas pack."

"I got it," Ren said. She retrieved Nya's support case and removed a spare recycling module. After moving behind Nya she pressed the release button on the suit and slipped the old module out, then quickly slapped the new one into place. "Good to go," she said with a pat on Nya's back. Kem opened her suit controls and restarted the processor.

"I'm okay, Sir," she said as she took a deep breath. "Thanks."

"You had me worried," Kem said. "From now on I want an extra helmet accompanying all trips away from the mine."

"Like I said, just another day."

"We need to contact the mine and let them know what we're up to."

"I'll do it," Ren offered. She climbed into the cockpit and activated the com. "Rover One to Mining Complex Alpha. Come in please."

"This is Alpha," Lues voice responded. *"Good to hear from you."* Kem squeezed between the seats and gestured for Ren to re-link his com.

"Lue, this is Kem. We've repaired the rover but we are going to be delayed a bit longer."

"Is everything okay?"

"We're fine, but the wind picked up the carriage cover and carried it away. We're trying to find it now."

"Anything we can do?"

"Have them access the grid," Nya suggested. "It should be able to detect the panel as long as it's not moving too fast."

"Can't we do that from the rover?"

"We are," Ren replied. "However, the rover only displays sensor data within a two klik area to reduce processing time."

"The panel must be farther way than that," Nya added.

"Hey, Lue. See if the grid can detect it. Even if you can't get a solid fix you may be able to point us in the right direction."

"Will do," Lue said. *"If we locate it I'll give you a call."*

"Thanks. Rover out."

"I hope they find it," Nya said. "We're way over our glitch quota now, so I'd like to get back before anything else happens."

"Maybe I need to stop bringing females on expeditions," Kem teased. "You seem to have all the bad luck."

"Hey. I'm not the one who got a transport stuck."

"Seriously, if it wasn't for the two of you we'd be stranded, or worse."

"I appreciate that, Sir, but you and Tam helped, too." She gave the Director a pat on the shoulder as he sat down, then leaned between the front seats. "Need me to take over?" she asked Tam.

"Can you even see through that mess?" Tam asked. "I don't mind driving if you need me to."

"I guess you're right." Nya stepped back and settled into the passenger seat. "This tape isn't as clear as I thought, anyway."

"I'll monitor the sensors," Ren said.

"Thanks." Frustrated, Nya buckled herself in with a sigh. "So this is what it feels like to be a passenger."

"Welcome to second class," Kem joked.

"Make sure you set the sensors for metal," Nya suggested.

"I know." Ren completed her adjustments and transferred the navigation and sensor data to the windscreen. "Nothing yet."

"With such strong winds that panel could be anywhere, even

behind us," Tam said as he remained focused on the driving.

"I've got the rear sensors on," Ren said with a quick glance at the large center screen. "We'll find it."

"Unless it finds us first."

* * *

After an hour of searching the explorers found themselves in the middle of a vast plain littered with modest-sized ice-boulders. Kem yawned deeply and was about to give up when the com came to life.

"Base to rover, come in."

"Go ahead Lue," Kem responded.

"We've detected an anomaly two point five kliks north of your position, directly between you and the mine. It could be the cover."

"Is it moving?"

"Not at present."

"Thanks. Let us know if it does."

"Will do."

"Rover out. Tam, let's go."

"Yes Sir." The rover snapped ninety degrees to the right and began weaving it's way through the rocks. After half a kilometer a faint blip appeared on the windscreen. "I think we found it!" Once they cleared the larger rocks Tam accelerated. "Shower and bed, here I come!"

"Let's not get ahead of ourselves," Kem cautioned as he stretched in his seat. He settled back and watched the yellow-orange landscape flash past the windows. After a few minutes Tam stopped the rover and leaned forward.

"There it is," he announced. Ren shut off the sensors and reset the windscreen to CLEAR. Just ahead of the rover lay the carriage cover, bent and battered from it's wind-driven journey.

"Try to position the rover so the panel is right behind us," Kem suggested.

"Yes Sir." Tam maneuvered the rover around the panel, then backed up to it. When he guessed they were in position he stopped and set the brakes. "That should do it."

"I'll get it," Nya volunteered.

"Are you sure?"

"Yes Sir. The tape is holding," she said. "Besides, if the wind grabs it again we won't be risking another suit."

"Speaking of wind," Tam began. "It's picking up again, so whatever you're going to do make it quick."

"Go," Kem said to Nya. He got up and opened the rear hatch and when the ramp lowered to the ground the panel was lying a few centimeters beyond it. "Never mind." He leaned out and grabbed the edge of the panel and dragged it into the cabin. Once it cleared the ramp he closed the panels and he and Nya both returned to their seats. "Let's go home."

"Yes Sir." Tam said, relieved. Ren reset the navigation and he began following the virtual line.

"How long will it take?" Kem asked.

"Less than an hour," Ren replied.

"Plenty of time for another nap," Nya teased.

"Very funny," Kem teased.

* * *

After another hour of driving a sharp jolt rocked the rover.

"Did we lose another track?" Kem asked.

"Sorry Sir, just a rock." Tam replied. "I've been doing my best to avoid them."

"How much longer?"

"We're here," Ren announced. Kem looked through the windscreen just as the rover entered the narrow gap leading into the mine basin.

"As soon as we stop we need to get Nya down to medical for a complete examination," he said.

"I'm fine," the driver insisted.

"We may not be in the military but I'm still ordering you to get checked out."

"Yes Sir." Once they emerged from the gap Tam guided the rover past the maintenance building and slipped between it and the gas pods. When he turned toward the habitat, though, everyone was surprised to see a shuttle parked on the landing pad, but instead of being white it was black with gray trim.

"Speaking of the military," Tam said. "Where did that come from?" He pulled the rover up to the habitat entrance and parked. "Do you think there was an enemy threat?"

"I don't know, but I'm going to find out," Kem said. "Let's get inside." He and Tam assisted Nya to the airlock while Ren opened the outer door. Once inside they activated the bio-cleanse and equalization processes and Kem switched to the habitat channel. "Kem to operations."

"This is Lue. Are you back?"

"We're back."

"You're probably wondering about the shuttle."

"That's an understatement. What's going on?"

"It arrived a few minutes ago."

"Where did it come from?"

"The Proelium."

"Proelium? I've never heard of it." Kem looked up, hoping for a glimpse of the orbiting ship but the fog had become too thick.

"Apparently, it's one of the new battle carriers. It arrived in orbit a short time ago."

"Who is the Commanding Officer?"

"Commander Orn."

"The name sounds familiar. Is he here?"

"No sir. He's waiting for you on the ship."

"Waiting for me?"

"Yes Sir. The Commander asked that the object be sent up right away. He also requested that you and Ren accompany it."

"Did he say why?"

"No Sir."

"I guess we better get inside and clean up then."

"The Commander wanted the shuttle to return the moment you arrived."

"Is that really necessary?"

"He was very specific about that."

"Fine," Kem sighed. "We'll get it transferred to the shuttle."

"Val is on his way with a transport."

"Copy that." Once the airlock pressurized Kem opened the inner doors. "Tam, make sure Nya gets checked out."

"Yes Sir." While Tam assisted Nya to the elevator Kem and Ren remained in the airlock and reversed the process. By the time they returned to the rover the transport was waiting next to it. They removed the object and carefully transferred it into the cradle.

"Should we strap it down?" Ren asked.

"It should be fine," Kem said. "We're only going thirty meters." They climbed into the cradle and crouched behind the object, then Kem slapped the fender and waved at Val. "Let's go."

"Yes Sir," the driver replied. The transport crawled across the frozen ground and ascended the ramp. When they reached the shuttle the landscape scrolled to the left as Val spun the transport into position and the cargo hold began to open. Other than being black and gray the shuttle was nearly identical to those assigned to the mining operation except for the small cannons recessed into the hull at key points fore and aft.

"Charming," Kem said he and Ren climbed out of the cradle. They lifted the object into the cargo hold and strapped it to the lower vehicle bracket between the two pod receptacles. As soon as they backed away the rear panel unfolded and lowered into place, sealing the hold.

"Shuttle Meki to Director Kem." a female voice called out over the radio.

"Go ahead," Kem replied.

"We're ready for departure as soon as you and Ren are on board."

"We're on our way." Kem waved at Val and the little truck pulled away. Once it left the landing pad Kem and Ren walked around the port winglet and up the ramp to the main hatch. Ren grasped the recessed handle and rotated it 90 degrees to the right, causing the seal to break with a faint *'hiss'*. The door swung outward and Kem followed Ren inside, then he turned the inside handle and the door closed. The airlock was the same as the civilian shuttles, but upholstered in grays and blacks. At the Starboard end of the airlock, opposite the outer door, was a storage closet with a hinged door, and centered on the rear bulkhead facing the inner cabin door was a shallow locker with a sliding door. The former contained emergency and protective gear while the latter contained two spare pressure suits. Kem could just make out the black helmets through the small window built into the upper part of the door. Once the airlock equalized Ren opened the hatch leading to the passenger compartment.

19

A New Presence

"Welcome aboard, Sir," the pilot said. Both she and the copilot were wearing the same Mark Ten suits as the miners, but instead of white with light gray trim they were black with dark gray trim, just like the shuttle and spare helmets.

"Thanks," Kem said as they entered the cabin. Like the airlock, the interior was also upholstered in black and multiple shades of gray. The passenger seats were similar to those in the rover but arranged in three rows of four across with an aisle down the center. Each row corresponded to one of the small round windows in the hull, while in contrast the only non-glass area of the cockpit was the floor, with the rest enveloped by the large multi-faceted bubble. The pilot seats were mounted on individual pedestals with only a modest console between that expanded into a 'T' in front of them. There were dozens of control switches and four display screens, one for each pilot and two arranged vertically in the center. The sparse design and large canopy provided a spectacular unencumbered view.

Kem approached the cockpit and placed a hand on the back of each seat. He leaned forward hoping to read the insignias on the pilots' pressure suits but his effort was unnecessary.

"I'm Lieutenant Pan and this is Ensign Cal," the pilot said.

"Glad to meet you both," Kem said. "Lieutenant, you wouldn't happen to have a sister, would you?"

"No Sir, why do you ask?"

"You sound just like my driver."

"I see. If you'll take your seat we'll be underway." When Kem returned to the passenger section Ren had already settled into the starboard window seat of the front row. Kem sat next to her and began buckling himself in.

"Did you want to sit next to the window?" Ren asked.

"No thanks." Kem turned the tension knobs, securing the restraints. "Ready when you are, Lieutenant."

"Copy that." The pilot pressed a couple of buttons, then gripped the control stalk in front of her and the thruster control to her side. "Mining Complex Alpha this is Shuttle Meki one nine six three, requesting departure clearance."

"Your kind of people," Kem said to Ren. "So formal."

"Shuttle Meki, permission granted for immediate departure. Follow vertical ascent pattern."

"Copy that Alpha." The pilot twisted the thruster control while pulling up on it and the landscape outside began to fall away. After a few meters the hum of the retracting landing gear could be heard for a few seconds. In spite of the strong winds outside the stabilization jets held the shuttle steady as the control tower passed by the window. Once it disappeared the pilot lowered the thruster control and pulled back slightly on the stick and the passengers were instantly pressed firmly into their seats by the powerful main engines.

"I love that part!" Ren said as she stared out the window.

"Uh huh," Kem replied.

"Are you alright, Sir?"

"I'm fine. I'm not really a fan of orbital flight."

"I love it," she said. "Nothing can match the view."

"Is it okay to remove my helmet?" Kem asked the pilot.

"No Sir. Regulations require a fully pressurized suit at all times during flights."

"Terrific." The pilot banked the shuttle to the right as she entered the spiral ascension pattern that would carry them into orbit. As the tilted horizon gradually slipped away the vibration also diminished until the flight became perfectly smooth. Once they left the thin atmosphere only a dull hum from the main engines and an occasional *'huff'* from the control jets could be heard resonating through the hull. The pilot turned off the interior lighting and the orange glow of the moon filled the cabin. As their eyes slowly adjusted the brightest stars eventually became visible through the windows. Kem loosened his restraints and leaned toward the aisle. From that angle he could see both center monitors but the lower one captured his attention. It displayed a grid of six live camera feeds showing the intakes, the outer door, the engines, and the lower half of the cargo hold cover.

"You keep your cameras on during flight?" Kem asked.

"Yes Sir." Kem turned his attention from the monitor to the canopy, but the view was short-lived when the pilot adjusted the shuttle's trajectory and the Gemisi filled the windows. The shuttle headed straight for the cargo ship's landing bay but then pitched up slightly and passed over the main hull, revealing the gleaming white battle carrier beyond.

"Whoa," Kem said.

"That's the Proelium, Sir." the Lieutenant explained. The carrier was almost as long as the Gemisi but far more intimidating. The hexagonal hull was slightly larger than that of the Gemisi and the landing bay was centered between two equal-length sections rather than being placed toward the front. Each section contained four rows of ten rectangular doors covering the fighter docks.

"How many fighters?" Kem asked the pilot.

"One hundred sixty, Sir."

"Impressive. What class is the Proelium?"

"Since it is the first one they designated it the Proelium class or Pro-class, for short."

"Amazing." Kem wasn't a fan of the military but the engineer in him couldn't help but marvel at the new ship. Instead of a small tapered nose like the Gemisi, the front of the carrier was capped by a huge multi-faceted wedge, which not only served as a shield for the rest of the ship but also gave it a far more menacing appearance. The aft end of the ship was made up of an even larger angular section containing the drive systems. Like the front, it also provided protection and a sense of overall size. Batteries of huge combination cannons were placed at key points all over the head, tail, and along the main hull. Each could emit a focused electromagnetic pulse from the fins surrounding the barrel, or fire any number of solid or self-propelled ordinance from the barrel itself. The EM cannons had been developed to eliminate the tons of excess flak that would end up floating around a battle zone, significantly reducing the number of post-shoot incidents. Like the Gemisi, a communications dish hung below the landing bay, but was complimented by the wing-shaped bridge directly above the bay on a rearward-swept pedestal. As they approached the bay Kem could finally see see inside the forward fighter deck. The individual docks also had doors on the inside, completely enclosing them when not in use to protect the fighters.

"The doors open in less than two seconds for rapid deployment," the pilot explained.

"That's a lot faster than the old Cernan class."

"Shuttle Meki one nine six three to Carrier Proelium two two five four. Requesting approach and docking."

"This is Proelium control." the response crackled. *"Shuttle Meki, permission to dock is approved for hanger station Alpha. Once aboard escort your guests to the bridge at once."*

"Affirmative Control." The pilot guided the shuttle into the landing bay, rotated it aft, and hovered over a glowing rectangle in the center of the floor. She deployed the landing gear and skillfully touched down with a muffled *'bumpf'*.

"Nice landing, Lieutenant," Kem said.

"Thank you Sir." The shuttle rocked gently and it began sinking into the landing bay floor. Once they reached the dimly lit hanger below the shuttle was moved by a conveyor crane into the front starboard berth and secured. "Let's go," the pilot said. Kem released his restraints and pushed himself up, instantly soaring to the top of the cabin where he banged his helmet on the forward bulkhead.

"Dammit."

"Did you forget already?" Ren asked.

"I told you I hate orbital travel." After activating her own attractors Ren grabbed Kem's boots and pulled him to the cabin floor. He magnetized his cleats and they followed the pilots into the airlock. The lieutenant opened the outer hatch and gestured for them to follow, then pulled herself out. After securing the hatch the copilot headed toward the back of the shuttle while the pilot led Kem and Ren around the front to a small tram waiting in the center of the hanger. It was basically a flat six-sided platform that traveled the length of the hanger along an electromagnetic track built into the floor. Lt. Pan stepped onto it, then tapped her boot against a slightly raised section in the center. It instantly popped up to waist height, forming a hexagonal handrail. Pan and Ren grabbed onto it but Kem was still taking in the unfamiliar space. In spite of the overall size of the ship the hanger was barely wide enough to accommodate four vehicles, with two on each side parked nose to nose. That configuration allowed cargo pods to be unloaded and attached to the adjacent bulkheads, then accessed from inside the pressurized fore and aft supply rooms, similar to the habitat. Two of the remaining three berths were occupied by identical shuttles, but the fourth contained a gray two-man fighter that Kem estimated to be at least 25 yeas old.

The craft shared many features with the shuttles, including the hexagonal main hull with an angled rear panel. The wings were longer, though, with additional control surfaces, and the main engines were mounted within them rather than against the hull. A rear-swept vertical stabilizer was also another difference, allowing more aggressive atmospheric maneuvering. As with the shuttles and Proelium it contained multiple cannons extending from the leading edges of the wings; one near the tip and two closer to the fuselage. Another pair were mounted on the trailing edges in between the hull and engines. The ship was covered with black scoring, but what caught Kem's eye was the large flared housing that had been added to the rear of the main fuselage.

"That's the Skoa," Lt. Pan explained.

"Why do you have such an old fighter on board?" Kem finally stepped on the tram and grabbed the handrail. The moment he did so it began moving toward the front of the hanger.

"It's our scout ship and emergency ride home, should we need it," she explained as they approached the forward bulkhead. "The extra housing contains an early version of a displacement generator and coil."

"Hard to fit an entire crew in their," Kem joked, but the Lieutenant didn't appear to find the comment funny. "I thought the Gemisi was the first ship with displacement technology."

"Not quite, but the Commander will explain everything once we reach the bridge." Kem accepted the answer, then turned to the shuttle they had just arrived in. The cargo hold was already open and the object they had found was being unloaded while the copilot supervised.

"What's going to happen to it?" Kem asked.

"It will be taken to one of the science labs just ahead of the supply rooms," Lt. Pan explained.

"Make sure they don't damage it," Ren said to the copilot.

"Affirmative." Kem thought the exchange odd but quickly dismissed it. They passed through a small opening and stopped between two sets of doors. Pan stepped off of the tram and pressed the UP button on the starboard shaft and the doors snapped open to reveal an elevator car inside the access shaft. Unlike the full elevators inside the spokes of the Gemisi's ring, this was a basic hexagonal capsule with an opening on each of the six sides. Outside the car Kem could see the padded walls lining the shaft and the electromagnetic strips mounted in each corner used to drive and stabilize the capsule. As they followed the Lieutenant inside Kem also noticed a larger purple-colored button below the call button.

"Why does the Proelium have elevators when there isn't gravity?" he asked. "The only reason the Gemisi has them is to make the transition to the ring easier and safer."

"Only the longer shafts have them. There is one at each corner of the landing bay which run between the hanger and the pilot quarters, allowing access to the fighter docks. The only other shaft with a passenger capsule is the one between the main ship and the bridge. It makes it more efficient to move groups together, rather than having them float single file."

"So what is the extra button used for?" Kem asked.

"That locks the capsule in place and opens both ends. That allows the shaft to be used traditionally."

"I'd hate to be inside it when someone reactivated the car."

"There are sensors that prevent it from engaging if the shaft is occupied," Lieutenant Pan explained.

"That's good to know."

"Remain inside the capsule," she instructed as the outer doors closed.

"Pilot *and* tour guide," Kem teased. "What else do you do here?"

"I am the Commander's personal pilot and assistant."

"Oh. Something else you have in common with my driver," Kem said. "I'd be lost without her."

After a brief ride the elevator stopped and the outer doors opened to reveal an airlock. As soon as they entered Lt. Pan activated the bio-hazard mist, followed by the equalization process. Once the airlock was balanced Kem reached up to release his collar latch but the Lieutenant stopped him.

"You can remove your suit when we get to the bridge. There is a changing and storage room next to the access shaft."

"Procedure, right?" Kem asked.

"Yes Sir. In case of attack all guests must be in suits when moving between hardened stations."

"I guess the fact that were are so far from home doesn't change that."

"No Sir. The Commander adheres strictly to the rules."

"I don't suppose the changing room has a shower."

"It does, Sir."

"Excellent." The airlock door opened, revealing the 84 meter long starboard observation deck directly above the landing bay. "This is a lot like the deck on the Gemisi." Kem stopped and looked across at the cargo ship floating silently above the moon. "What a view."

"Except this deck also contains the pilot mess and recreational areas," Lt. Pan explained. "This way." She leaned forward and pushed off, allowing herself to float alongside the expansive stretch of glass. Kem and Ren did the same but Kem found himself heading toward the ceiling. He quickly grabbed one of the recessed handholds and launched himself toward the far end.

"I didn't realize how accustomed to gravity I'd become," Kem said as he skimmed along the ceiling. "Where do the pilots sleep?"

"Our quarters are on the deck directly above us." As they approached the center of the observation hall Kem noticed an identical airlock at the opposite end. "There are airlocks at both ends of each halls," Lt. Pan explained as she turned down the side hall. Once the guests followed her the port observation deck became visible at the far end. They floated to the center of the crossover hall and she stopped at yet another access shaft and planted her boots on the floor. "The Landing Bay's Flight Control bubble is directly below us," she explained while Kem and Ren oriented themselves upright. The doors opened and they followed the Lieutenant into the capsule. She pressed the top button and the outer doors closed and they began moving upward. Eight decks later a set of doors opened on either side, revealing two small vestibules, each with a door to a changing room on the opposite wall.

"The officers' locker room is on the port side," Lt. Pan explained. "You can use the starboard locker room."

"Thank you." Kem said. He turned and instantly jerked backward when he found himself staring directly into a pair of dark red eyes set deep into the round translucent-gray face of the Commander.

20

The Sazin

"Welcome to the Proelium," the man said with a series of grunts and gurgles from his roughly hexagonal snout. "I'm Commander Orn." He held up his left hand with all three fingers extended and touched the thumbs on either side together.

"Thank you, Commander," Kem said as he mirrored the gesture before removing his helmet. "I apologize for my behavior. I've gotten so accustomed to wearing suits that I almost forgot what we look like without them." In spite of Kem's reaction the Commander looked very much like any Sazin man, except at 2.5 meters he was a full 10 centimeters taller than Kem. His intimidating presence was further augmented by his neatly formed dark gray uniform and red and blue rank insignia. It featured a cluster of multiple-sized hexagons above his name and commander rank. As far as the man's facial features, the six sides of his snout were less defined and his heavy brow drooped closer to his eyes, indicating he was a bit older than Kem. The small angular spots that began on each side of his face and wrapped around the back of his head had also faded to a light reddish-brown color, as opposed to Kem's, which were still dark red. That made the Commander's multiple auditory inlets more visible among the spots. The two rows of six nostrils running along his snout up to his brow twitched in sequence and the Commander scrunched his face.

"Speaking of suits, It's about time you got out of yours."

"That sounds like a good idea," Kem said just as a glob of snot oozed from his lower nostrils. Embarrassed, he quickly wiped it away with his sleeve before it could detach and float away. "Sorry. Space travel doesn't always agree with me."

"You and me both," Commander Orn said. "Lieutenant Pan, show our guests to the changing room."

"Yes Sir." The lieutenant removed her helmet, revealing her spots to be deep yellow, then stepped through the changing room door. "This way." Ren removed her own helmet, revealing her spots to be a medium green, and she and Kem followed the pilot. When they entered the changing room there were individual stalls, each with a locker large enough for two pressure suits and several uniforms, as well as a set of zero-gravity showers and toilets. "I'll make sure your suits and uniforms are cleaned while you freshen up."

"Thank you, Lieutenant," Kem said with a friendly grunt and snort as she left the room.

* * *

"Between the atmo problem and our expedition it feels good to be out of that suit." Kem said as he ran his hands down is freshly cleaned white and gray uniform. He and Ren returned to the bridge but the Commander was nowhere to be seen. The rest of the bridge staff were busy staring at data screens or communicating with crew in other parts of the ship. There were three long control consoles arranged in shallow 'V' formations, all facing the large screen mounted to the wall separating the bridge from the elevator shaft, with the vestibules exiting on either side. Each console contained several stations, including communication, navigation, weapons, and sensor control. Behind the consoles there was a raised platform with a single chair. It was occupied by a female officer staring intently at a control pad. Her medium blue spots were much brighter and crisper, indicating she was considerably younger than the Commander and Kem. Using the attractors to walk across the floor, Ren led him around the last row and they both stepped onto the platform. While they waited patiently Kem scanned the rest of the bridge until he spotted Lieutenant Pan standing against the back wall next to a lone door. Her helmet was off but she still wore her pressure suit. Kem was about to mention it to Ren when the officer finally looked up.

"You must be Director Kem," she said while displaying the standard gesture. "I'm Sub-Commander Tev."

"Good to meet you," Kem replied. He was about to introduce Ren when the First Officer interrupted.

"Good to see you again Ren," she said. "How is your assignment going?"

"I-It's going well, Ma'am," Ren replied.

"Excellent. The Commander is waiting for you both in his private office." She swept her arm toward the door Lt. Pan was standing next to.

"Thank you," Kem said. He and Ren stepped down from the command platform and walked to the back. The Lieutenant pressed a button to open the door and she and Ren exchanged nods as the linguist entered the room. When Kem passed the pilot he stopped and leaned closer to her. "You may sound like my driver but you sure don't look like her." As he entered the dark office Pan scrunched her snout and furrowed her brow, unsure whether the comment was an insult or a compliment. By the time the office door closed she decided it must be the latter and her frown was quickly replaced with a look of satisfaction.

Once inside Kem's eyes strained to penetrate the dark room, but all he could see were two huge angled windows he guessed were at least 30 meters wide. They provided a spectacular view of the wing-like tail section of the Proelium.

"Care to enlighten me?" Kem asked Ren quietly as he waited for his eyes to adjust. "I don't like being lied to."

"Don't be too hard on Ensign Ren," the Commander's disembodied voice said.

"Ensign?" Kem asked.

"Yes. Her Mining Guild rating is a cover."

"That explains a lot," Kem said under his breath. The overhead lights came on, revealing him standing to their right, next to a large screen on the port side wall. The office was 12 meters deep and the full width of the huge windows. Below the screen there was a low cabinet with a control console built into the top. The starboard end of the room was mostly empty, except for a large desk facing outward, another low cabinet against the wall behind it, and a vertical sleeping berth to the side. The center of the room was occupied by a U-shaped conference table surrounding a computer display table similar to those in the control tower, but much larger. "Please, have a seat." The Commander gestured toward the near side of the table where four metal bottles waited, two large and two small, each held in place on the metal table by weak magnets in their bases. "I took the liberty of having some food brought in for you."

"Thank you," Kem said. As he and Ren moved to the table and sat down he noticed the Commander's right hand trembling. As if sensing Kem's observation the man began rubbing it firmly with his other hand. Kem quickly shifted his gaze to the windows but the view had been replaced by a reflection of the room. "This is your office?"

"Well, obviously it also serves as a conference and briefing room, but yes."

"Impressive." Kem picked up the smaller of the two bottles in front of him and began suckling on the feed tube. The re-hydrated blend of plant proteins and extracts lacked the flavor of the Gemisi's fresh produce but he felt it prudent to be respectful of his host. "Not bad," he said with an exaggerated slurp.

"When I assumed command the Proelium I asked for the finest food preparers in the service," the Commander said. "Between you and me, though, it's still slop." Kem almost choked on his food and quickly changed the subject.

"So why all the secrecy?" he asked.

"You don't waste any time, Director. I like that." The Commander approached the table, took a sip from his own food bottle, then set it down. "We're not naive enough to believe we are winning any popularity contests among the civilian population, so we thought it would be less *irritating* if Ren was presented as a mine employee."

"We might have a better opinion of the military if you didn't keep so many secrets," Kem argued.

"Perhaps."

"So why were Ren and her team assigned to the Gemisi?"

"They weren't. We transferred Ensign Ren to the Gemisi right before she and the rover were flown to the surface. It was necessary to maintain the illusion of her being part of the mining team."

"I'm confused," Kem said. "I thought you had just arrived."

"Actually, we arrived right after the Gemisi, but this isn't our first visit to this system," the Commander explained. "We were sent here before to make sure it was safe."

"Safe?"

"You never know who may be out there," Orn said, prompting Kem to look over at Ren.

"I think the two of you have been out here too long," Kem said. "Ren said the same thing."

"It's just a statement of fact, but I'll get to that later. Our mission demanded the presence of a team like Ren's, with highly trained specialists in linguistics, biology, geology, and engineering."

"Ren already explained that part, too," Kem said. "I'll ask again, why all the secrecy? The military has never cared what civilians think about them, so there has to be more to it than just that."

"You're very perceptive, Director."

"Does the Captain know?"

"She was aware we were here, and she facilitated the blackout needed to transfer Ensign Ren to the Gemisi. Beyond that she has not been informed of our entire mission, only instructed by the Mining Guild and your administrative Board to remain at our disposal."

"At your disposal?" Kem asked. "The Guild is a civilian organization."

"True, but you were correct about there being more to our secrecy." The Commander picked up a small control pad from the console and activated the display table. "What I'm about to show you must not be discussed with anyone. Not even your second in command."

"Of course," Kem agreed. While he resumed slurping his liquified plants the Commander called up a three-dimensional model of their home solar system, showing all thirteen planets orbiting the red dwarf. Sazi, the second planet, and Asell, the third planet were both highlighted by a pulsing aura. He pressed another button and the image switched to an isolated view of the two planets. "As you know, the people of Sazi became united after the discovery of intelligent life on our sister planet, Asell. However, soon after that revelation there were disagreements over which nation should represent us when dealing with our newly discovered neighbors. New fighting began and continued until fifty years ago when the Aselli became a genuine threat by developing interplanetary travel. It was that threat to our way of life that led to the unification we still enjoy to this day."

"I'm familiar with our history," Kem said. "Ren and I had an interesting discussion about it."

"Of course. I simply want to emphasize the importance of our mission."

"Many have argued that the Aselli threat was exaggerated to justify invading them first to take their resources," Kem said. "They said their ships were barely capable of interplanetary travel and had no weaponry."

"I'm well aware of the pacifists' claims," the Commander said. "Believe me, the threat was real. Even before they had long-range ships they were more than capable of launching weapons powerful enough to reach Sazi."

"But they never did, nor did they attack us with warships until after the war began." Kem's comment prompted the Commander to clench both thumbs of his right hand and punch the table, challenging the attractors on his boots to keep him secured to the floor.

"The Aselli are barbarians!" The Commander straightened up and took a deep breath through all twelve nostrils. By the time he continued it was as if the outburst had never happened. "I apologize. It was never our intention to take control of Asell, for resources or any other purpose. The goal was to always to ensure our safety as we searched our own solar system for an answer to our methane shortage."

"We could argue exopolitics all day," Kem said. "Is there a point to your presentation?"

"There is."

"What exactly is your mission?"

"I'll get to that momentarily," Commander Orn said. He

switched the 3D display back to their entire solar system. "Once the war with Asell began it wasn't long before every planet in our system other than Kreela was being mined by one side or the other, further adding to our shortages. That meant every one of those mines were under constant attack by the other side."

"I experienced that first hand," Kem said. "I was on Gezen when the mine there was attacked."

"I heard that was a bad one," Ren said.

"It was."

"That incident is one of the reasons you were selected for this mission," the Commander explained. "From the reports I read you repelled the Aselli attack almost single-handedly, and with nothing but hand weapons."

"It was more than just me, and we did have the roof cannons," Kem said.

"Ah, modesty. Was it not that incident that led to your promotion to Director."

"That was just a rumor," Kem said. "I had already been offered the promotion when the attack occurred."

"Well, regardless of the circumstances it was well earned. That's why I asked for you specifically."

"You asked for me? Since when does the military get involved with civilian mining operations?"

"Since we discovered this system," Orn explained. "We are in relatively uncharted space now, so all mining operations must be secured at all costs."

"Are you expecting an attack way out here?" Kem asked.

"Not from the Aselli," the Commander replied. "Our intelligence tells us they are many years away from interstellar travel." He walked around and sat on the edge of the table next to Kem. "The mine is safe, I assure you. As far as your other question, we needed someone who is willing to do whatever it takes to keep the methane flowing. I believe that person is you, Director Kem."

"I'm flattered, I guess."

"We're not the bad guys, I assure you. We just want what's best for our people." The Commander returned to the console and leaned on it, lost in thought for a moment.

"There's something you're not telling me, isn't there?"

"Yes," the Commander said with a sigh.

"The war is not going as well as the general public believe," Ren said.

"How bad is it?" Kem asked as he adjusted his gaze from her back to the Commander.

"Very bad," Orn replied. He opened the front of the cabinet, revealing a dozen rows of hexagonal data drives about the size of a flashlight. He pulled one out and inserted it into an empty slot on the console, then brought up a chart on the wall display. "Without a long term solution our experts estimate we will run out of methane within ten years."

"That can't be right," Kem said. "Once the mine on Gezen was operational again it was producing more methane that Malis and Terman combined."

"I'm afraid all three have fallen to the Aselli," the Commander explained.

"When did that happen?"

"Shortly after your departure."

"I can't believe it. Were there any survivors?" Kem asked. "I had friends at all three facilities."

"The reports we received before leaving stated most of the workers were evacuated." The Commander opened the cabinet and removed another drive, then held it up. "This drive contains everything we have on the attacks. You're welcome to go through the lists of names."

"I'd appreciate that, Commander." Kem stared at the drive, stunned.

"That's why this mission is so important," Ren said. "We need you."

"But with those three mines gone this moon isn't going to provide enough methane, even after the beta complex is built."

"Not on it's own," Commander Orn confirmed. "But, thanks to a new technology we are confident we will have a much larger source of methane within two years."

"What source?" Kem asked. The Commander switched the screen image to that of a single planet with modest land masses surrounded by abundant water oceans. A heavy covering of clouds swirled over the planet's surface, giving it an overall blue and white color. "I don't recognize it."

"That's because it's the third planet of *this* system."

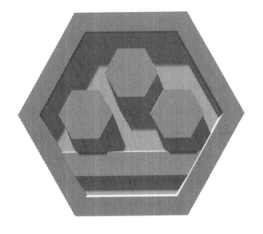

21

The Target

"I'm confused," Kem said. "I was under the impression this moon was the only viable source of methane in this system."

"As of right now that's true," Commander Orn replied.

"Then what are you proposing?"

"Surely you don't think we spent the last fifty years and half our defense budget developing displacement drive technology, then traveled forty light years from home just to mine one little moon."

"I guess that wouldn't make much sense, but how are we going to mine a planet if there isn't methane there?" Kem asked. "What new technology were you talking about?" The Commander switched the display table to show a model of a ship that resembled the Gemisi, but without the gravity ring. As it rotated laterally Kem realized the panels on the port side were perforated with thousands of small holes, but the starboard side panels remained smooth. "What kind of ship is that?" Kem asked. "It looks a bit like a Muso class corvette, but more plain and with a displacement drive."

"You have a good eye, Director. It used to be the Engano before it was refit with the new drive and a full compliment of next generation launch tubes."

"I thought the Engano was destroyed during the battle of Surnat."

"That was the official report, but in reality it was only moderately damaged, so it was towed to the same secret shipyard where the Proelium and Gemisi were built." Commander Orn explained. "Most of the gun batteries were also removed, but that won't be an issue. Once the refit was completed it was renamed the Reaper."

"Where is it now?"

"The Reaper arrived in this system shortly after we did and is currently in orbit on the far side of the planet," Orn explained. "We transferred a small crew aboard to perform the initial start-up procedures. Once those have been completed we will bring it around for final checks, then both the Reaper and Proelium will jump to the launch coordinates."

"What exactly does it launch?" Kem asked.

"It launches these." The Commander switched the 3D display to that of an object consisting of a long black shaft with an inverted bowl attached to one end, while the other end tapered to a point. A floating set of specifications indicated the object was 2.5 meters long and 20 centimeters wide at the flat side of the bowl. "After a spectral analysis of the target planet we began developing these," Commander Orn explained. "We call them arosils." Kem stood up and leaned across the table for a better look. Up close he could see that the object wasn't actually black, but a deep red color, like their eyes. The surface was also lightly textured rather than smooth. The Commander pressed another button and like the previous model the arosil began to rotate laterally. As the flat side of the bowl swung around it appeared to be covered with a transparent membrane, protecting a set of radially arranged vanes.

"What exactly does it do?"

"It's the delivery package for an organic methane generator," the Commander replied. "The shaft is formed out of billions of highly compressed genetically engineered seeds and the tail piece is a dormant organic plant designed to convert the environmental composition and then begin generating methane."

"How do they work?"

"These things are amazing," Ren said. "The Reaper will shoot millions of them to the surface where they will start to grow."

"Grow?" The Commander switched the wall screen to an animation showing one of the projectiles arcing across the screen until it struck a circle representing the planet. Then the shaft broke down, covering the surface. While the seeds sprouted into a mold-like material, the inverted bowl increased in size and multiple vines appeared from underneath, growing outward in a radial pattern. By the end of the animation the dome had grown to 60 centimeters across and had become elevated by the vines, which formed a central stalk to support it.

"The tail forms a protective shell for the plant inside," Ren explained. "Once fully grown it will remove the water and most of the gases other than the nitrogen and use them to manufacture the methane."

"And how does it do that?"

"Simple. The planet is rich with both water and carbon. The vines absorb the water and separate it, then the plant feeds on the oxygen while combining the hydrogen and carbon into methane."

"You're going to turn the entire planet into a methane farm."

"Exactly," the Commander replied. He switched the image to that of the Reaper with one of the arosils below it.

"So how will the Reaper deploy them?" Kem asked. The Commander switched the screen to another animated model as he narrated.

"There is an asteroid belt between the fourth and fifth planets. It's mostly empty space so the Reaper will be positioned near the inner edge where it will launch sequential waves of arosils toward the planet, altering the speed and trajectory of each wave so they land in opposition to the planet's rotation. That should guarantee even distribution of the groups."

"The launch has to be precisely timed and angled," Ren added. "The arosils are passive so they have no way to correct themselves."

"I'm guessing that's why we are collecting the extra nitrogen."

"Exactly. In fact, the Corona and Horizon should be departing in a few minutes to pick up the pods."

"What happens to the arosils that land in water?"

"The shell will serve as a flotation vessel as the shaft dissolves and the plant grows," Ren explained. The Commander switched the display back to the single arosil. "Rather than the appendages supporting the dome, the dome will support the appendages as they absorb the water."

"That's an ambitious plan," Kem said as he stared at the model, admiring the engineering. "What do I have to do with this? If it's technical advice you require then you should be talking to the engineers."

"Correct me if I'm wrong, but your background is strong in engineering."

"Yes, but I've been out of that since shortly after I joined the Mining Guild."

"True, but that doesn't mean your education and experience is any less valuable."

"That's kind of you to say, but I still think you'd benefit from speaking with engineers who are familiar with modern systems."

"Modesty," Orn said as he took another draw from his food bottle. "I like it."

"I'm simply being practical," Kem said.

"Of course. You're correct that I don't need another engineer. That part is done. What I need is a miner who knows his job inside and out and knows how to get things done."

"Continue."

"Once the arosils have been deployed and the plants are producing methane we want you to oversee the entire operation as Supreme Director," Commander Orn explained. "Not just one facility, but all of them."

"How many mines are you planning to build there?"

"By the time the methane production reaches full capacity we will have one hundred processors spread across the planet." Orn switched the screen back to the image of the planet.

"That's impressive, but how are you going to build all those mines and get all that methane home with only one ship?"

"The Gemisi may be the only ship of it's kind right now, but in less than a year we will have a fleet of ships just like it," Orn explained. "The first to launch will be it's sister ship, the Uzai, which will deliver the materials and workers to build the Beta complex. Then both ships will remain stationed here."

"Why isn't the Mining Board handling this operation?" Kem asked. "No offense, but I still don't understand why the military has gotten involved when there isn't any threat. The Guild runs hundreds of facilities. Surely they can handle the farming in this system."

"Actually, we've been involved since the day this system was discovered."

"But that was forty years ago, when we first started looking for resources outside of our own solar system."

"Correct."

"But why?"

"At first we mainly provided technical advice and hardware. There were three agendas when we began searching for other systems." Commander Orn switched the display back to the image of the target planet. "The first was finding a planet that could support us. The second involved looking for intelligent life advanced enough to become allies in our fight with the Aselli."

"And the third?"

"If the first two goals failed but a suitable planet was located, then it was decided we would develop it for farming methane."

"I didn't realize we were looking for a second home."

"Not a second home, a *new* home," the Commander said.

"Surely things aren't *that* bad."

"The war has escalated since you left," Ren explained. "It's far worse than losing the three mines."

"I had no idea." Kem bent his knees, pulling himself onto the chair, then stared silently at the image for a full twenty seconds.

"No one outside of the governing and scientific communities knows about this," Orn explained. Kem emerged from his state of disbelief and read the list of technical data accompanying the image. "We must increase our methane production while continuing to search for a new home."

"According to the specifications it looks like the atmosphere of your target is very similar to home, with only a few minor differences."

"That's correct."

"Then why focus on the arosils? Why aren't we developing this planet to live on?"

"Unfortunately, it simply isn't suitable for us, in spite of the atmospheric similarities."

"What's wrong with it?" Kem asked as he squinted to read the smaller text.

"For one thing it's far smaller than Sazi, only about twelve percent the size."

"That means a much weaker gravity and magnetic field," Ren added. "We would have to build huge domes for protection, further limiting the number of people it can support."

"It's significantly cooler, also," the Commander said. "Their sun may be larger but it's also considerably farther away."

"*Their?*"

"I'll get to that later."

"Okay," Kem said guardedly. "Didn't we know all this when the spectral analysis was performed?"

"We did."

"If we knew we couldn't live there why didn't we launch the arosils decades ago?" Kem asked.

"That was the plan, until more advanced scans revealed the presence of new compounds, making the planet unsuitable for restructuring."

"What kind of compounds?"

"Hydrocarbons, nitrogen oxides, sulfur dioxides, both carbon monoxide and dioxide," Ren explained. "The list is quite extensive."

"Why not simply re-engineer the arosils?" Kem asked.

"They tried, unsuccessfully," the Commander replied. "To accelerate their deployment the arosils had to be engineered based on our original analysis of the planet's environment."

"Due to the extreme complexity of the genetic coding every time we tried to modify them to be resistant to the toxins that code became unstable," Ren explained. "They simply didn't work."

"If they don't work why are we still talking about it?"

"Things have changed," the Commander replied.

"How?"

"With no other potential planets available to us the scientific community refused to let this one go. Thirty years ago we finally developed a prototype displacement drive and outfitted a small scout ship to send here to investigate."

"Not the one in your hanger," Kem said. "It's not that old."

"As I said, you're very perceptive," Orn said. "No, the Skoa came a bit later."

"I hadn't heard anything about this."

"The mission was performed in secret to avoid raising the hopes of the Sazin people prematurely."

"That was very thoughtful," Kem said with a hint of sarcasm.

"The scout ship was supposed to obtain more detailed readings of the planet and return with the data."

"I can't believe the public was kept in the dark. Interplanetary travel has been celebrated as the greatest achievement in the history of the Sazin people, and you're telling me we did it thirty years earlier than most people know."

"The trip was going to be announced once they returned a few months later, without the mission details of course."

"So why wasn't it?" Kem asked.

"Well, everything went well until a glitch in the computer miscalculated the deceleration sequence. The displacement bubble collapsed prematurely and crushed the ship and everything in it, including the data they had recorded."

"Not even a posthumous celebration of their achievement?"

"If this all goes well they will both be honored publicly," Commander Orn said. "We simply have more important things to focus on right now."

"So when did we come back?"

"The technology was refined and twenty years ago the Skoa was modified to perform another data gathering mission. Like the prior mission they were supposed to return a few months later."

"And?"

"And they never returned."

"But the Skoa is in your hanger."

"Yes. I'll get to that shortly." The Commander called up an image featuring dozens of calculations and several crude ship designs. "After the failure of that mission the Council commissioned a new ship to be built that was designed from the ground up with a displacement drive. That would allow it to handle the stresses involved and complete the mission. That ship eventually became the Proelium, which was completed just over eight years ago. After a year of tests the ship was sent to locate the Skoa and complete the study of the target."

"And you were appointed Commander."

"No. My original position aboard the Proelium was as Sub-Commander," Orn explained. "Unfortunately, my former Commander fell ill near the end of our mission and I was forced to assume command. Tev was promoted to Sub-Commander and assigned to the Proelium right before our current mission."

"How long were you out here the first time?"

"Five years."

"That's a long time without gravity," Kem said.

"Indeed," Orn said as he again rubbed his right hand.

"What happened to your original Commander?" Kem asked. "Was it Zero-G Dementia?"

"A logical assumption, but no." Orn took a long draw from his water bottle before continuing. "No, nothing so spectacular as that. Apparently, one of the bottles of ferment Commander Olu brought aboard was tainted. The ship's Doctor did everything he could but it was too late."

"I'm sorry to hear that," Kem said. "Was anyone else affected?"

"Luckily the Commander chose to enjoy that particular bottle alone in his quarters."

"Were you able to complete your mission?"

"Yes, we were."

"So what did you find?" Kem asked.

"Well, we performed numerous scans of the planet while we searched for the Skoa, and after several years we finally located it near the fourth planet."

"It was during that mission that they also discovered your moon," Ren added. "As I told you before, that is why I volunteered for this mission."

"Quite the happy accident," Commander Orn said.

"Then I guess I have you to thank for my job, again," Kem said.

"Nonsense. As I said before, you earned it."

"Did you find out what happened to the Skoa?"

"As far as we could determine the ship was struck by a micro-meteoroid. It damaged the port engine and left them stranded."

"What a way to go."

"They made a valiant effort to repair the ship but were ultimately unsuccessful and perished."

"At least you were able to retrieve the ship, and pilots."

"Correct."

"I didn't notice any damage to the port engine when we arrived."

"After we returned home it was fully repaired and I requested it be kept on board the Proelium."

"A trophy?"

"A reminder."

"Fair enough. So no public acknowledgment of the Skoa crews' accomplishment, either."

"Sadly, no. Not yet."

"What about their mission?"

"Fortunately, they had completed most of their mission before the incident, so we retrieved the data and found some interesting changes," Orn explained.

"What kind of changes?" Kem asked.

"The crew found that the particulate and toxin levels of the planet had decreased significantly."

"Do we know the source of the toxins or why they were

decreasing?" Kem asked. The Commander switched the wall screen to a live feed from an isolation lab aboard the Proelium, where several pressure-suited technicians were busy studying the object Kem and his team had found on the surface.

"You're telling me it's from the planet we're going to mine?"

"Correct."

"That would mean it's inhabited."

"Also correct. We discovered their existence shortly after we arrived and began scanning the planet. Is there a problem?"

"Did you know about this?" Kem asked Ren.

"All the science team is aware of the plan," Orn replied. "As are most of my senior officers."

"So the rest of the crew is kept in the dark in case they disagree."

"Not at all. It's merely a question of logistics. The entire crew simply does not need to know the mission details to perform their duties. Regardless of their knowledge, they are soldiers and will follow orders."

"If you wish to discuss logistics, is starting a war with another race the best idea if we're already losing one?" Kem took a drink from his water bottle as the ramifications played out in his head. "Surely this will only serve to divide our resources even further."

"I'm not sure I appreciate your tone," Commander Orn said.

"I'm just considering all the options," Kem hastily replied. "I didn't get to become Director by making uninformed decisions."

"A valid point," the Commander said. "Continue."

"If one of the goals was to search for allies then why aren't we trying to make friends with them? We know they are advanced enough to send probes to other worlds."

"That's true, but they simply aren't advanced enough to provide any real tactical value," the Commander explained. "The probe you discovered is not very old, but the technology is ancient compared to ours."

"That's why it used a parachute rather than descenders," Ren added.

"Ensign Ren is correct. They have an impressive collection of satellites in orbit, but they all seem to be used for scientific discovery or communications. The only real progress they've made is a failed attempt to mine their own moon. Beyond that all they've managed to do is send a few robotic probes to other worlds."

"Like the one we found."

"Not very promising. The good news is, that also means they don't pose a threat. I assure you Director Kem, there will be no war."

"If you already knew where the probe came from why did we bother going out there?" Kem asked Ren.

"We had to be sure," Ren replied. "It wasn't until I got a good look at it that I was able to confirm not only it's origin but it's purpose. Once I had determined it was not a threat I filed my report."

"But you said you couldn't get through because the grid hadn't been completed."

"The grid only has to be completed for navigation and civilian communications," Ren explained. "Once a satellite had been deployed over the area I was able to call the Proelium by relaying a signal through the Gemisi."

"Does the Captain know?"

"What she knows won't hurt her," the Commander said.

"This species may not be as advanced as we are but if they have so many satellites how did the Skoa crew obtain such detailed data without being detected? Surely they didn't have long range sensors on such a small ship."

"The same way we gather intel on the Aselli bases. They

attached sensor arrays to stray asteroids and sent them past the planet." The Commander seemed suddenly amused. "A couple of them even passed between the planet and their satellite network."

"I can't believe the Council approved this." Kem said.

"I can assure you they did," Orn said firmly. "Once we returned home we reported our findings to the Council and Mining Guild. The terms of this mission were agreed upon and once the parameters were set then construction of the Gemisi began, followed by the Reaper refit."

"Maybe I misunderstood. When you said farming would take place if the first two goals failed I assumed you meant only if the planet was uninhabited."

"I think the Council's mandate is quite clear," Orn said. Again he gripped his right hand in his left. "Shall we continue going over the plan?"

22

The Alien Race

Commander Orn switched the display table to a rotating model of the target planet, including it's relatively large moon orbiting obediently. "As I was saying, from what we observed they've been polluting their home for decades."

"If that's true then why have the toxin levels been decreasing?" Kem asked.

"We believe they simply weren't intelligent enough to develop manufacturing and energy production techniques that weren't toxic, but as their technology has advanced they've finally improved their methods."

"Isn't that reason to make them an ally rather than wipe them out?" Kem asked. "Or at least leave them alone."

"We believe a species like this will always find a way to destroy themselves," Orn said impatiently. "Based on our data we believe their carelessness has already triggered a change in their climate. A change that has little chance of being reversed at this point."

"But we could help them with that."

"Even if we tried, what could they offer in return?" Ren asked. "Certainly not a home, resources, or weapons."

"They simply aren't worth the effort," Orn added. "As far as the Sazin people are concerned, as long as they don't know where their precious methane comes from we will be able to maintain order."

"What about the construction and mining crews? Won't they know when they see cities and satellites and dead bodies everywhere?"

"Once the process is complete most of the indigenous life will have been broken down by their own bacteria." The Commander switched to rendering of a landscape covered with the blackish mold and seemingly endless domes. "Then our spores will finish off the bacteria, leaving nothing but our plants. By the time our workers arrive there won't be any indigenous life remaining."

"So the carbon source is the life forms."

"Exactly. This planet is rich with the materials we need."

"It makes Sazi look downright barren," Ren added. "Think of it as recycling."

"And the structures?" Kem asked.

"Each facility will be located in an undeveloped area and accessed using standard vertical flight paths and topographic sensor blackouts. As far as the satellites, they will be destroyed and mine sweepers will be used to collect the debris."

"If secrecy is so important then why tell me?" Kem asked. "I could have been brought in after it's done just as easily."

"That goes back to your engineering background. You were chosen because of your education and hands-on expertise, not just your administrative skills. Because of the limited choice of locations we want you to accompany the survey team to determine the best place to construct each mine."

"So how do we launch the arosils without being detected?" Kem asked, prompting the Commander to call up the model of the Reaper again.

"The asteroid belt is well beyond the aliens' detection capability. That is also where our scout crews obtained the asteroids they used for their sensor platforms. The only way for the aliens to detect the Reaper is if they aim an optical sensor directly at it, but the odds of that happening are virtually zero."

"Won't they detect the arosils as they approach their planet?"

"We don't believe so, for the same reason the Gemisi hasn't been able to detect their transmissions," Orn explained. "They use completely different radio frequencies for communications and detection, but we were able to replicate enough of them to develop countermeasures and integrate them into the arosil design. Their surface will scatter the signals enough to avoid detection until it's too late. Then they will take out their satellites and disrupt ground communications."

"The arosils were originally designed to be aerodynamic, but that has an added benefit," Ren added. "When they land they will act as spears, killing anything they strike during the initial seeding process."

"Oh, that's much better," Kem said. "And what about those who survive the initial attack?"

"As the spores grow and spread they *should* make the surface too toxic for the remaining life to survive. Should any of them manage to live beyond that point then their atmosphere will simply lose the ability to support them."

"They can't hide forever," Commander Orn said. "Our plan is foolproof."

"So what else can you tell me about the inhabitants?" Kem asked.

"Thanks to Ensign Ren's ability to decipher some of their communications, quite a bit."

"They aren't dissimilar to us," Rem replied. She stood up and moved to the console, pulling up a crude rendering of a human male on the screen. "Bipedal, so two arms and legs, hands, feet, a distinct head with a brain and sensory organs. Given their similarity to us and the Aselli we believe there is at least one universal model for intelligent life, as long as the environmental conditions are relatively similar."

"So you're saying any planet like Sazi or Asell will eventually develop intelligent life to look like us?" Kem asked.

"Perhaps."

"More for us to conquer," Kem said under his breath.

"What was that?" Commander Orn asked.

"Nothing. I'm just trying to take it all in." Kem raised an apologetic hand toward Ensign Ren, prompting her to continue.

"Their hands have five digits, the same as ours, but they only have one that is opposable, with the other being replaced by a small but mostly useless finger. Their feet are long and narrow, providing more forward but less lateral stability."

"Senses?"

"Are you sure you want to know all this?" the Commander asked Kem. "You already seem uncomfortable with the plan. Knowing them intimately will only make it more difficult."

"I'm fine. As I said, if you want my help I need to know all the variables."

"Very well." Orn motioned for the Ensign to continue.

"Senses, right. As far as we can tell they have stereoscopic optical vision similar to ours, but it's shifted more toward violet. Olfactory is evident, but they only possess two receptor passages facing downward, just above a flattened mouth containing two rows of calcified structures. We believe they are used for breaking down solid food."

"That's weird. What is their diet?"

"Apparently, everything. They eat plants, of course, but also other species of animals, as well as a host of artificially produced foods."

"That's disgusting."

"It makes our dehydrated plant proteins seem downright

appealing," Commander Orn added before suckling the straw of his food bottle.

"Imagine having to smell all of that as you eat it," Ren said. She scrunched her snout in disgust, then took a sip of water. "Auditory receptors are indicated, but probably within a far narrower range, given that they only have two, one on each side of their head."

"They must be practically deaf," Kem said as he ran his right hand across the back and side of his head.

"Their skin color ranges from pale yellow to dark brown and is practically opaque. Strangely, many of them are covered with millions of tiny fibrous strands."

"For what purpose?" Kem asked. "Warmth?"

"I don't think so," Ren replied. "The length and density varies wildly, not just between individuals but also between regions of their bodies. They may be another type of sense that responds to physical changes in their environment. Possibly a second form of vision that some have lost over time."

"Fascinating."

"I can't tell you much beyond that."

"How big are they?"

"That's one of the more interesting differences between us. Every adult Sazin is between two hundred forty and two hundred fifty centimeters in height, but this species seems to range anywhere from one hundred twenty to two hundred twenty centimeters once they reach adulthood."

"Imagine if *we* were that different," the Commander said. "Clothes, uniforms, and environment suits would all have to be custom fitted."

"Are we sure they are all one species?" Kem asked.

"As far as we can tell. It's possible the variance is due to genetic malfunctions brought on by their toxic environment."

"A good reason not to bestow pity on them," Commander Orn added. "As I said, if left alone they will certainly destroy themselves anyway. The curse of intelligent life is to make mistakes and then repeat them. Survival depends on doing whatever it takes to overcome those mistakes."

"By making new ones."

"Perhaps. We have certainly made plenty of mistakes ourselves, but as long as I have a way to prevent it I refuse to allow the Sazin race to become extinct, either by war or depletion of our natural resources."

"Of course."

"Have we answered all of your questions?"

"I think so. On a technical level your plan is brilliant, but I have to admit it relies heavily on supposition," Kem said. "I'm still not convinced the arosils will kill everything. What if they have filters, or self contained shelters or environment suits like ours?"

"Should all of this fail and they still manage to survive then we will switch to plan B."

"And what is plan B?" The Commander called up an animated model of the Proelium from the display table. The rows of doors quickly retracted into the hull, revealing the fighters.

"Then it's my turn." With that statement Kem became visibly agitated as he carefully considered how to proceed with the conversation.

"I'm still a bit surprised the Council approved such a plan."

"Is that hesitation I'm detecting?" Commander Orn asked. "I was assured by your Board that you were loyal." Kem composed himself and looked into the Commander's eyes with all the confidence he could muster.

"I am absolutely loyal to my people," Kem said. "I'm simply expressing concern for them. If word ever got out about this plan it would make the protests against the war with Asell look like a family gathering."

"Indeed. Now you fully understand the need for absolute secrecy."

"Of course." Kem took another sip from his food bottle and stood up. "Is there anything else? I'd like to return to the surface as soon as possible," he said. "We're at a critical stage of the operation and I really should be there."

"I think that about covers it," Commander Orn said. He pulled the data drive from the console and the Proelium model vanished. After placing the drive in the cabinet below he stood up and faced Kem. "As soon as you change I'll have Lieutenant Pan return you to the surface."

"Thank you, Commander." Kem stood up and turned toward the door.

"Good day, Director Kem."

"Good day." The door opened and Kem stepped out of the office. After it closed Orn continued to stare at it for a few seconds.

"Damn," Orn said softly. After a few more seconds he adopted a more pleasant demeanor and turned to face Ren. "You did well, Ensign."

"Thank you, Sir."

"I'm particularly impressed with your ability to adapt and improvise. Helping them solve their atmo problem and restoring communications during your expedition certainly assisted with your integration into their group."

"I appreciate that, Sir."

"So, what do you think of the Director?" Orn asked.

"He's not a fan of the military, that much is certain."

"I can hardly fault him for that. Not liking us isn't a crime, Ensign, and only a fool believes there is only one viewpoint. I admire the Director for not being afraid to speak his mind, especially when surrounded by that which he is so strongly opposed to."

"I still think he's weak, Sir. He values our enemies more than his own people."

"Nonsense," Orn said firmly.

"Sir?"

"Valuing life of any kind is never a weakness, and I believe the Director wouldn't hesitate to give his own life to save his people."

"You're not actually considering going through with his promotion to Supreme Director, are you Sir?"

"Of course not," Orn replied. "Director Kem wouldn't hesitate to defend his people against extinction by an enemy's hand, but it's clear he could never justify preemptively destroying that same enemy to achieve the same goal."

"You agree with him?"

"Partly, but make no mistake, Ensign, I will do whatever it takes to insure the survival of the Sazin people. That being said, had we found these aliens under different circumstances I would have been the first to extend the hand of friendship."

"Yes Sir. I still don't understand why you wasted time bringing him up here. You heard my report."

"That's true, but I wanted to see for myself how he reacted to the details of our mission. There was still a chance he would join us, and the Director is a very capable man. He would have been a valuable asset."

"If you say so, Sir, but as I was saying, you could have gone down to the surface and determined that."

"Also true, but even though I hoped for a different result the possibility of the Director reacting as he has made it necessary to bring him aboard to facilitate his accident."

"What accident?"

"Space travel is dangerous, Ensign," Orn said coldly. "You never know what might happen out there."

23

Flight

In the changing room Kem finished slipping into his suit, but then stopped and activated the com.

"Kem to base, come in." There was no response so he switched channels. "Kem to Gemisi, please come in." Kem looked at the control pad on his arm, but everything appeared normal. "Either I'm out of range or they are blocking the signal." He pulled his helmet on and latched it but then paused and stared at the control pad.

When Kem entered the vestibule Lt. Pan was waiting for him.

"All set, Lieutenant."

"If you'll follow me, Sir." She pulled her helmet on and entered the capsule facing forward. Kem followed but made a point to stand behind her.

"So how long have you been a pilot?"

"Since before the academy. I flew dusters for my father growing up."

"You must be pretty good to fly one of those death traps," Kem said just as a random voice blared from his helmet's internal speaker. He quickly used his pad to turn down the volume as other transmissions began to overlap the first.

"Did you say something?" Pan asked.

"No, nothing. Flying a modern shuttle must be easy for you."

"Yes Sir. Here we are." The outer doors opened to the

crossover hall and the Lieutenant lead Kem out, then launched herself toward the starboard side of the ship. Kem waited a full second, then followed.

"So how did you end up as Orn's personal pilot?" Kem asked as they floated down the hall.

"The Commander wanted the best pilot in my class," she replied confidently. Kem strained to mentally filter the voices inside his helmet but when the Commander's voice came on he was able to isolate the channel and listen.

"... must look like an accident," Orn's voice said. *"No mistakes."*

"Yes Sir," Pan replied after switching channels. "Should I broadcast the accident on general channels?"

"No, let's make it look as real as possible. Once the Director is dead go ahead and broadcast a distress call."

"Yes Sir." Kem had to force himself to remain calm and continue following the pilot as his mind raced to come up with a plan. "Shall we leave him out there?" she asked the Commander.

"No. Retrieve the body and bring it back on board. We will return it to his crew once the investigation determines the decompression was caused by a failure of the airlock window."

"Yes Sir." Kem could hardly believe what he was hearing as his rage surged out of control. When the Lieutenant reached the observation hall she looked back just as the bottom of Kem's boot slammed into her face shield. She sailed across the hall and struck the thick glass window, yet still managed to unclip her sidearm. Kem gripped the handhold even tighter and launched himself toward her, knocking the weapon from her hand and again slamming her into the glass. When she didn't move right away he desperately pulled himself toward the forward airlock. Pan finally recovered and reached for the floating gun but Kem had already made it inside and initiated the equalization process. *"Sir, he got away!"* she reported.

"What do you mean he got away?" Orn asked. *"How would he know?"*

"He must have realized you had no intention of bringing him in on the plan."

"Get him! If he makes it off this ship alone he could cause a lot of trouble for us."

"Yes Sir!" While Kem listed to Orn call for security reinforcements the airlock door opened and he entered the access tube. He positioned himself head down and pushed off with his legs, floating toward the hanger deck below.

When he reached the bottom of the shaft he hit the button and the doors snapped open, revealing Cal, the copilot. Kem grabbed the bar over the door and kicked him back, then pulled his legs in and hit the button with his boot, closing the doors. His mind raced through possible solutions when he looked up and realized the elevator was shooting toward him at a high rate of speed, and with the floor panel closed.

"Safety sensors my ass!" Kem shouted. The copilot had recovered and reopened the doors, so without thinking Kem flung himself toward the approaching car. As he shot upward he rotated his body into a prone position but when he reached the next level he missed the grab bar and continued floating up. He gently tapped the toe of his boot against the back wall and when he reached the next level he slammed his hand against the door button, propelling himself backward, then planted his feet on the opposite side of the tube and thrust himself through the opening doorway just as the elevator car streaked by. Kem slammed against the end of a cage and bounced around until he was able to grab onto a handhold and stabilize himself. Once he stopped tumbling he realized the cage extended into the cavernous forward flight deck and ran along the outside of the access tube. Each side of the huge open space held four rows of ten inner doors where the fighters were docked, but the top and bottom rows were stepped inward to accommodate the angle of the exterior hull. Full-length observation halls spanned the center of each side but Kem didn't see any crew members inside. The roof and floor of the flight deck each had a recessed track running down the center, with branches toward each column of doors. The tracks led to a set of huge full-height doors at the far end that concealed an automated docking crane used to park the fighters when they returned. Once Kem was done marveling at the engineering he realized he was standing on top of the bottom row of docks and directly even with the second row, with the doors stretched out before him on his right.

Kem knew it wouldn't take long for the Proelium crew to find him so he quickly scanned the space for any possible escape. Finding nothing useful he turned around and found himself looking out over the open landing bay, with the floor a few meters below him. Even if he could get into the shuttle hanger he knew by then it would be guarded. In desperation he turned around and surveyed the entire fighter deck one more time. His visual sweep ended on the 5 by 12 meter door directly in front of him. A small panel next to it contained two buttons. One was blank and the other had the standard fire suppression symbol molded into the surface.

"Surely these things are locked," Kem said aloud, prompting a wince as he realized he was also broadcasting. He quickly disabled his microphone but kept the speaker active. With no other options he slapped his gloved hand against the blank button and to his surprise the door slid straight down into the floor, revealing the fighter nestled inside the dimly lit space. The craft was similar to the Skoa below, but being a single seat fighter meant it was shorter overall and the section of canopy behind the access panel was missing. The wings and tail were also shorter but the weapons were far more modern. The only other significant difference was the rail attached to the landing skid housing, which fit into a keyed slot mounted to the dock floor. The design served as both a restraint system to keep each fighter in place during storage, but also allowed for faster launches by not requiring the pilot to maneuver out of the dock. Instead, they simply applied full power to the engines and allowed the rail to guide the fighter out of the tight space. Beyond that the design hadn't changed much since the Skoa was new.

Kem pulled himself over the port wing toward the front of the fighter. The three combination cannons were similar to those mounted to the Proelium only much smaller. Just as Kem reached the cockpit the dock was plunged into darkness. He looked back and realized the door had closed. *I hope that was automatic*, he thought. With renewed determination he opened his control pad, casting a green glow on his suit and helmet. He activated his helmet lights and turned to face the angled glass panel of the cockpit just in front of the main hull. Kem grasped the recessed release handle below the panel and turned it, causing the panel to hinge upward.

"I don't suppose you left the keys in it," Kem said as he poked his head inside and looked around. The keys he spoke of were the electronic identification chips molded into the pilots' insignias, linking them to their particular fighter. Kem's comment was a joke, since he knew that even with the correct badge he was not trained to fly a fighter. Instead, he searched the cockpit for a weapon or anything else he might be able to use to avoid capture and get off the ship. The seat was in the entry position so Kem pressed a button on the left-hand armrest and it slid forward into the flight position, revealing a small door in the rear bulkhead. He leaned farther in and opened it and inside he found a neatly organized set of tools and emergency gear, but no weapon. Kem let out a disappointed sigh and backed out of the cockpit. He was about to give up when the beams from his helmet lights reflected off of something tucked under the seat.

* * *

On the bridge Commander Orn paced impatiently while his crew scanned the sensor and camera data. He was about to call for his First Officer when she appeared by his side.

"Nothing yet, Sir," Tev reported.

"Why is it so difficult to find one man?" Orn shouted.

"We will, but I still don't understand why the Director attacked Lieutenant Pan like that."

"I told you. He believes we should only mine natural sources of methane like his precious moon, rather than re-engineer planets for our needs."

"But we are depending on that methane," Tev said. "Without it the Sazin people won't survive."

"Exactly, which is why the Director must not make it back to the surface. If he does he could turn his entire crew against us, and that would set us back years."

"Don't worry, Sir. There isn't any way for him to get off of this ship."

"Sir, I have an inner door alarm in the forward hanger," one of the security technicians announced.

"Which one?" Orn asked.

"Docking bay thirty."

"Close it."

"Yes Sir." The tech pressed a button and the indicator on his screen disappeared.

"And inform the search team in that area that we have him trapped."

"Right away, Sir."

"That's close to where Cal lost sight of him," Tev said. "Is he trying to steal a fighter?"

"Not without the pilot's badge," Orn said. His confidence suddenly waned, though, and he straightened up and turned to the Flight Operations officer. "Flight, find out who pilots that fighter and make sure their badge is accounted for."

"Yes Sir!" The officer pressed a few buttons, then activated his com, speaking softly with some unseen voice. After a few seconds he turned toward the command platform. "Lieutenant Gro reports her key is with her suit in the pilot changing room."

"Have the Lieutenant double check, just to be sure."

"Yes Sir."

"And have two fighters readied, just in case."

"Sir, I think it's too late," the security tech announced. "I have an outer door warning for that same dock."

* * *

Kem stood on the very edge of the open fighter dock and stared across at the Gemisi. He felt as if he could reach out and touch it, yet at the same time it seemed to be a thousand kliks away. He looked down but there was nothing below him other than the orange mist of the moon's atmosphere. Knowing the bridge would have detected the opening door he reactivated his microphone.

"Director Kem to Gemisi, come in!" he called again but there was still no answer. *They must be jamming the signal*, he thought. *I'll have to wait until I'm away from the ship.* He finished slipping on the escape pack he had retrieved from beneath the fighter's seat. It consisted of a small backpack and a series of straps to secure it. In addition to the main thruster on the face of the pack there were multiple micro jets placed at key locations along the straps for precise maneuvering. The packs were designed to allow a fighter pilot to abandon the craft and make their way back to the support vehicle. Kem opened the control pad on his sleeve and linked it with the pack, and once the two were synchronized he issued a short burst from the main thruster and gently drifted forward, away from the ship. After a few meters he pressed the halt button and the jets stopped his forward movement.

* * *

Orn again leaned over the tech's shoulder. The monitor displayed an exterior view of the ship from a camera looking back along the rows of doors. With the shallow angle they couldn't see the door in question, but the pressure-suited Director was clearly visible, gently lit by the distant sun as he hovered next to the ship.

"What is he doing?" Orn had barely finished the sentence when he realized Kem was wearing the escape pack. The Commander pressed a button, mirroring the image to the main screen.

"He must have taken it from the fighter." Tev said. "Where does he think he's going to go with it?"

"He must be trying to get to the Gemisi," Orn said. "I want the suppression field expanded now! We can't allow him to contact them."

"Yes Sir," the Communications tech replied.

* * *

"Director Kem to base," he called again but there was still no answer. "Look out the damn window!" Kem yelled out of frustration. He composed himself and stared at the Gemisi beckoning from across the void. "It looks like I'm really doing this." He took a deep breath, then activated the main thruster.

* * *

Orn stared at the screen as the pack thruster fired, propelling Kem out of view of the camera.

"Flight, is Lieutenant Pan cleared for departure?"

"Yes Sir."

"Good. Tell her to bring Director Kem back. Now."

"Do you really think he would turn his crew against us?" Tev asked quietly.

"I don't know, but I refuse to let one misguided crusader interfere with our plan before we even get started."

"The Shuttle is departing now, Sir." Flight Control announced.

* * *

"Director Kem to Gemisi, come in!" Even after reducing the distance Kem was still unable to contact the cargo ship. Unsure how far he had traveled he activated the yaw control to turn himself around. He expected to see the Proelium but instead found himself staring at the rapidly approaching canopy of a shuttle.

24

Ejection

"Whoa!" Kem activated the escape pack in time to avoid being struck by the solid vertical section of the shuttle canopy near the bottom, but the sloped glass above caught his legs and he tumbled over the top of the bubble and drifted toward the back as the craft passed below him.

"That should have shaken him up," Lt. Pan said. "I'm coming around." She jerked hard on the controls, sending the shuttle aft-over-nose while also rolling. When it came to a stop they were in the same spot but facing the Proelium. Both pilots searched the immediate area but there was no sign of the defiant Director.

"Where is he?" Cal asked as he shifted his gaze back and forth. He reached over to activate the landing lights when Pan placed her hand on his forearm.

"Leave them off," she said. "We don't want to draw any attention."

"Right. So what do we do?"

THUMP

"He's on the hull," Lieutenant Pan said as she activated the external cameras. Most of the images were clear, but with the sunlight behind them the sides of the hull in front of the intakes were cast in shadow, including the outer door.

"What do we do?" Cal asked again.

"He's probably unconscious and hung up on something. Go

out and get him."

"Why me?"

"Because the rank insignia on my suit says so," she said firmly.

"Fine." Cal released his restraints and pushed up, drifting out of the seat, then grasped the headrest to pull himself toward the back of the cabin. As he did Pan rotated the shuttle 90 degrees to the right so the outer door was facing the Proelium, causing Cal to float into the starboard hull. "What are you doing?"

"Sorry! I was making sure no one on the Gemisi can see what we're up to."

"Good idea, but next time wait until I'm secured before you do that." Cal opened the inner door and entered the airlock.

"Ready your sidearm, just in case." Cal nodded and closed the inner door, then activated the pumps. Once the airlock depressurized he grasped the inner release and turned it. As the door swung out he drew his weapon, then removed the clip from the front of his suit and began pulling out the tether. He attached it to the inside anchor and nervously approached the open door until he was standing right on the edge. "Amazing," Cal said quietly when he looked down.

"What is it?"

"Nothing. Just admiring the view."

"Hurry up, or he won't be the only one getting jettisoned into space."

"Right." Cal grasped the handhold and leaned out. "So why don't we just leave him out there?"

"We need to make sure he's dead, otherwise he could call for help and tell them everything."

"That makes sense." Cal leaned farther out for a better view when his head was pulled hard to the right. Whatever had grabbed him let go just as quickly, but before he could turn to look he was launched up and away from the shuttle. "Whoa!" As he slowly rotated heels over head he caught sight of Kem standing on the side of the hull just above the outer door, gently waving. "Help me!" Cal's heart raced, but panic hadn't fully set in until he realized Kem's other hand was holding the small gray antenna from the copilot's helmet. The copilot's tether finally reached the end and he snapped to a stop still facing the shuttle.

* * *

"What's going on?" Pan asked. She glanced at the camera image but saw nothing. Annoyed, she was about to remove her restraints when the outer door indicator went out and the airlock began to equalize. "Did you get him?" She spun her seat toward the back of the cabin just as a black helmet appeared in the small window of the inner door. After a moment it was replaced by the back of a gloved hand displaying the three-fingered 'all clear' sign. "Is he dead?" There was no response. She looked again and the right half of the helmet reappeared with a finger tapping the antenna. Pan let out a frustrated sigh and unbuckled herself, then floated back to the airlock and opened the door. "What are you doing?"

The answer came in the form of a streak of black filling her vision as she was struck in the face. Kem pulled the spare helmet back for another swing but the Lieutenant recovered and drew her weapon. He managed to knock her arm away, but she again recovered and pulled herself into the airlock. Her attention was momentarily diverted by Cal's unconscious body so Kem let go of the helmet and grabbed her by both wrists. He began slamming her hand against the bulkhead, desperate to knock the gun loose, but her vise-like grip maintained control. He tried again and the gun went off, burying a projectile in the rear bulkhead.

"You're going to kill us both if you don't stop!" Kem yelled.

"So be it," she replied. "At least I'll save the mission!"

"Your mission is going to destroy an entire planet! How can you go along with that?" Kem asked as they continued to struggle.

"Because I want to save my people!" The Lieutenant drew her knee up between them and kicked out hard, pushing Kem back against the outer door. Pan aimed her weapon at Kem's head but he jerked to the side just as she fired. The projectile grazed his visor before striking the window, lodging itself in the layers of composite material. Both Kem and Pan breathed a deep sigh of relief, but when she opened the inner door and flicked her weapon toward the cabin the damaged outer window suddenly vanished. The rush of air pinned Kem to the hull and began dragging him toward the breech when Cal's body was thrown hard against the door, followed by Pan's. The sudden lack of air prevented any sound but Kem could imagine the 'crunch' of the young copilot being crushed by his superior. The double impact also damaged the latching pins and the door finally failed, swinging out and sending both pilots hurtling into space, followed by the spare helmet. Kem tried to hang on but lost his grip and was also forced out of the shuttle. After tumbling for a few seconds he managed to hit the escape pack stabilizers and then watched as the two pilots drifted toward the Proelium.

"I want to save my people, too," Kem said quietly. He used the pack to spin around and realized the rapid decompression had sent the shuttle drifting toward the Gemisi in a slow flat spin. "Oh no." Kem activated the main thruster and chased the crippled vehicle. "Kem to Gemisi, come in!" He waited, but there was no response. He decided saving the cargo ship was more important than his escape and switched channels. "Director Kem to Proelium, come in!" Still nothing. "Dammit! Isn't anyone watching?" As he approached the shuttle he reduced his speed and waited until the port side came around, then fired the thruster at full power. He was thrown toward the shuttle, clipping the open door before entering the airlock, which by then was lit only by the dim emergency lights. Kem shut down the pack but his momentum caused him to skim along the bulkhead and slam into the storage closet on the opposite side. The impact caused the door to fly open as he bounced off of it. Dazed, he grabbed the nearest hand hold and waited a few seconds to recover. Once he was able to focus he made his way back to the outer door and tried to close it but the damage was too great. "Dammit." He thought about blowing the hinges but decided one runaway object was better than two. He moved back to the inner door when he noticed the shuttle's camouflage cover spilling out of the storage closet. He paused, then continued into the main cabin.

Kem closed the inner door and hurriedly made his way to the cockpit as the approaching Gemisi passed across the view outside the canopy, followed by the receding Proelium. He buckled himself into the left seat and checked the status display. The shuttle seemed to be intact other than the damaged door but the unexpected decompression activated the fail-safe and shut down the main power. Kem pressed the override and the radio came to life.

"*...Meki one nine six three, this is Gemisi Control, come in!*" a voice crackled.

"*Shuttle Meki, you're heading directly for us!*" Kem recognized the second voice as that of the Captain.

"This is Director Kem. Mat, I've lost atmo and am trying to restore control." He looked out the canopy just as one of the huge spokes rose into view a few meters in front of the shuttle. Kem braced for the inevitable impact but the spoke swung out of the way just as the shuttle passed silently through the inside of the ring. As he drifted away from the Gemisi the flat spin kept it in view. "I don't believe it," Kem said, relieved.

"Kem, what is going on?" the Captain asked in a much more even tone. *"Why are you in a military shuttle drifting through space?"*

"Mat, they tried to kill me."

"Who?"

"Commander Orn and his pilots."

"What are you talking about? Why would he...?" The signal suddenly went dead.

"Dammit! Mat, come in. Kem to Mat, please come in." Kem checked the radio even though he already knew what the problem was. "That bastard extended the suppression field." He grabbed the stick and reached down for the thruster control when he stopped himself. Having passed the Gemisi he knew he could safely eject the damaged outer door, which would be necessary if he was going to have any chance of making it to the surface in one piece. Kem unbuckled the restraints and returned to the airlock. First he attached his tether to the inside anchor, then carefully moved toward the open doorway as the receding Gemisi and Proelium drifted past it. Kem knelt down and opened a small panel on the rear bulkhead, revealing a yellow handle not unlike those for the habitat airlock. Hoping the door wouldn't hit the shuttle he grabbed the handle and twisted it hard to the right. He felt a mild vibration accompanied by three puffs of smoke as the explosive bolts fired and the door darted away from the shuttle. He winced when it looked like the canopy might rotate into the door's path, but to Kem's relief it cleared with a meter to spare.

Kem returned to the cockpit and strapped himself in. He again reached for the controls when the shuttle lurched violently. Without air he couldn't hear anything, but a warning light on the control console indicates a port engine failure. He activated the cameras and when the shifting sunlight finally illuminated that side of the shuttle it revealed a column of smoke pouring from a large hole in the engine casing. Kem scrambled to initialize the engines but the damage was too great. Another round struck the shuttle and the starboard wing image went blank. Kem slammed his hand on the auto-stabilization button. The shuttle had barely straightened out when it shuddered as the moon's gravity took hold and the damaged craft began falling toward the surface. *Think, Kem. Think.* Without the main engines there was no way to control the shuttle's descent. As it entered the orange veil Kem remembered the storage closet and had an idea.

25

Recovery

"Why have you fired on Director Kem?" Captain Mat asked Commander Orn, her snout twitching angrily as she waited for a response.

"Director Kem is a sympathizer and traitor," the Commander replied. *"I explained our plan to reform one of the planets in this system and just because it happens to have basic life on it he went crazy, claiming we can't just take what we want."*

"Basic life?" Captain Mat asked.

"Yes," Orn replied. *"Nothing but primitive plant and animal life, I assure you. Nothing worth saving."*

"Nothing worth saving?"

"Captain, we're wasting time. I've already been over this with the Council. They approved this mission two years ago." The Captain gestured to the communications tech to mute the com.

"Traitor my ass," Mat said to her first officer, Cru. "Whatever is going on has nothing to do with farming an uninhabited planet."

"What do you think they are up to?" Cru asked.

"I don't know, but I'm sure it's not good." She signaled to reopen the com. "Commander Orn, I've known Kem most of my life and he is one of the most level headed and loyal people I've ever met."

"I don't know what to tell you, Captain. Director Kem was being flown back when he attacked my pilot for no reason. He

then killed the copilot and ejected them both into space and stole the shuttle. We had no choice but to destroy it."

"Kem would never do anything like that." Before the Commander could respond the Captain continued, hoping to keep him off balance. "Don't give me that crap about being a sympathizer, either. Kem is one of the most loyal and dedicated people I know. Besides, this facility is under the jurisdiction of the Mining Guild. Any judgment or punishment directed against a miner must be determined by us."

"This moon is mine!" the Commander shouted. *"Correction, this entire system is mine and I will do whatever is necessary to insure the success of my mission."*

"Captain!" the tracking officer shouted. Mat gave the mute sign and stepped over to the tracking console.

"What is it?"

"The shuttle. It's entering the atmosphere."

"Is it being controlled?" Mat asked.

"No Ma'am. It's falling."

"Oh no." She reached out and switched the tracking image to the main screen, then watched as the shuttle slowly vanished into the haze. Feeling helpless the Captain fell back into the command chair and wiped her snout on her uniform sleeve, then signaled for the com to be reopened. "Well, congratulations, Commander. You just killed our best hope of this mine being successful."

"Nonsense! Director Kem was only one man, and can easily be replaced."

"Is that how you justify murder, Commander, by simply replacing people with the next in line?" The Captain slowly stood up and took a moment to compose herself before continuing. "Commander Orn, I don't know what's going on here, but I guarantee the Mining Guild and the Council are going to hear about it."

"Let me remind you, I am operating under the authority of the Council, and the Guild, Captain."

"We'll see about that."

"And what exactly do you think you're going to do, send a message and wait eighty years for a response?"

"You're not the only one with a ship that can jump, Commander."

"Captain Mat, if you move the Gemisi so much as one centimeter out of position I'll blow it out of orbit."

"You wouldn't dare."

"I told you I will do whatever it takes to protect my people, Captain, and there are more ships like yours under construction as we speak. Don't think it can't be replaced."

"You claim to be protecting your people yet would so casually murder two hundred of them?"

"An acceptable sacrifice to preserve our way of life."

"You're insane."

"No, Captain. Unlike your undisciplined miners, I am loyal."

"We're done." Captain Mat signaled the tech to end the transmission and slumped into her chair, lost in thought as the bridge crew looked on. After giving her a minute First Officer Cru stepped over and knelt next to her.

"What do we do?" he asked quietly. The Captain placed her hand on his arm, then sat up straight.

"Tracking, where is the shuttle now?"

"It just impacted the surface twenty five kliks from Alpha Complex."

"Satellite Control, I want a complete scan of the crash site, now!"

"Yes Ma'am."

"I know Director Kem was a friend of yours, but there is no way he survived that," Cru said.

"You're right, Kem *is* a friend," Captain Mat said as she stood up again. "That's why I'm not giving up on him."

"Of course."

"The scan is complete, Ma'am."

"Any signs of life?" the Captain asked, hopeful.

"No Ma'am. No ID signal, no movement, not even a heat signature."

"Now what?" Cru asked.

"Ma'am, Commander Orn is calling again," the Com tech announced.

"Put him on."

"Captain, I understand you've scanned the site and found no survivors."

"How did...that's correct."

"I'm sorry it had to come to that. It is not my desire to engage in any kind of conflict with our own people."

"Isn't it a little late for that?"

"Excuse me, Captain. As soon as we retrieve our pilots I'll be moving the Proelium over the crash site to perform a full scan of my own." The channel closed abruptly.

"Com, get me Assistant Director Lue right now!" Captain Mat ordered.

"Yes Ma'am."

"And make sure the channel is encrypted!"

* * *

The Rover skimmed across the frozen surface as fast as Nya could push it without losing control. Tam held on tightly, in spite of being strapped securely into the seat.

"How much longer?" Ula asked from the right-hand passenger seat. "We need to get there before the Proelium can image the site."

"I know, I know," Nya said. Ula sat back and forced herself to relax. The left-hand seats had already been folded into their medical bed configuration and a spare pressure suit had been strapped on top, just in case. Even though the rover was already well stocked Nya also insisted on bringing two extra cases of medical supplies, which were stowed below the bed.

"How long?" Ula asked again.

"We're almost there," Nya replied.

"Is there anything on the scanner?"

"No," Tam answered after a quick check of the screen. "Nothing."

"There!" Nya shouted. A swirl of black and gray rose into the orange sky, eventually fading into the stratosphere.

"That must be it," Tam said.

"Don't get your hopes up," Ula warned them both. "We all know this is most likely a recovery mission, not a rescue."

"I'll believe that when I see it," Nya said. As the dark cloud approached they began to pass pieces of wreckage. Nya slammed on the brakes, throwing everyone against their restraints, then proceeded forward slowly. "Keep your eyes open." She carefully navigated the debris field while scanning it both visually and with the sensors set to FULL.

"Nothing yet," Tam reported. "Wait."

"What is it?"

"I'm picking up something large, five degrees to the left." Nya turned and continued toward the object. As they penetrated the heavy fog and smoke the main hull of the shuttle appeared, lying on it's roof. The canopy was missing and the cockpit had been shoved into the passenger cabin.

"It must have landed nose first," Ula said.

"If it was dead shouldn't it have come down ass first?" Nya asked as she slowly circled the wreckage. The starboard engine was still attached but the winglet was completely gone, replaced by a scorched hole.

"That's not from the crash," Ula said. When they passed the cargo hold the entire hatch was also missing. "That answers your question," Ula said to Nya. "With the hold empty the shuttle would have been balanced enough for aerodynamics to take over." They continued around to the port side. The winglet was hanging by the upper skin but all six pairs of eyes were immediately drawn to the large hole in the engine casing.

"That's not from the crash, either." Nya said as she fought to keep her emotions in check.

"They knew exactly where to hit it."

"What do we do?" Tam asked.

"The main hull is mostly intact," Ula said as they approached the cockpit again. "If Kem made it to the airlock he may have been able to strap himself into one of the spare suit berths. That's what I would have done."

"Even if he did, that would have been a lot of force to endure," Nya said.

"I know, but it's something." The main hatch came into view, revealing the open airlock and missing outer door.

"Maybe he was blown out when the outer door failed," Tam said excitedly. "He could still be in orbit." Nya stopped the rover next to the front right corner of the shuttle so they had a clear view of both the crushed cockpit and the airlock.

"I don't think so," she said. "The Gemisi would have seen him on their sensors."

"What if he was blown out on the way down?"

"Then the grid sensors would have picked up his residual body heat or the signal from his suit."

"Nya is right," Ula agreed. "Besides, from the look of the hinges I'd say the door was blown deliberately."

"It's definitely worth checking out," Nya said as she unbuckled herself.

"I agree," Ula said as she removed her own restraints. "We should let Lue know what we're doing."

"Right." Nya activated the com. "Rover to Alpha, come in."

"This is Alpha, go ahead rover."

"Lon, is Director Lue available?"

"One moment." There was a brief pause before Lue's voice replaced Lon's

"Have you found the crash?" Lue asked.

"We have, but there are no life signs," Nya reported. "We found the main hull. It landed pretty hard but is mostly intact. We are going to check it out."

"I want you to record everything inside and out," Lue requested.

"Yes Ma'am."

"Be careful."

"Rover out. Are you coming Tam?" Nya asked.

"Of course." The trio migrated to the back of the rover and Ula opened the panels. Nya grabbed one of the medical kits and they stepped into the constantly shifting haze. After activating their helmet lights and video recorders they each prepared themselves for what they may find, then approached the shuttle cautiously. Ula led the way as one by one they pulled themselves up to the open airlock and climbed into the dark interior.

"Watch where you step," Ula warned. "There is a lot of debris and sharp edges in here." She stepped carefully across the airlock ceiling until she reached the suit storage. "One of the spare helmets is missing but the suits are empty." Disappointed, she stepped over the inside door frame and entered the main cabin. As she moved forward her boots crunched on the broken pieces of the canopy. She looked up and the beams from her helmet illuminated the passenger seats hanging from the floor above like upholstered stalactites.

"Anything?" Nya asked from the airlock.

"No! No pilots, no Kem."

"So where is he?" Tam asked.

"We'll have to search the entire debris field." Nya said. "Come on." The trio climbed out of the shuttle and returned to the rover. Nya activated the sensors, then drove around the wreckage once more hoping for any sign of their leader. "Nothing."

"If Director Kem wasn't in the shuttle there is no way he survived the fall." Tam said. "Not even in this gravity."

"We still need to find his body," Ula said.

"Agreed." Nya continued driving in a spiral pattern away from the shuttle, but even after reaching a radius of nearly one kilometer there were still no life signs or heat signatures on the readout. "Now what?" Tam asked.

"What is that?" Ula asked as she stared intently out the right-hand window.

"What?" Nya asked. She rotated the rover to face where Ula was pointing.

"Right there. That tall thin formation." Nya eased the rover forward and the object became more visible. It was about two meters tall by a meter wide and was the same yellowish color as the frozen ground.

"It's just a rock," Tam said.

"Are you sure?"

"Yes, why?"

"Because I'm sure I saw it move."

"The weather is playing tricks," Tam said. "The water here is frozen solid."

"There! It moved again!" Ula shouted.

"I don't see anything," Nya said. She activated the forward

sensors and looked down at the screen. "That's weird."

"What is it?" Tam asked.

"According to the sensors that rock isn't there."

"How can that be? We're looking right at it."

"That's not a rock," Nya said and suddenly sat up straight. She twisted the throttle and drove straight toward the object as her emotions began to overwhelm her. When it looked like she was going to drive straight into it she suddenly spun the rover 180 degrees so the back end was no more than two meters away from the rock. "Open the back!" she shouted to Ula.

"I'm on it." The engineer jumped up and opened the panels as the object suddenly moved toward them. It entered the cabin and Ula closed the hatch. Nya purged the gases as the thing moved forward and slipped into the rear passenger seat.

"I thought you were going to sit there and stare at me forever," Kem's voice said from beneath the camouflaged shuttle cover.

26

Pursuit

"How soon before we have an image?" Commander Orn asked.

"We're in position now, Sir."

"Let's see what's down there." The sensor tech activated the main screen but all it showed was orange haze. "Switch to thermal and radiographic."

"Yes Sir." The image shifted colors and the entire crash site came into view.

"Focus on the main wreckage." The tech obeyed and the inverted shuttle grew to fill most of the screen, along with the rover. "Zoom in on the hatch."

"Yes Sir." The image shifted again, revealing a pressure-suited figure climbing out of the shuttle, followed by two more. The Commander and crew watched as all three returned to the rover, which then began circling the wreckage in an outward spiral.

"What are they doing?" Tev asked.

"Looking for their precious Director," Orn replied. His confidence waned slightly when the rover suddenly stopped, then pivoted to it's right. After a few seconds it began moving forward until it suddenly spun around and stopped.

"Did they find him?" Tev asked.

"Sensor Control, magnify."

"Yes Sir," the tech replied. The image zoomed in on the rover and the two officers watched intently.

"What are they doing?"

"They are just sitting there," Tev said. "Wait, now they've opened the back. Why aren't they getting out?" After a few more seconds the panels closed and the rover took off at a high rate of speed.

"They must have thought they found something, but it looks like it was nothing."

"Let's hope so."

"It doesn't matter," Orn said. "Tev, send two fighters down to sanitize the entire crash site and destroy that rover."

"The rover, Sir?"

"Is there a problem?"

"No Sir. I just don't understand why we need to fire on more civilians when the Director has already been eliminated."

"They are clearly loyal to their former Director and could still pose a threat to this mission." Orn said sternly. "I want that rover destroyed at once!"

"Yes Sir."

"Nav! Return us to standard orbit and get me the Reaper."

* * *

"It's good to have you back, Sir" Nya said as she continued to beam with joy from behind her face shield.

"It's good to be back," Kem said from underneath the shuttle cover.

"What exactly happened up there?" Ula asked as the rover raced across the landscape. "What is this about?"

"I'll tell you when we get back," Kem said. "I want the entire senior staff to know what's going on."

"Fair enough. Can you at least tell us how you survived the crash?"

"I wasn't in the crash."

"Sir?"

"I bailed out."

"I know the gravity is weak here, but it's not that weak," Tam said.

"Haha. That is very true." Intrigued, Nya switched the rover to auto-drive and all three crew members waited anxiously to hear the story.

"Nya, how far have we gone?" Kem asked.

"Ten kliks."

"I think that's far enough." Kem began pulling at the cover until it his helmet and shoulders were uncovered.

"Good to actually see you again, Sir," Ula said. "You were saying?"

"Right. I thought I might still be able to perform a controlled reentry but the outer door had been damaged when the shuttle pilots tried to kill me. I blew the hinges so it wouldn't be ripped off during reentry."

"You were right," Tam said to Ula. "About the door."

"Go on, Sir." Ula urged Kem.

"The shuttle was too badly damaged, especially after the second shot, so I had to think of another way out. I had seen the camouflage cover in the storage bin but it didn't register until I remembered the probe we found." Kem held up the cover and began passing the edge through his hands to show the attached cables and clips. "These go under the shuttle to hold it on even in the strongest winds, so I clipped them together and attached the bundle to my tether."

"You made a parachute," Nya said.

"Exactly."

"That was a huge risk." Ula said. "You didn't have any way to know if it would work."

"That's true, but if I stayed in the shuttle I was dead for sure."

"That's quite clever, Sir," Tam added. "I still have one question. Why didn't the sensors detect you?" Kem continued to pull the edge of the cover through his hands until he reached the corner, then flipped it over to reveal a 3 centimeter disc embedded in the yellow fabric. He turned it back over and pressed it to his leg and within two seconds the entire cover changed to match the color and pattern of his suit.

"Active camouflage," Kem explained. "It's also sensor neutral."

"I've never seen that," Ula said.

"I have," Nya said. "Before I quit the academy they were experimenting with it."

"How did you know about it?" Tam asked Kem.

"The Guild held a send-off party for the mission and one of the members mentioned it. I guess they were hoping to apply it to the mining facilities to make them harder to spot by enemy bombers."

"I don't remember a party," Ula said.

"It was really for themselves," Kem explained. "Mat and I were the only two from the actual mission who were invited. Anyway, I didn't remember the camouflage part until I landed and it automatically matched the color of the ground."

"I wonder why the Guild didn't put it into use," Ula said.

"Probably because the locations of the existing mines were already known by the Aselli, and ours is out of reach," Nya guessed.

"No doubt," Kem agreed. "How much farther?"

"About five kliks." An explosion erupted just ahead of the rover, rocking it violently and showering it with ice and dust. Nya grabbed the yoke and swerved to avoid the crater that had likely been created. As soon as they cleared the debris she hit the brakes and the rover slid to a stop just as two fighters passed overhead. Everyone strained to look through the front windscreen as the two craft peeled off in opposite directions.

"They're coming around!" Nya said. She gripped the yoke even tighter and twisted the throttle hard. "Hang on!" The rover leaped forward as two rows of plumes erupted from the ground heading toward them. Nya managed to swerve at the last second and the hits passed safely by.

"Why are they shooting at us?" Tam asked. "If they want us to stop they could use their EM cannons."

"I don't think they are here to talk," Kem guessed. "Nya, can you get us out of here?"

"There is no way I'm outrunning fighters," she said as she struggled to evade the two craft.

"What do we do?" Tam shouted.

"Shut up!" Nya turned toward Kem. "Sir, open that rear ceiling panel." Kem spun his chair around and grabbed a small recess molded into a boxed section of the headliner. When he pulled on it the panel dropped down and a small yellow yoke with a screen in the middle unfolded, accompanied by low hum that seemed to come from the roof. When a targeting image appeared on the screen Kem understood.

"Your just-in-case?"

"Push the button on your armrest marked AUX." Kem did so and his seat began to move, following the track built into the floor until he was sitting in the center of the cargo area facing the gun control. The rover jerked sideways as another missile exploded nearby. "Any time would be good, Sir."

"Right." Kem gripped the yoke, which swiveled in all directions on a central gimble and had a trigger button under each inside thumb. "Won't I shoot the dish?"

"No! The dish automatically folded forward when you

activated the gun."

"Good to know!" Kem moved the yoke around to get a feel for the aiming, then lined up the cursor with one of the approaching fighters. "What kind of ammo do I have?"

"Right is ordinance, left is EM!" Nya replied as she dodged the rounds striking the ground nearby.

"Got it!" A flurry of rounds streamed from the fighter as Kem pressed the right trigger and a loud but muffled 'whump' resonated through the cabin. "I thought you said right was ordinance!"

"Sorry Sir, *Left* is ordinance. Right is EM!" As the second fighter began another run at them Kem again lined up the cursor and pressed the left trigger. A hail of rounds streaked toward their target, clipping the port wing.

"Yes!" Kem shouted, but his celebrating was cut short when he realized the fighter was still coming toward them. He lined up the cursor again and pressed the right button.

Whump!

The fighter stopped firing and began to tumble wildly toward the ground.

"Punch it!" Kem yelled. Nya twisted the throttle and the rover accelerated just as the fighter slammed into the frozen ground right behind it. Kem leaned back to relax when another explosion hit to their right, showering the rover in more debris and coating the windscreen.

"Dammit!" Nya yelled. She activated the wipers but the ice and hydrocarbon mix only streaked the glass. She then switched to sensor imaging and activate the wire-frame view. "He's coming back!"

"Where?" Kem asked.

"Behind us!" Kem moved the cursor around until the remaining fighter appeared on the screen.

"Can you shake him for a second?"

"I'll try!" Nya jerked the yoke to the right, then left, forcing the pilot to realign his shot. As he did so Kem release another burst of ordinance toward the starboard wing. The pilot avoided them but Kem had already anticipated the maneuver and moved the cursor to the right. The fighter drifted right into his sights and he pressed the right trigger.

Whump!

The fighter tumbled out of the air and crashed less than 10 meters to the left of the rover. Nya again slid to a stop, then drove slowly around until the section of the fighter that used to be the cockpit was visible. The pressure-suited body of the pilot was slumped over the side, unmoving.

"Is he dead?" Kem asked. Nya checked the signal from the pilot's suit.

"Yes Sir."

"*What* is going on?" Tam suddenly yelled. "Why is the military trying to kill us?"

"Let's check the other pilot and get home before more show up," Kem said. "Then I will tell you everything."

27

Reaction

Kem stood at the head of the modest table with his pressure suit lying in front of him. The senior staff, along with Nya and Lon, did their best to squeeze into the cramped conference room next to the Director's private quarters. Once he finished his account of recent events he allowed them a few minutes to absorb the news.

"This is disgusting," Cas finally said. "We discovered intelligent life in a new system and our first response is to wipe them out and take over their planet?"

"I can't believe our own government could be capable of committing global genocide," Lue agreed.

"I'm still having trouble believing it myself," Kem said.

"Based on what you've told us this race doesn't stand a chance," Ula added.

"Which is why we need to find a way to stop the launch and inform the Council."

"But when I spoke with Captain Mat she told me the Commander was acting on behalf of the Council, and the Guild," Lue said. "If we try to stop him we could all end up in prison."

"I'm not convinced he is acting with the Council's approval."

"What makes you say that?"

"When the Commander told me about the mission he said they had three main goals: The first was finding an uninhabited planet to relocate to and the second was to look for intelligent life advanced enough to be turned into an ally."

"Relocate?" Ula asked. "Why would we need to do that?"

"I guess the war isn't going very well," Kem said. "At least according to Orn."

"You mean according to the bastard who just tried to kill us," Tam said.

"Yes."

"So what was the third goal?" Lue asked.

"If neither of the first two were successful but a suitable planet was found, then we would convert it and farm it for methane."

"But the planet is inhabited."

"It's my belief that Commander Orn has reinterpreted the mission parameters to mean that the planet was to be converted no matter what life may be present."

"But how could he do that on his own?" Tam asked. "The military isn't the most ethical organization but I've always believed their goal was to protect us, not wipe out any new life we discover."

"I think in his own way the Commander believes he *is* protecting us," Kem replied. "He's obsessed with obtaining the methane we need, no matter the cost."

"Obsessed?"

"Maybe even delusional."

"What makes you say that?" Doctor Rue asked.

"When the Commander was going over the plan I noticed his hands were shaking and he rubbed them several times like he was trying to make it stop."

"You think he could be experiencing Zero-Gravity Dementia?" Doctor Roe asked.

"Maybe," Kem said. "It could simply be a nervous tick, but the Commander doesn't strike me as the type to be nervous about anything."

"I thought you didn't believe in gravity dementia," Ula said.

"I didn't, but what else could it be?"

"It's certainly possible after being out here for so long," the Doctor said. "That's why the Gemisi was designed with the ring."

"Why wouldn't the Proelium have a ring if it was sent on such a long mission?" Tam asked.

"Can you imagine a battle carrier with a huge spinning target?" Nya answered.

"We're getting a bit off topic," the Doctor said. "If Director Kem is right the commander could be extremely unpredictable."

"I agree," Kem said. "We need to be extra cautious."

"Were there any other indications of dementia?"

"You mean other than him changing his mandate and sending two fighters to kill a group of civilians?"

"Yes. Anything with his personality?"

"Well, when I mentioned the original attack on the Aselli he became very angry for a moment, then resumed the presentation as if it never happened."

"Abrupt fits of rage are one of the advanced symptoms."

"He also mentioned the original Commander of the Proelium fell ill during their first mission."

"Did he say what from?" the Doctor asked.

"He claims the Commander brought aboard a tainted ferment and it made him sick."

"But you don't believe him," Lue said.

"No," Kem replied. "I think Orn was already suffering from early stages of the dementia when they discovered the alien race. When the Commander called off the mission Orn must have believed he was traitor and took him out."

"What a cold bastard," Tam said.

"This is still all speculation," Lue added.

"It does fit, though," Dr. Rue said. "ZGD doesn't simply

render the suffer insane. They become fixated on a specific goal to the point where any attempt to discourage them from achieving it is met with resistance. That resistance is often violent." The doctor paused before continuing. "I recall studying one case of a pilot becoming so determined to shoot down enemy fighters that he eventually saw all other fighters as the enemy," the Doctor continued. "He killed three of his own squad before his ship was disabled."

"Oh, great," Tam said. "So we have a madman on our hands who believes he has the support of the council."

"Not exactly. If Director Kem is right he would have had to lie to the Council about the planet being occupied."

"How could he lie to them but still think he's following their orders?"

"Once Orn altered the original mandate he would see anyone going against him as a traitor, even the Council members themselves. He would have no problem lying to them and his entire crew to achieve his goal."

"Once they returned to this system he knew there would be no way to contact home to confirm his orders," Kem added. "That being said, Council approval or not I can't just sit by and allow this to happen."

"I'm not sure which version is more frightening," Tam said. "Orn having the support of the Council or being delusional and going against them."

"Can't we just have him removed as Commander?" Lon asked.

"How are we supposed to do that?" Ula said. "We're a civilian operation."

"She's right," Nya replied. "Only the Sub-Commander and the Ship's Doctor possess the authority to relieve the Commander."

"But if he's gone rogue wouldn't they be obligated to do so?"

Tam asked.

"Not if they believe he's still acting under Council orders. Then neither would have reason to do so."

"Unless one of them didn't know the actual plan and was operating under the Councils original orders," Kem said.

"What do you mean?" Lue asked.

"What if Sub-Commander Tev doesn't know the planet is occupied?"

"Wouldn't she have to know? The rest of the officers certainly seem to."

"Don't forget, Orn was the Sub-Commander during the first mission," Kem said. "Once he took out the Commander and assumed control he didn't have a sanctioned first officer until they returned, then Tev was appointed to the Proelium by the Council right before they left home on this mission."

"If you're right do you think she could be convinced to remove the Commander?"

"I'm not sure. She's very young, so even if she believed our theory I doubt she would go against a new commanding officer. It's definitely worth keeping as a backup plan, but for now we have to assume the entire crew is loyal to the Commander."

"How loyal are they?" Lue asked.

"Enough to kill me," Kem replied. "At least his pilots were."

"Shouldn't we let the Captain of the Gemisi know you're alive?" Cas asked. "Maybe she can help."

"Not just yet," Kem replied. "First we need to come up with a plan. Then we can bring the Captain up to speed."

"We better come up with one fast then," Lue said. "If you're right about the launch schedule we don't have much time."

"It's too bad we didn't know about this earlier," Ula said. We could have made up an excuse to delay the nitrogen pods, but they have already been delivered."

"No sense dwelling on that now," Kem said. "We need to focus on disabling the Reaper and getting a message back to the Council."

"And how do we do that?" Tam asked. "As you pointed out we can't send a message home."

"We will have to obtain hard evidence and jump home with it."

"Where are we going to find that kind of evidence?"

"The presentation he showed me is stored on a data drive in his office," Kem explained. "We'll have to send someone in to steal it."

"Oh, that should be easy," Tam said, but his sarcasm was lost on Kem as he stared off into empty space. "Why don't we just declare war on the military while we're at it?"

"You have an idea, Boss?" Ula asked.

"What is the military's biggest weakness?" Kem asked.

"Being nuts?" Nya asked.

"Guns."

"I'm not sure you understand what weakness means," Tam said. "Guns are anything but a weakness."

"They are when you rely on them to solve every problem," Kem said "Since the rover managed to escape the Commander is certainly anticipating a response. Tam is right, though, we don't have the means to launch an assault against them, and even if we could the crew is simply following orders. I refuse to kill anyone if we don't have to."

"So what are you thinking?" Lue asked.

"We need a more subtle way to infiltrate the ship."

"We would need a distraction," Ula said. "Something simple that would create a lot of confusion."

"Even if we manage to get someone aboard and onto the bridge, anyone who isn't supposed to be there would be spotted immediately," Lue said.

"What if they were all wearing pressure suits?" Ula asked.

"In case you forgot their suits are black and gray," Tam added. "That would make one of us stand out even more."

"We could borrow a couple," Nya suggested.

"And where are you going to get two military pressure suits?"

"From one of the shuttles."

"Nya's right," Kem said. "If all of their shuttles are equipped the same they should have two spare suits in the airlock storage of each remaining shuttle."

"Assuming we can, what would it take to get the crew into their suits?" Tam asked. Before anyone else answered Kem's face suddenly lit up.

"A sensor malfunction!"

"Exactly," Ula said. "We could duplicate the problem we just experienced in the habitat."

"Will that work?" Tam asked. "I doubt they are going to be fooled by the computer telling them the bridge atmosphere is made up of hydrocarbons."

"It should give us enough time to steal the drive," Kem said. "It would be helpful if whoever does it could also gather video evidence."

"So how do we recreate the sensor error?" Lue asked.

"We could fabricate a small spray bottle and fill it with a compressed version of the natural gases from outside," Ula explained. "All you'd have to do it spray at least three sensors, let it dry, and you'll trigger a warning."

"That might work," Lue said.

"How small can you make the sprayer?" Kem asked.

"I'm sure we can get it to fit into the thigh pouch of your suit," Ula replied. "Unfortunately, that means you will have to give up your flashlight."

"One stupid pouch. Who designs these things?"

"Not me, that's for sure," Ula said.

"We don't have much choice, but I think I can manage with my helmet lights. Which sensors would have to be targeted?"

"The more widespread the alarm the harder it will be to lock it down, but they will have to all be in the same atmo controlled space," Ula explained. "I assume the bridge is isolated from the rest of the ship."

"No. There is an airlock at both ends of the observations halls. Once we passed through it there was atmo all the way up to the bridge."

"There will be a sensor above every airtight door, inside of the room it isolates, just like other ships. To get the widest alarm whoever does this should start with the sensor above the airlock door."

"You said they will need to spray three?" Kem asked.

"Correct. One or two will be seen as individual sensor malfunctions and simply trigger a request for service. Once three or more are reporting a problem then the actual alarm is triggered and protocol will require pressure suits."

"If we can't use the spray is there another way to disable atmo?"

"The processors could be shut down, but that comes with it's own challenges."

"Where would they be?"

"I'm not too familiar with the Proelium's bridge design but if I had to guess I'd say the processors are either in the neck or in the bridge module itself. Probably on the floor directly below the bridge."

"That may be easier to get to," Lue said.

"Maybe." Kem said. "The next task is preventing them from launching the arosils. Can we disable their com link to the

Reaper?"

"I doubt it," Lon said. "They probably have multiple redundant systems and frequencies."

"What about disabling the entire console with EM guns?" Ula asked. "They were designed to shut down faulty equipment, but there's no reason they wouldn't work on a control console."

"Would that really stop the launch?" Kem asked.

"I honestly don't know. They could have com stations all over the ship."

"Even if they didn't, the other problem is sneaking one onto the bridge," Lue said. "Even if you weren't already carrying the sprayer and EM gun won't fit in the pouch, and if you replace your black sidearm with a white EM gun it will stand out."

"Whoever does it could use their sidearm to shoot the console," Nya suggested.

"Then they'd be arrested and wouldn't be able to retrieve the data drive."

"That's true."

"We will have to try something else," Kem said. "Speaking of sidearms, would the EM guns disable them?"

"Their sidearms are shielded against EM," Nya explained.

"Is there any other way we can use them?"

"Not unless you need to disable a control pad or a suit com," Ula replied.

"We'll add that to the backup list."

"We're back to the original problem," Lue said. "How do we disable the Reaper?"

"What if we could get someone on board?" Kem asked.

"I doubt we would be able to pilot it, and we have the same issue with the EM guns, but it shouldn't be too difficult to disable the ship with a few carefully placed charges," Ula said.

"Who would know where to set them?" Lue asked.

"You said it's a converted Muso class?" Ula asked Kem.

"That's right."

"I worked on several Musos when I apprenticed at the Juunto shipyard. It shouldn't be a problem."

"How will Ula get back once she's disabled the ship?" Cas asked as she rubbed her head.

"I can slip off before it jumps and then wait for someone to pick me up," the Chief Engineer replied.

"It won't take you with it?" Lue asked.

"Not unless I'm in the path of the ship. Then it would flatten me so thin I'd be two-dimensional."

"Then make sure you're far enough away," Kem said as he placed a hand on her shoulder. "So, assuming this all works, how do we get the data drive into the hands of the Council?"

"What are our options?" Cas asked.

"We can't use the Gemisi," Kem said. "It's the main lifeline for the mine."

"Besides, Commander Crazy already threatened to blow it up if the Captain tried to leave," Lue said.

"I'm not convinced he would follow through on that threat," Doctor Rue said.

"Are you certain?"

"Not completely, but if the Commander is obsessed with obtaining methane to send home I doubt he would destroy the only ship capable of achieving that goal right now."

"But like Kem said, we need the Gemisi here, so it's a moot point."

"So how do we send someone home?" Kem asked.

"I doubt he's going to let us borrow the Proelium, and we're going to disable the Reaper." Ula said.

"That leaves the scout ship, which makes more sense anyway," Kem concluded.

"How will we get it out of the hanger?"

"Ula's right," Nya said. "The hanger lift will be locked down the moment you're discovered."

"Ula, how many rope charges do we have left?" Kem asked.

"Six, why?"

"What if we made our own exit? The hull can't be that thick."

"I'd guess two layers four to six mil each with insulation in between," Ula said. "The problem is removing the section."

"What do you mean?"

"The rope is a cutting charge. The explosion will separate the section of hull but you will still have to remove it from the opening."

"Can't I just kick it out?"

"Unless you blow it out."

"How would I do that?"

"Open one of the interior hatches and depressurize that room."

"And if it's occupied?" Kem asked. "Like I said, we're not killing anyone else if we don't have to."

"I'll see if I can come up with another way to clear the breech." Ula said.

"Even if you manage to escape, what then?" Tam asked. "The Commander may not fire on the Gemisi but the scout ship is another thing, especially if he thinks you pose a real threat to him. I doubt you'd get more than a klik away before he blew you up."

"We will have to create another diversion," Kem said. "If anything goes wrong, though, we'll have to abandon the plan and steal a shuttle."

"So how do we get someone aboard the Proelium and Reaper?" Lue asked. "It's not like we can send a shuttle over and say 'Hi there! We're here to sabotage your plan'."

"Maybe whoever goes can hitch a ride on a shuttle," Nya said.

"What do you mean?"

"All we have to do is come up with a reason to send one over and let you tag along, Sir."

"You realize they are going to know I'm there."

"Exactly," Nya said.

"You've lost me."

"If we send a shuttle they are going to be suspicious, so we let them search it and have them come up empty."

"If it's empty then what is the point?" Tam asked.

"It'll only be empty by the time they dock."

"So we get off before the shuttle docks," Kem said.

"But how?" Cas asked.

"Simple," Nya said smugly and turned to Ula. "Do you think Ari could fabricate two sets of magnetic handles and tether anchors?"

"Ari can make anything."

"I get it," Kem said. "Whoever goes will hang onto the back of the shuttle, out of view of the Proelium. When it approaches the ship they will let go and float to their destination."

"Exactly," Nya said. "The ships are so close to each other the acceleration will be minimal. I doubt they will push the engines above five percent."

"Won't their suit signals be detected?" Lue asked.

"Only if they decide to scan the shuttle."

"That's a chance we will have to take," Kem said.

"And what happens if the stowaways miss their target?" Tam asked.

"I'm sure the Captain will let us borrow a couple of EVA packs," Nya replied.

"Their use will have to be kept to a minimum to avoid detection but that should work," Kem said.

"Maybe we can come up with another distraction," Ula said.

"Maybe. Ula, I want you and Ari to get to work right away on those handles and the sprayer."

"Yes Sir."

"There is another problem we haven't addressed yet," Kem said.

"What's that?" Lue asked.

"There is a good possibility they will be able to listen to our transmissions even if we encrypt them."

"How?"

"The same way I knew they were planning to kill me and make it look like a decompression accident." Kem picked up the sleeve of his pressure suit and opened the control pad. He entered the Onslaught code and the helmet's interior speakers began to buzz.

"It actually worked?" Lon asked. He picked up the helmet and turned it over to listen to the overlapping chatter.

"It saved my life," Kem replied with a shudder.

"So how will any of this work if they can hear our transmissions?" Tam asked. Kem thought for a moment, then turned back to the communications tech.

"Lon, would it be possible to install a small button in the glove of a pressure suit that can toggle between preset radio frequencies?"

"I think so," Lon replied. "Do you want it to change the channels you're listening to, or talking on?"

"Can you make it do both?"

"No problem, but it won't do much good if the military can listen to every channel."

"We have to take that chance. Assuming they can, will they also be able to locate us?"

"Outside the ship, sure. Once they detect the telemetry from the suit they can narrow it down with a sensor sweep. Aboard the ship they will only be able to determine your general location."

"How general?"

"One hundred meters, tops." Lon replied. "Unless..."

"Unless what?"

"Unless that ship has internal tracking sensors."

"How would we know if it does?"

"Do you remember seeing any additional sensors on the walls?"

"No, but I wasn't looking for them."

"Does it matter?" Ula asked. "Sensors or not they will know which section of the ship you're in."

"Is there a way to disable the telemetry signal?" Kem asked Lon.

"Not without also disabling your com."

"There must be something we can do."

"The telemetry is built right into the hardware as a fail-safe," Lon explained. "The only thing you can do is switch between live and previously recorded data, but it's always going to transmit something when it's powered up."

"We will have to work around that."

"Do you think they are aware that *we* know about the code?" Ula asked.

"I doubt it or Orn wouldn't have used the com to order Pan to kill me," Kem replied. "I just hope he didn't figure it out by my reaction."

"You're making an awful lot of assumptions," Lue said as he checked the clock. "We're almost out of time."

"Then we need to be ready to go as soon as Ari's parts are completed. Once they are it will be time to let the Captain know I'm still alive."

"We still haven't addressed one important issue," Lue said.

"What's that?"

"Who is going to do it?"

254

"There is still an element of risk, even if we pull it off," Kem replied. "Since I can't order any of you to participate I will do it myself. Besides, that bastard has tried to kill me *three* times now." His deep red eyes darted in Tam's direction for a split-second.

"You're still going to need help," Ula said.

"Yes, but it has to be voluntary." Kem scanned the translucent gray faces staring back at him in anticipation. "So, who is it going to be?"

28

Peace Offering

"I knew that bastard was lying about the Council," Captain Mat said as she retrieved two bottles of ferment from the small refrigerator in her private office. She pushed one of them over to Kem, then held hers out in front of her. "To a successful mission," she said and took an extended draw from the tube. Kem raise his to his mouth but paused. "Don't worry, I didn't poison it." Kem laughed and slurped the contents through the tube.

"It's good," he said and took another sip. "This mission is definitely not what any of us signed up for."

"You said you have a plan?"

"I do, but I can't ask you to put yourself or your crew at risk."

"Are you kidding? There's no way I can stand by and allow an entire planet full of life to be destroyed."

"Are you sure?"

"What do you need me to do?"

"Well, we need a way onto the Proelium and Reaper, so a distraction would be nice."

"What did you have in mind?" Captain Mat asked.

"I think it's about time you and the Commander make up and be friends again."

* * *

"Captain Mat. To what do I owe the pleasure?"

"I wanted to apologize for my earlier behavior, Commander. Once the ground crew fired on your escort I realized you were right about Director Kem. His selfish behavior was *unexpected*, to say the least. I guess I didn't know him as well as I thought."

"Nonsense, Captain. You were simply being loyal to a trusted associate who betrayed you. I don't feel any better about the situation, I assure you."

"Thank you for understanding."

"So what can I do for you?"

"Actually, there is something I can do for you."

"And what might that be?"

"Our crop production is well above average so I thought you and your crew might enjoy eating fresh produce for a change, instead of that dehydrated pre-mix."

"I believe it's safe to say the entire crew would appreciate that," Orn replied. *"I'll send a shuttle over as soon as you're ready."*

"It's no problem for me to send a shuttle to you," Mat said hastily. "The mine isn't quite ready for us."

"Nonsense," Orn replied. *"Besides, thanks to Director Kem my pilot has been forced to break in a new copilot so it will give them some flight time."*

"Of course, Sir. We should have the pod ready in an hour. Gemisi out." Once the channel was closed Mat turned to her guests. "I hope you know what you're doing."

* * *

"Shuttle Corona one six two nine to Gemisi Control, requesting permission to board."

"Shuttle Corona, you are cleared for Pad One."

"Copy Control." The shuttle entered the landing bay from the

port side and pulled through until it settled onto the starboard pad, facing outward and perfectly centered within the glowing yellow square. Once the skids magnetized and the main engines shut down the cargo hold cover began to rise. At the same time the outer door of the starboard berth opened and the little transport backed out. It shuffled over to the wall of supply pods and back up to one near the center with a flashing blue light.

Captain Mat used the bridge's main screen to keep an eye on the black and gray shuttle. Once the pod transfer began the outer door opened and the ramp extended out from below it. Passengers could simply float between the shuttles and airlock, but protocol required the ramp to be deployed to provide a continuous contact point, since even a minor bump could send a passenger sailing into open space. Two black-suited figures emerged, then walked down the ramp and across the landing bay toward the open berth, eventually disappearing from view. Shortly after, two figures in white suits appeared, each carrying a small case and an EM gun as they moved toward the shuttle.

"Imaging," the Captain snapped. "Bring up the aft view of the ring on the main monitor and the nose and engine cones on the secondary monitors."

"Yes Ma'am." As soon as the images had been switched the Captain turned to face the entrance to the bridge. Within a minute the door opened and Commander Orn appeared, accompanied by Lieutenant Pan.

"Welcome about the Gemisi," the Captain said cheerfully.

"Thank you, Captain." Orn said as he and Pan removed their helmets. "It's good to be here."

"I have to admit, I wasn't expecting you to accompany the shuttle."

"Well, I never got a chance to see the Gemisi completed before we began our mission, so I thought I'd take advantage of your hospitality and have a quick look."

"Of course."

"It's an impressive ship."

"Thank you Sir, but it's nothing compared to the Proelium."

"You flatter me, Captain. Did you know I assisted in the design?"

"I did *not* know that."

"Just a few basic suggestions based on my previous commands. Yes, the Proelium is impressive, but the Gemisi has one major advantage over it."

"What is that?" Mat asked as the Commander walked right up to the main screen.

"Gravity, of course." He stared longingly at the image of the slowly turning ring as he rubbed his right hand. "What I wouldn't give to feel my boots actually pressed against the floor for a change, rather than just stuck to it."

"It definitely makes a difference," the Captain said. "I don't know how you managed without it for so long." She couldn't help but glance at the Commander's trembling hands but quickly looked away. "Would you like a tour?"

"Perhaps another time." The Commander glanced at the smaller monitors, then resumed staring at the main screen. "I thought you would be monitoring the pod transfer."

"My people know what they are doing."

"Of course."

"Besides, we've detected an anomaly in our radiation absorption readings, so I've been monitoring the effects of the solar radiation on the ring."

"Are you having a problem?"

"Not specifically, but I've been considering turning the ship around to even out the exposure."

"Is that necessary?" Orn asked. "The tiles on these ships have been designed for that very reason."

"That's true, but the greenhouse glass was made with less shielding to maximize the natural light."

"I see." Commander Orn turned around and looked at Mat with a deep, calculated gaze. "Well, Lieutenant, if the Captain's crew are as good as she claims they should have her gift to us loaded by now. Shall we?"

"Yes Sir." They headed toward the exit when Mat interrupted.

"Uh, Commander. Could I interest you in a vintage ferment?"

"Another time, perhaps."

"It would really mean a lot to me," Mat said. "A token of goodwill."

"Very well," Commander Orn sighed. "Lieutenant, get the shuttle prepped for departure."

"Yes Sir." Once Lt. Pan left the bridge Mat gestured toward the door to her private office.

"Shall we?" She led the Commander inside and moved straight to the refrigerator. "I had intended to give this to you when you first arrived, but we've been so busy."

"A very nice space," Orn said as he looked around the room. There were no windows, but a screen on each wall provided an exterior camera view in the corresponding direction. In between those, artists' renderings of the ship as well as landscapes of Sazi's reddish surface provided a sense of home.

"It does the job." Mat removed a tall, thin metal bottle with green and purple swirls around the thickest part, with the rest left bare and brushed. "It's nothing like *your* office, though," she said.

"You're familiar with the Proelium?" Orn asked as he took the bottle from her.

"Oh no," Mat said quickly. "I meant it must be as impressive as the rest of the ship."

"I see. Well, if there is nothing else I better get back. We have a lot to do and very little time to do it."

"I know the feeling," the Captain said softly. "I'll see you out." She led the Commander back to the bridge and accompanied him to the exit. "Have a safe flight, Commander Orn."

"Good luck with your rotation," he replied. "I'll be monitoring it with great interest." Commander Orn stepped through the doorway and the panels closed with a faint *'schwip'*.

"I'm counting on it," Mat said to herself. She returned to her command chair and pulled herself into it. "Imaging, show me the landing bay."

"Yes Ma'am." The picture changed, revealing the Commander's shuttle along with two figures in black pressure suits clinging to the upper half of the cargo hold cover using Ari's anchors. Mat watched nervously as the Commander finally appeared from the airlock and made his way to the shuttle.

"Clever, Boss," Cru said. "Putting them on Pad One and using the starboard airlock."

"You can praise me all you want *after* we pull this off," Mat said as they both stared at the screen. Commander Orn boarded the shuttle without reacting, but even then she found it impossible to relax. "Good luck," the Captain said softly as the shuttle lifted off and drifted out of the landing bay.

29

Infiltration

"Lieutenant Pan, why is your approach so low?" Commander Orn asked his pilot.

"Sorry, Sir. I wanted one more look at the Reaper before it leaves."

"She is a thing of beauty, isn't she?"

"Yes Sir."

"Just think, in a couple of hours the final stage of our mission begins, and thanks to the Captain we will have fresh food and a bottle of ferment to celebrate with."

"Yes Sir."

"That reminds me. Lieutenant, contact the Proelium and have Sensor Control keep a close watch on the Gemisi."

"Yes Sir." While the pilot called the ship she happened to glance down at the camera feeds and for a split-second thought she saw something dark dip into the top of the cargo cover image before disappearing out of frame. "Sir, I think we may have a problem."

"What is it?"

"Stand by." As they approached the Proelium she pitched the nose of the shuttle up sharply toward the landing bay, then checked the image again. "I thought I saw something on the hull."

"Proceed with your approach. We'll check it out once we're safely aboard."

"Yes Sir. Shuttle Corona one six two nine to Proelium two two five four. Requesting approach and dock."

"This is Proelium docking control." the response crackled. *"Shuttle Corona, permission to dock is approved for hanger station Beta."*

"Copy that Proelium." The pilot guided the shuttle into the landing bay and rotated it to face forward. She deployed the landing gear and touched down with a firm *'thud'*.

"Interesting technique, Lieutenant," Orn said as he removed his restraints. "Within specs, but not exactly your usual landing."

"Sorry Sir, I guess I got used to the Meki."

"Not to worry," the Commander said. "It was still superior to most." The floor lowered the shuttle into the hanger and it was moved into it's dock with a series of muffled *'thumps'*.

"Control to Shuttle Corona, stand by for pod transfer."

"Negative Control," Lt. Pan said. "Belay transfer until my order."

"Affirmative. Standing by."

"Well," Commander Orn began. "Shall we have a look?"

"Yes Sir." Both pilots removed their restraints and floated out of the cockpit and back to the airlock. The copilot, Sim, stepped through first but stopped and placed his back against the rear bulkhead, allowing Lt. Pan to pass by and open the outer door. She gripped the handhold and pulled herself out, followed by the Commander, and finally Sim.

After closing the hatch Pan unclipped her sidearm and quickly surveyed the entire shuttle and surrounding area, then pointed her weapon upward. The copilot pushed himself up and over the shuttle, then used the overhead structure to pull himself toward the back. At the same time, the pilot and Commander floated around the port side until they were even with the back edge of the winglet. Pan looked at the copilot and held all three fingers up, then folded them one by one. When her last finger dropped they both launched themselves toward the back of the shuttle. "Don't move!" Pan shouted, but there was no one there.

"Are you certain you saw something?" Commander Orn asked.

"Yes Sir. It looked like a boot." She raised her eye line slightly and used her weapon to point to the two sets of anchors, which had been colored black to blend into the shuttle surface. "Someone *was* here."

"You're right, but where did they go?" Commander Orn asked. "Search the hanger at once."

"Yes Sir." The two pilots separated and systematically worked their way through the dimly lit space, mindful of the multitude of hiding places in and around the ships and structure. When they reached the far end they repeated the procedure until they had rejoined the Commander. "Nothing sir," Pan reported. "They must have already made it out of the hanger somehow."

"They are probably after the Reaper data," Orn guessed aloud as he activated the general com. "Security, we have two intruders aboard. They may be headed toward the bridge."

"Copy that Sir."

"Flight Control, lock down the hanger."

"Yes Sir." The Commander looked around the hanger one more time, then pointed at the new copilot.

"Ensign Sim, if I'm right they will need a way off the ship. Stay here in case they return."

"Yes Sir."

"And make sure the pod is scanned before they open it."

"Yes Sir."

"Lieutenant, come with me. We have to protect that data."

* * *

When the capsule reached the bridge Commander Orn pulled off his helmet.

"Get changed," he said to Lt. Pan. "I'm going to check my office."

"Yes Sir!" The Lieutenant turned toward the locker room while Orn stepped out of the small vestibule onto the bridge.

"Status!"

"Sir, the Gemisi is moving," the tracking tech reported. The Commander stepped around the console and leaned over the technician's shoulder.

"Where is it going?"

"Nowhere, Sir. It's turning in place."

"The Captain told me she was going to turn it around to limit solar exposure. Monitor it closely and let me know if it moves out of it's current position or launches any shuttles."

"Yes Sir."

"Welcome back, Commander," Tev said. She vacated the command chair but Orn set his helmet on the seat and continued past her without a word. When he entered his office he went directly to the display console and opened the data cabinet. All the drives were present but he pulled the mission drive out and plugged it in. Once he activated the display table the Reaper model appeared, and after a quick check of the data log he confirmed it had not been accessed since he had shown it to Kem. Relieved, he removed the drive and placed it back in the cabinet, then returned to the bridge. He pulled himself into the command chair and removed his gloves, then promptly began rubbing his trembling right hand.

"Communications, I want all transmissions monitored!" the Commander ordered.

"Yes Sir!" The technician tapped his console and the speakers erupted with cross-chatter from on-board transmissions, but one voice caught the Commander's attention.

"...in the atmosphere processor room..."

"Filter out standard channels."

"Standard channels are off, Sir."

"I'm ready to disable atmo on the bridge," the female voice continued.

"How long will the processors be offline?" a male voice asked.

"I'm not sure, but long enough to get into the Commander's office."

"Do it." After a few seconds the conversation continued.

"Atmo has been disabled."

"Good work. Get to the bridge."

"Engineering, can you confirm the status of the bridge processors?" Orn asked.

"Processors are at one hundred percent and functioning normally, Sir."

"What are they talking about?" Orn asked Tev. "There's nothing wrong with our atmo." The atmosphere alarm nearly cut him off as the wailing tone began to echo throughout the bridge and the strobes flashed.

"Sir, sensors report bridge atmo is failing!"

"Everyone get your suits on!" the Commander ordered. He picked up his helmet and started to put it on when Pan appeared from the locker room and raised her hands out of confusion. He motioned for her to join him and she quickly squeezed past the stampede of crew members heading toward the locker room. "Lieutenant, watch my office," he said as he slipped his helmet on. "I don't know what game our intruders are playing but I want that drive protected at all costs."

"Yes Sir." Lt. Pan moved to the office door and positioned herself directly in front of it, then drew her sidearm. Orn had just pulled himself back into the command chair when the communications console activated.

"Supply room to bridge," a voice called over the com. With the crew changing Orn glided over to the console.

"Go ahead Supply."

"Sir, we have a problem in Supply Room Beta."

"What is it?"

"We found an unidentified case inside the pod you brought back from the Gemisi. It was hidden in a container of produce."

"Is everyone evacuated?"

"Yes Sir."

"Isolate that section and alert the emergency crew. Is Ensign Sim with you?"

"No Sir."

"He was supposed to oversee the pod scan personally."

"I haven't seen him, Sir, and we found the case when we opened the container."

"What is going on?" Orn asked himself.

"Sir?"

"Nothing. Call me when you have something new to report."

"Yes Sir."

"And send someone to the hanger to find Ensign Sim."

"Yes Sir."

"Another problem?" Tev asked as she and the other bridge crew began emerging from the changing room.

"I don't know. It could just be a trick, or another attempt to sabotage the ship." Once the techs returned to their stations Orn moved back to the command chair.

"Tracking, what's the status of the Gemisi?"

"It stopped, Sir."

"Any other activity?"

"No Sir."

"What is she up to?" Orn asked.

"You just said the Captain was going to turn the ship to reduce solar exposure," Tev reminded him.

"That's true, but something about that keeps bugging me."

"What's that, Sir?"

"I'm not sure. Wouldn't they have thought of solar exposure when they designed the glass for the greenhouses?"

"Maybe this sun is stronger than they originally thought."

"Maybe." Orn stared blankly at the main screen for a few seconds. "Sensors. Have you detected *anything* usual about the Gemisi?"

"No Sir. All sensors have been focused on it since you gave the order."

"Dammit!" Orn shouted as he slapped the arm rests.

"What is it?" Sub-Commander Tev asked.

"Sensors! I want a full sweep around the Proelium. Two klik radius."

"Yes Sir!"

"Solar exposure my ass. She *wanted* me to think she was up to something."

"But why?" Tev asked.

"Sir, I'm picking up two signals directly to port."

"Who is it?"

"We're receiving suit telemetry but no identification signals, Sir."

"They took their badges off so they can't be identified," Orn concluded. "What is their heading?"

"Directly toward the Reaper, Sir."

"They're attempting to disable it. Imaging, put the Reaper on the main screen. Tracking, how close are the targets?"

"Thirty meters to contact, Sir."

"Proelium to Reaper."

"This is Reaper, go ahead."

"We believe there are two intruders attempting to board you. I need to you jump now."

"Yes Sir. Initializing displacement drive."

"Tracking. Distance of targets to Reaper."

"Twenty meters, Sir."

"Drive is set. Initiating countdown to jump."

"Ten meters."

"Five, four, three."

"Five meters!"

"One." All eyes moved to the main screen just as the Reaper vanished.

"Tracking and Sensors, do you still have the targets?" Orn asked.

"Stand by." Everyone on the bridge waited anxiously for the reply. "Targets remain, Sir."

"Sorry Boss," a second female voice said over the com. *"Mission One is negative."*

"You did everything you could," the male intruder's voice said. *"Stand by for extraction."*

"Copy that."

"Ha!" Orn shouted in triumph. "Com, can you locate who they are talking to?"

"Somewhere in E section, but I can't narrow it down more than that."

"Security, find them!" The Commander again slammed both hands down on the arm rests, pushing himself to his feet.

"Shall I have the others picked up?" the flight controller asked.

"No. Let them sit out there and watch until they run out of air."

"Sir, we can just leave civilians to die," Tev said.

"Those people stopped being civilians the moment they declared war on us!"

"Yes Sir."

* * *

Down in the hanger Kem lowered his head, dejected. He had just finished applying five rope charges to the inside of the hull when the two officers began arguing, giving him hope that Tev might relieve the Commander. Once that didn't happen he removed the initiator from the silver case and began attaching it to the end connector of the rope. He pressed the small box against the hull, then turned to close the case when he realized there were two boots standing next to him. He looked up slowly to see Ensign Ren standing over him.

"Really," Ren said. "An atmo sensor error?" She raised her sidearm and aimed it at Kem. "Stand up, Director."

"Crap." Kem said. "How did you know it was me?"

"Do you recall what my primary job is?" Ren asked.

"To be a scumbag spy for Orn?" Kem didn't intend to be quite so snarky to the Ensign while she was pointing a gun at him, but that was how he reacted under stress.

"No, I am a linguist, remember?" That means I have an excellent memory when it comes to accents and vocal inflections, so I never forget a voice.

"Congratulations! Maybe you'll get a promotion."

"Quiet!" Ren took two steps back without taking her eyes off of Kem. "Ensign Ren to Commander Orn."

"Go ahead Ensign."

"Commander, I found your intruder."

"Who is it?"

"Director Kem, Sir, and he's wearing one of our spare suits."

"It seems the Director is more resourceful than I imagined,"

Orn said. *"Maybe I should go ahead and promote him."*

"Sir?"

"Never mind. Where did you find him?"

"In the hanger. He was planting rope charges on the inner hull."

"That must be how he planned to escape. Is there any sign of Ensign Sim?"

"No Sir."

"Good work, Ensign. Detain the Director and secure the hanger. Then try to locate Sim."

"Yes Sir. One more thing. His driver, Nya is probably the one responsible for your atmo problem and is planning to steal the data drive."

"Not to worry, Ensign. No one is getting into my office."

"Yes Sir."

* * *

Orn turned around and pointed at Lieutenant Pan. She opened the door and entered the office, then reappeared after a few seconds shaking her head.

"All drives are accounted for, Sir."

"Ensign Ren, can the Director hear me?"

"Stand by. Go ahead, Sir."

"Well, Director Kem, I'm not sure how you survived but you should know your plan has failed."

"Well, you can't win them all." Kem replied.

"Sir, we'll have to jump soon if we're going to make the launch window." Tev reminded the Commander.

"You don't want to miss your opportunity to wipe out an intelligent species." Kem said.

"What does he mean by that, Sir?"

"Didn't you know, Sub-Commander? That planet you're about

to destroy is full of life, including a race of intelligent beings."

"Is that true Sir?"

"It doesn't matter," Orn said. "Our mission comes first. Our people are depending on us and I will not let them down."

"But how could the Council go along with this if they knew there was advanced life there?"

"Tell her the truth," Kem goaded. *"You and I both know you never had the Council's approval."*

"Sir?"

"The Council is a bunch of pacifist cowards who couldn't even adhere to their own mandate!" Orn suddenly shouted. "They didn't have the courage to order a preemptive strike sixty years ago when the Aselli first became a threat and they didn't have the courage to go through with this mission. I was the only one willing to save my people, not them."

"You can't just alter orders," Tev argued, prompting Orn to unclip his sidearm and point it at her face shield.

"I will not tolerate insubordination aboard my ship!" Orn shouted as his hand began to shake.

"I'm simply asking for clarification," Tev said as she remained focused on the weapon.

"The only clarification you need is that I am the field Commander and we are cut off from home out here!" Orn pressed the trembling gun closer to Tev. "That gives me the authority to adapt orders to the current conditions as I see fit! Does anyone have a problem with that?"

"No Sir," Tev said meekly. "I apologize. As I said, I only sought clarification."

"I hope so, for your sake *Sub-Commander.*" Orn slowly lowered his sidearm and snapped it into the clip on his leg. "I would hate for your first assignment as first officer to be your last."

"What about the Director's partner?" Ren asked.

"Where is she, Director?" Orn asked Kem.

"Nya? She could be anywhere," Kem replied. *"That girl has a mind of her own."*

"She must have planned to slip into your office and steal the data after she disabled the atmo," Ren speculated aloud.

"Except she didn't account for Lieutenant Pan and myself still having our suits on." Orn agreed. "Where would she go once the plan failed?"

"Since I caught him trying to blow the hull she's probably on her way back to the hanger."

"And then what, steal a shuttle?"

"I don't think so, Sir. The only way the data would be of any use to them is if they gave it to the Council."

"The Skoa."

"Yes Sir. Even without the data that's how I would escape. It's a lot faster than the shuttles."

"That makes sense." Orn thought for a moment and turned toward the security officers stationed outside the elevator vestibules. "Ensign Lee, relieve Lieutenant Pan."

"Yes Sir!" As Lee made his way to the office door Pan stepped forward.

"Lieutenant, return to the hanger and don't let the Skoa out of your sight."

"Yes Sir!" Pan pushed off and glided to the side wall, then repeated the move toward the exit and left the bridge.

"Ensign Ren."

"Go ahead Sir."

"I'm sending Lieutenant Pan down to relieve you and keep an eye on the Skoa."

"What would you like me to do?"

"When she arrives take Director Kem to the brig and continue the search for his partner and Ensign Sim."

"Yes Sir."

30

Extraction

"Don't move," Ren barked at Kem. She flicked the gun toward the center of the hanger. "Get on the tram."

"You said not to move."

"Don't get cute. You know what I meant."

"Fine," Kem groaned. He picked up the case and began walking, planting each step deliberately as he made his way between the scout ship and shuttle. "So you knew the real plan all along."

"Quiet."

"Tev didn't, did she?" Kem feigned a sigh as he reached the tram. "It's a shame, really. I was hoping she would relieve your boss of his command and put an end to this madness."

"I said quiet. Commander Orn is a great man."

"Is he, or is he a delusional nut?" When Kem reached the tram he stepped onto the platform and turned to face Ren. "Now what?"

"Now you tell me where your partner is, where you got that suit, and what you did with Ensign Sim."

"Well, I borrowed the suit from your shuttle, Ensign Sim is taking a break from the military, and Nya is standing behind you." Ren spun around but no one was there.

"Nice try." As she turned back toward Kem he slapped his boot onto the tram's retracted handrail, causing it to pop up and knock the gun from Ren's hand. When she shifted her gaze to follow it Kem gripped the explosives case tightly and swung as hard as he could, striking her across the lower front of her helmet. As she drifted backward he launched himself upward in pursuit of the weapon. He reached out as it bounced off of the underside of the landing bay floor but he was suddenly pulled straight down until he was once again facing Ren. She had wedged her right foot under the tram to keep herself in place, allowing her to grab Kem's arm and spin around, slamming him against the frame of the transfer crane. Dazed, Kem planted his boots against the strut and launched himself toward her, but she managed to grab him again and pulled him down hard against the tram.

"I give up!" Kem shouted as he grabbed the handrail and started pulling himself off of the floor. "Stop."

"Not until I teach you a lesson, traitor." Ren reached out to grab him again but he kicked her square in the chest, sending her flying between the shuttle and Skoa, finally coming to rest against the hull. Before she could recover Kem removed the detonator from his thigh pouch, opened the cover, and pressed the top button. The rope charges flashed, sending a mild vibration through the floor as the Ensign was instantly enveloped by a ring of smoke. The rope had cut a clean hole but as Ula had predicted the section of hull remained in place.

"You fool!" Ren shouted as she planted her boots against the hull for another attack. "I guess you forgot there's no atmo in here!"

"Actually, I didn't." Kem pressed the bottom button and the end of the supply pod exploded outward, followed by a rush of air, fresh produce, and other debris from the evacuated supply room. The escaping mass slammed into the separated section, sending both the panel and Ren hurtling into space.

* * *

"Ensign Ren, what's happening?" Orn asked as more alarms blared. "Ensign Ren, come in."

"Sir, this is Lieutenant Pan. The intruders blew a hole in the side of the hanger and are escaping in one of the shuttles."

"Which one?"

"The Horizon, Sir,"

"Lieutenant, what happened to Ensign Ren?"

"I don't know."

"Dammit! Imaging, put it on the main screen."

"Yes Sir." The technician switched the image to a live feed of the port hull just as the shuttle cleared the breech.

"Should we launch fighters?" Tev asked.

"I can get to them a lot faster in the Skoa," Pan said.

"Stay put, Lieutenant," Orn barked. "Launch control, prepare two fighters."

"Yes Sir."

"Sorry about Ren," Kem's voice said. *"I guess she wasn't feeling well and stepped out for some air."*

"Argh!" Orn growled. "Lieutenant Pan, go after them!"

"Yes Sir." The bridge crew continued to watch the main screen as the Skoa eventually drifted through the breech. Once it cleared the hull the main engines fired and it shot out of frame.

"Tracking, shift to port. Show me the Horizon and Skoa."

"Yes Sir." The screen displayed a computer-generated overhead view of the scout ship speeding toward the lumbering shuttle, which was headed directly toward the spot where the Reaper had been.

"Sir, I have the Horizon in sight." Pan announced.

"Disable it."

"Locking EM."

"Shouldn't we try ordering them back first?" Tev asked but Orn ignored her.

"Lieutenant, disable that ship."

"Yes Sir!" The Skoa zipped past the shuttle, then snapped around 180 degrees and stopped directly in it's path, but the shuttle continued toward it. *"Sir, I don't think anyone is in control of the Horizon,"* Pan reported.

"Sensors, scan that shuttle."

"Sir! Sensors are showing no life signals."

"What? Lieutenant Pan, can you verify?"

"Stand by." The Skoa waited until the two ships were barely two meters apart and then began flying backward, matching the shuttle's speed. Pan activate the landing lights, illuminating the inside of the Horizon cockpit. *"Sir, it appears to be empty."*

"Another decoy?" Tev asked.

"That explains why it didn't change course."

"They must still be aboard the Proelium."

"I'm tired of this game," Orn said. "Lieutenant, can you stop the shuttle without damaging it?"

"I believe so." The Skoa slowed just enough for the flat noses of the two ships to bump together, then used the maneuvering jets to bring both craft to a stop. *"Forward motion zero. Horizon is stable."*

"Good work, Lieutenant."

"Sir, the two signals are gone!"

"What?"

"They were stable until the Skoa and Horizon approached, then they vanished."

"They must have panicked and moved away. Increase to three kliks."

"Three kliks, but we're still only picking up the Skoa, Horizon, and Lieutenant Pan."

"They didn't just disappear!" Orn shouted. "Lieutenant, can you see them?"

"Negative, Sir."

"I want you to perform a full sensor and visual sweep of the area."

"Yes Sir."

"Tracking, standard radius."

"Sir, the other shuttle has been launched," Sensors reported.

"What?" The repositioned tracking image showed the Corona on a direct heading toward the Gemisi. "Life signs?"

"Two signals, but no identification."

"Who do you think it is?" Tev asked. "The two saboteurs Pan is looking for?"

"They couldn't have gotten back to the Proelium that quickly," Orn concluded. "It must be Director Kem and his driver trying to escape."

"Sir, I can bring them back." Before Commander Orn could respond, Lt. Pan moved the Skoa away from the lifeless Horizon and accelerated under the Proelium toward the Corona. "Locking EM."

"Lieutenant, stand down." Orn said.

"Sir?"

"You heard me. This one is mine."

"Sir, I can disable them."

"Get out of there Lieutenant!" Orn barked. "Weapons, destroy the Corona!"

"Yes Sir!" A single missile erupted from the starboard side of the Proelium and raced toward the shuttle. The pursuing Skoa barely had time to bank out of the way as the missile struck the port engine of the Corona, blowing a huge chunk out of the main hull and sending debris in all directions. The Skoa banked hard again but the detached winglet struck the belly pan, sending the scout ship tumbling out of control. "Lieutenant, are you alright?" Commander Orn asked.

"I'm okay but I've lost power. Stand by."

"We'll send a retrieval team out right away."

"Sir, if we don't jump soon we will miss the launch window." Tev reminded him again. Orn glanced over at the launch control monitor and focused on the mission clock in the upper right corner.

"Damn." Orn thought for a moment, then sat back. "Tracking. Is the Skoa in any immediate danger?"

"No sir. The trajectory will carry it away from the moon."

"Sit tight, Lieutenant. We'll have to come back for you after we complete the launch."

"Don't forget about me, Sir."

"I won't. Launch Control, how much time?"

"Five minutes, Sir."

"Weapons, finish off the Corona, then lock a missile onto the Gemisi coil but don't fire until I give the command."

"Yes Sir." Another missile left the Proelium and struck the damaged shuttle, causing it to erupt into a huge fireball. Once it faded there was nothing left larger than a fist.

"Corona destroyed, Sir."

"Com, get me Captain Mat."

"Yes Sir. Proelium two two five four to Gemisi, come in."

"Go ahead Proelium." Captain Mat replied.

"Captain, this is Commander Orn. I don't know what you hoped to accomplish, but I'm calling to let you know your plan failed."

"I don't know what you're talking about. What was that explosion?"

"Spare me, Captain. I've had to deal with enough deception for one day. The launch is on schedule, the data drive is still in my possession, and that explosion was your would-be saboteurs."

"How dare you fire on unarmed civilians!"

"How dare I? How dare *you*, Captain. I can assure you once my mission here is completed the Council will hear about this."

"Not if I have anything to say about it." Captain Mat replied. "Commander Orn, if you were under the authority of the Sazin Mining Guild I would place you under arrest."

"Then it's a good thing I don't answer to the Guild. Excuse me, Captain, but I have an appointment and I don't want to be late."

"Missile is locked, Sir," the weapons tech announced.

"Oh, and in case you get any ideas about jumping home I have a gift of my own." Orn pointed at the weapons tech and a missile raced toward the Gemisi."

"We need to go, Sir," Tev said.

"Jump the ship."

* * *

"Incoming!" the Gemisi tracking tech shouted.

"How many?" Captain Mat asked.

"Just one. It's headed for the tail."

"Navigation, ninety degrees to port! Imaging, show me the impact point."

"Captain, the missile is already locked," Cru said. "Turning won't keep it from hitting the ship."

"No, but a shallower angle might direct part of the blast away from us."

"Impact in three, two, one." There was no sound and only a slight vibration passed through the hull, but the image on the screen showed a mild explosion on the largest part of the tail shroud as an alarm began repeating throughout the ship.

* * *

The Proelium appeared at the edge of the asteroid belt,

although the vast distances between individual bodies belied the label.

"Security, begin a search for Ensigns Ren and Sim," Orn said.

"Yes Sir."

"Tracking and Sensors, get me a picture."

"Yes Sir," the two techs replied in unison. The combination image came up on the screen showing the relative positions of the two ships. "The Reaper is five kliks to port."

"Obstacles?"

"None, Sir."

"Switch to visual and contact the Reaper."

"Proelium two two five four to Reaper one nine five eight."

"This is Reaper. Go ahead Proelium."

"Reaper, initiate launch position." While the bridge crew watched the screen the Reaper began to rotate on three axes until it appeared almost vertical in relation to the Proelium.

"Reaper in position."

"Initialize the sequence," the Launch tech relayed.

"Sequence initialized."

"Prime the launch tubes."

"Tubes are primed."

"Send the authorization code." Commander Orn instructed the tech.

"Code sent sir."

"Proelium, authorization has been accepted and confirmed. Stand By."

"We are about to make history and hopefully put an end to this war," Commander Orn said proudly. "Send the final launch code."

"Launch code sent. Stand By." The entire crew remained fixated on the main screen as the Reaper's computer calculated the precise launch time. After almost a minute the entire starboard side of the vessel erupted with thousands of bursts of nitrogen.

"Proelium this is Reaper. The first wave is away." The bridge crew cheered in unison as the mist dissipated. *"Tubes are reloading for the second wave."*

"Good work, everyone," Commander Orn said as he settled back in his chair. "Security, is there any news on Ensigns Ren or Sim?"

"No Sir."

"Where could they be?" Tev asked. "What did the Director mean when he said she stepped out?"

"I'm not sure," Orn said. "Something about this doesn't seem right. Their plan was destined to fail, so why did they even try?"

"I don't know what to tell you, Sir. They definitely had us running in circles." The idea didn't sit well with the Commander but he also knew his first officer was correct.

"Yes they did, but what was all that talk about them having the drive?" Orn asked.

"A final desperate attempt to confuse us after their plan failed," Tev suggested. "We know they didn't get the drive because Lieutenant Pan checked it herself." Orn straightened up and stared at the Sub-Commander for a few seconds, then pushed out of the command chair and himself launched toward his office. He opened the door, then pulled himself to the control console and opened the data cabinet. His eyes were immediately drawn to the silver spray canister resting in the slot where the mission's data drive had been.

Conclusion

The tumbling Skoa had drifted well beyond the moon's orbit when the stabilization jets suddenly fired and it came to a stop. The pilot restored atmo, then unlatched her helmet and pulled it off.

"Well, that was fun," Nya said. Directly behind her the blackness began to undulate until another helmet appeared.

"That was some fancy flying," Kem said as he pulled the camouflage shuttle cover all the way off. "I'm glad your flying skills are as good as your driving."

"It's all in the wrist." Nya held up the small control pad from the rover and wiggled it. "I've never flown two different vehicles with the same pad before. All while flying this antique."

"I'm very impressed."

"I can't believe that lunatic blew up another shuttle. I was sure once they detected our telemetry recordings they would let me disable it. Then it would have been a simple matter of simulating a malfunction and playing dead."

"We make have pushed Orn a bit hard," Kem said as he finished removing the camouflage cover and stuffed it behind his seat. "Did we sustain any damage when the wing hit us?"

"Hang on." Nya initiated a systems check and read the results. "All systems are functioning but it looks like the starboard landing gear door is damaged."

"Can we still get home?"

"Yes, but we won't be able to enter the atmosphere."

"I'm not sure this bucket is capable of reentry anyway. Did you get the package?" Nya pulled the data drive out of her thigh pouch and handed it over her shoulder. "And the video?" Kem asked as he took the drive from her. Nya turned her helmet around and grasped the hexagonal protrusion on the back. She pulled it out, revealing it to be another, smaller data drive.

"Here you go, Sir. Everything the helmet recorded while I was on the bridge."

"This should be more than enough to get the council to act," Kem said. "I just hope it won't be too late."

"Don't be too hard on yourself. We knew our chances of stopping the launch were slim at best."

"I know. I still wish we could have done more to help those people."

"At least Lon's channel toggle worked," Nya said. "I was so nervous. Every time I used it I was sure they were going to figure out it was me guarding the office."

"I'm glad they didn't."

"I do feel bad for Ren. Don't you?"

"Maybe a little, but there is still a chance she made it."

"What a way to go if she didn't."

"Let's finish up before Commander Wack-job comes back."

"Yes Sir." Nya adjusted her seating position and activated the com. "Skoa to Gemisi."

"Good to hear your voice, Nya," Captain Mat said. *"How did it go?"*

"We've got the packages."

"That's great. I hope it will be enough to convince the Council to take action."

"Are you okay?" Kem asked the Captain. "It looked like he fired on you."

"We're fine," the Captain said. *"It's only minor damage to the displacement coil, so we should have it repaired in a day or two. I think you were right about him not being delusional enough to destroy the Gemisi.*

"How about the other team?"

"Ula and Ari are already on board."

"That's good news."

"Ula says tell Nya thanks for the lift to the Horizon. That was quite a maneuver."

"No problem," Nya said. "I'm just glad he didn't blow that one up too."

"He would have if they hadn't used the shuttle cover," Kem added. "Mat, how are your two guests holding up?"

"Oh, Pan and Sim aren't too happy, but at least they are comfortable. I have a feeling the Commander won't be as accommodating once we return them."

"Are you going to be okay?"

"I'll be fine. He'll threaten me for a while, then I'll return his shuttle along with the pilots and promise to play nice."

"I hope so."

"You better get going before he returns."

"Right."

"The coordinates are set Sir." Nya announced.

"Mat, we are ready to go."

"Good luck. We'll see you soon, I hope."

"You too." Kem placed a hand on Nya's shoulder and spoke softly. "Are you sure this ship actually works and the Commander wasn't just keeping it aboard as a historical antique?"

"As long as he was telling the truth about having it repaired."

"That doesn't make me feel any better. Assuming you're right, how long will it take to get home?"

"Well, my math is a bit rusty, and as you pointed out this ship is as old as I am, so I have no idea what the specs are."

"How about an educated guess then?"

"Based on the size of the coil and the approximate mass of the ship, I'd say four to six hours."

"That's good enough for me," Kem said. "Let's go home."

Acknowledgments

My deepest appreciation to the following:

Christiaan and Constantijn Huygens

Carl Sagan and Bishun Narain Khare

Wikipedia

Space.com

Thales Alenia Space

Planetary Habitability Laboratory

and the acronyms:

ESA

NASA

JPL

ASI

Arbor Day and Titan Mine title font:

'WLM Poster Type' created by Wolf Lambert

Finally, a special thanks to Pierre Boulle.

About The Author

After publishing Arbor Day B.L. Alley soon began writing his second novel, The Diamond. During that time he realized the back-story for Arbor Day had the potential to make an interesting follow-up novel. Not wanting to create a traditional series, he chose to make Titan Mine a prequel that could stand on it's own while complimenting Arbor Day. While intended to be read after Arbor Day, it is structured so that it can also be read before.

With the publication of Titan Mine B.L. Alley began work on Plan B, the third novel in the series, as well as research for yet another story.

41494631R00173

Made in the USA
Lexington, KY
15 May 2015